The RED BLAZER GIRLS

THE vanishing Violin

Michael D. Beil

Alfred A. Knopf
New York

THIS IS A BORZOI BOOK PUBLISHED BY ALFRED A. KNOPF

Visit us on the Web! www.randomhouse.com/kids

Educators and librarians, for a variety of teaching tools, visit us at
www.randomhouse.com/teachers

Library of Congress Cataloging-in-Publication Data
Beil, Michael D.
The Red Blazer Girls : the vanishing violin / Michael D. Beil. — 1st ed.
    p. cm.
Summary: Seventh-graders Sophie, Margaret, Rebecca, and Leigh Ann follow
a trail of cryptic clues to locate a rare violin, catch the person sneaking into
St. Veronica's School for late-night cleaning and redecorating, and outsmart
a conniving classmate.
ISBN 978-0-375-86103-1 (trade) — ISBN 978-0-375-96103-8 (lib. bdg.) —
ISBN 978-0-375-89627-9 (e-book)
[1. Puzzles—Fiction. 2. Friendship—Fiction. 3. Catholic schools—Fiction.
4. Schools—Fiction. 5. Mystery and detective stories.] I. Title.
PZ7.B388234953Reg 2010
[Fic]—dc22
2009023984

The text of this book is set in 12-point Bookman.

Printed in the United States of America
August 2010
10 9 8 7 6 5 4 3 2 1

First Edition

My, isn't *this très* puzzling?

For my parents, Bill and Nan

In which the true nature of detective work is revealed to be full of cobwebs, beady-eyed critters, and something sticky

Like a plaid-skirted Jedi Knight, I wave my trusty lightsaber—okay, really it's just a flashlight—back and forth in front of my face, carving a swath through a tangle of spiderwebs. Convinced that my eight-legged enemies have been cleared from my immediate path, I aim the beam at the jumbled piles of broken desks and God only knows what else lurking in the far corners of the school basement.

"There's definitely something dead down here," I announce.

"It's not the dead things I'm worried about," Leigh Ann says. "There might be rats."

Rebecca laughs deviously. "Might be? Um, Leigh Ann, this is New York. Just keep your feet moving and they won't bother you."

In spite of Rebecca's sensible advice, Leigh Ann freezes. "Are you serious?"

"Rebecca. Sophie. Stop scaring her. There are no rats, and nothing is dead," Margaret says.

I shine my light at a shelf just above my head and detect two beady eyes sizing me up. He's so close I can see his whiskers moving. "Nah. There wouldn't be rats down here. This is our neat-and-tidy school, after all." I brush aside a few more spiderwebs and charge ahead.

Margaret pats me on the shoulder. She has spotted my furry friend, too. "All right, let's concentrate. We have a job to do."

Ah yes, the job.

After our triumphant recovery of the Ring of Rocamadour, we became minor celebrities at St. Veronica's School. Malcolm Chance, the ex-husband of our first client, and someone all my instincts were absolutely, 100 percent wrong about, told the neighborhood newspaper, the *East Sider,* all about us. They sent a reporter to the school for an interview, and we ended up splashed across the front page, with a picture and this story:

"Red Blazer Girls" Solve Local Mystery

It seems that Sherlock Holmes, Nero Wolfe, and Hercule Poirot have some competition right here on the Upper East Side.

Four St. Veronica's School students solved a 20-year-old mystery when they discovered one of the famed Rings of Rocamadour in its hiding place beneath the floor of St. Veronica's Church on Lexington

Avenue. The students—Rebecca Chen, Margaret Wrobel, and Sophie St. Pierre, all of Manhattan, and Leigh Ann Jaimes, of Queens—followed clues, cracked a devilishly clever mathematical code, and outwitted a pair of fiends who appear to have taken lessons from Boris and Natasha of *Bullwinkle* fame.

The ring, hidden by the late noted archaeologist Everett Harriman as part of a birthday puzzle for his granddaughter, dates back to the first century and is alleged to have certain mystical powers—including the power to make dreams come true—according to the girls, who refer to themselves as the Red Blazer Girls in honor of their St. Veronica's School uniforms.

"These girls have done the city, and the whole world, a huge service," says Malcolm Chance, professor of archaeology at Columbia University, and the son-in-law of Everett Harriman. "The ring is priceless—and it almost certainly would have been lost forever without their intelligence and persistence." Professor Chance reports that the ring has been donated to the Metropolitan Museum of Art and reunited with the other of the pair, believed to be wedding rings given to a young couple in France by St. Veronica herself. According to Catholic tradition, St. Veronica was the woman who wiped the face of Jesus as he carried the cross to the site of his crucifixion.

"It was an awesome experience," Miss St. Pierre says. "We were happy to help out Ms. Harriman and her family, and then finding the ring, holding it in our hands—it's like we're part of its amazing history now. Which is pretty cool."

The drama began in September, when Ms. Elizabeth Harriman, Everett's daughter, found a letter he had written the day before his death, nearly 20 years ago. The letter contained the first of many clues, and after a chance meeting between Harriman and the girls, the hunt for the ring was on.

What does the future hold for these crime-fighting tweens?

Miss Wrobel, acknowledged by the other girls as the "true brains" of the outfit, reports that for now she is concentrating on school and the violin.

Her eyes light up, however, when Miss St. Pierre suggests that there are always new mysteries to be solved.

So, Upper East Side miscreants and ne'er-do-wells, take heed. The Red Blazer Girls are in your neighborhood, and on the case.

So we are famous. Sort of.

The day after the article appeared, Margaret showed up at school with a box of business cards personalized for each of us. Here's one of mine:

Red Blazer Girls Detective Agency
No Case Too Small
Reasonable Rates

Sophie St. Pierre

And just like that, we were in business. Two days ago, Sister Bernadette, the principal at St. Veronica's, dragged Margaret and me into her office, a place that was becoming all too familiar to us.

"Miss Wrobel and Miss St. Pierre. Sit."

You have to love Sister Bernadette's just-the-facts-ma'am style.

"Hey, you rearranged the furniture," I said. "This is much better—and now you can see out the window."

"Humph."

I guess she didn't want to talk about it.

She continued: "Let me preface my remarks by saying that I have not forgotten about the week's detention you owe me. Just because you and your friends have become the darlings of the local media does not mean that all your past offenses have been pardoned. Quite the contrary. As I learn more and more about this recent adventure of yours, I am more and more convinced that I was far too easy on you. Sneaking into the church at all hours, digging up the altar's floor. Good Lo—er, my goodness."

"But, Sister—" Margaret started.

Sister Bernadette held up her hand. "Stop. I'm not going to add to your punishment. I want to do business with your, er, agency." She held up one of Margaret's cards.

Margaret and I looked at one another, eyebrows at attention.

"I have a little case for you, if you're interested. Of course, there will be no fee, but if you do this for me, I will remove your names from next week's detention list."

"That seems totally fair," I blurted out.

"Sophie, wait. We haven't heard what's involved yet," replied my more pragmatic friend.

"Indeed. I like you, Miss Wrobel," said Sister Bernadette, resting her chin on her interlocked fingers, but without even a hint of a smile. "I'm starting to understand how you managed to do whatever it was you did over there in the church. This situation is nothing like that. It's a matter of a few . . . unexplained events. I merely want you to seek—no, I demand—an explanation."

"Ooohh. What kind of unexplained events?" I asked, sliding forward on my chair. My brain ran riot: sinister spies, ghastly ghosts, evil extraterrestrials.

"Calm down, Agent St. Pierre. These are the kinds

of events that can be explained—they simply have not been. Put simply, someone has been cleaning and straightening up around the school—after hours. Things that the janitor is not responsible for. Take the refrigerator in the teachers' lounge. Please understand that this is not just a refrigerator, but more a biology experiment gone horribly wrong. In my twenty years here at St. Veronica's, no one has ever cleaned it voluntarily, and if a teacher did, he or she would rightfully expect a medal, and perhaps a hazmat suit.

"And every night, someone is loading paper into every single tray of every copy machine, getting it ready for the next day. They're stacking the reams of paper neatly in the supply closet, instead of merely leaving them scattered around the room, as is the usual practice. The other day, Sister Eugenia jammed the machine in the faculty room so badly that we had to call a repairman, but when he showed up the next morning, somehow it had been fixed.

"Last night was my turn. As Miss St. Pierre so astutely pointed out, all the furniture in my office was rearranged. Nothing missing, not a paper on my desk is out of place. And do you know what I find the most vexing? This arrangement is much better. Now, I do believe in miracles, but I also believe that the good Lord has more important things on his mind than cleaning nasty refrigerators and redecorating offices. I want an explanation, and you girls are going to find it for me. You may snoop around to your hearts' content. So, do we have a deal?"

Margaret stood up and shook hands with Sister Bernadette. "You came to the right place, Sister."

"Satisfaction guaranteed," I added.

"I'll be counting on that, Miss St. Pierre."

Gulp.

Which explains, more or less, why we are spending a Friday afternoon in the subterranean rat kingdom that is St. Veronica's basement. Murder and intrigue. Espionage. Missing persons. Heck, even a lost dog. But tracking down some misguided do-gooder who is sneaking into the school at night to clean and straighten? Oy.

"I guess this is what we meant by 'No Case Too Small,' eh, Margaret?" I grumble, spitting out a mouthful of cobweb.

"Not all detective work is glamorous," she replies. "The real world isn't like TV."

"Yeah, on TV you miss out on the funky smells of places like this," Rebecca says. "Hey, how come nobody ever came up with smell-evision?"

Margaret forges on and then stops abruptly in front of a refrigerator-size pile of old textbooks. Rebecca and I clunk into each other and then into Leigh Ann, who wobbles like a bowling pin before regaining her balance.

"Why are these down here?" Margaret asks. "Do you know how many trees it took to make these books? I'm going to talk to Sister Bernadette about recycling these."

(Please add "environmental activist" to Margaret's

résumé, right after "straight-A student" and "violin prodigy.")

Meanwhile, my flashlight reveals something chromey bright on the other side of the books, and I move closer to investigate. "Hey, a doorknob."

Margaret, Leigh Ann, and Rebecca crowd around me as I shine my light around the edge of the door.

"Where do you think it leads?" Leigh Ann asks.

"It's just a storage room," Margaret says. "Probably full of more textbooks like these. In fact, that probably explains why these are stacked right here. They're going to go in there. Try the door."

I reach for the knob, and just as I am about to put my hand on it, Rebecca gasps really loudly right in my ear. I almost have a heart attack, and she laughs hysterically.

"Oh, you are just a regular riot, Miss Chen," I say, and stick out my tongue. I try the knob, but it doesn't budge. When I put my shoulder against the door and shove, nothing happens.

"They don't make 'em like this anymore," Rebecca says, pushing against it with me.

Margaret shakes her head sadly. "Well, your first problem, geniuses, is that the door opens out."

Becca and I look sheepishly at each other.

"What do you think about that lock, Becca?" Margaret asks, still smirking at us. "Think you can pick it?"

Becca, whose lock-picking skills came in handy in our previous case, takes my flashlight and kneels down for a closer look. "There are two locks. I could probably open the one connected to the knob with my school ID. But this one up here is a dead bolt. I'll need a few tools."

"Can't we just ask Sister Bernadette for the key?" Leigh Ann asks.

Za-zoink. A perfectly reasonable question, no?

Margaret slaps her palm to her forehead and says, "Jeez, I keep forgetting that we have permission to be doing this. Okay, let's take a quick look over there and then get out of here. Soph, lead the way." She points to the darkest, creepiest corner in the basement.

"I am oh-so-happy to get my recommended daily allowance of spiderweb gunk." I step forward, swatting madly at the scurrying spiders, and completely miss what is on the floor right in front of me—a gooey puddle oozing out from beneath a set of metal shelves. As my stomach does a double backflip with a twist, I point my flashlight at my brand-new Chuck Taylor. I pry it loose—icky-ick-icky-ick. The ooze I'm standing in is red—blood-red.

Chapter 2

But whose shoes left those too-few clues?

"Ohmigoshohmigoshohmigosh."

"What's wrong?" Margaret grabs me by the shoulders and shakes me.

"I—I just stepped in . . ."

"Blood," says Rebecca.

A mere step behind us, Leigh Ann swallows loudly enough for me to hear her. "Bl-blood?" Her voice is barely a whisper.

"Nobody move!" Margaret orders.

I drop my lightsaber, something I have an unfortunate history of doing in stressful situations. Rebecca gasps, and poor Leigh Ann's death grip on my arm is cutting off my circulation as she starts to say a Hail Mary.

"Wh-what is it?" I manage to stammer.

Margaret shines her light on our faces and giggles. That's right—Miss Wrobel is giggling. Margaret will smile frequently, chuckle occasionally. But until this moment, she has never giggled.

"It's paint! Sorry, I didn't mean to scare you more. I just didn't want anyone to disturb the evidence."

"We oughta—" I start.

"Kill you," Leigh Ann says.

"Twice," adds Rebecca.

"Is that so?" Margaret says, stifling another giggling fit and crouching down to find the source of the puddle. "Look, here's the paint can." She points to it, lying on its side behind the bottom shelf.

"Now, since it is still wet, we have to assume that it must have been very recently knocked over. Maybe the someone we're looking for was just here and heard us. Let's survey the crime scene before it's completely compromised."

For someone who supposedly doesn't watch a lot of television, Margaret sure knows all that *CSI* lingo.

"Crime scene? Compromised?" Rebecca sputters. "You just took a month off my life. Someday I'm gonna need that time."

Margaret is already busy "surveying." "See these footprints in the dust? Definitely new." She lifts the overturned paint can and gives it a good shake. The lid is on, but there is a dent in the top, where paint continues to ooze. "Still quite a bit left. It would be empty if it had been knocked over more than a day ago. Ah, I bet that's what they were after." She stretches her neck to get a look at the top shelf. "Cleaning supplies. Whoever it was doing the reaching had to stand on the bottom shelf to reach up to the top. When they did that, their feet must have pushed this can right off the back of the shelf. It landed on that pile of rags, so they never heard it fall."

"Which could explain why a person who's obviously a neat freak didn't pick it up," I say. "Assuming this was our guy—or girl."

"Right." Margaret claps her hands together, shaking off the dust, and turns to Leigh Ann, the "new kid" at St. Veronica's we got to know during our first case. "Okay, based on what we have observed, what do we know about our suspect?"

"Um, he's clumsy?"

"And?"

"He's short. Or she's short. For a grown-up, anyway. I mean, I'm only five foot six and I can almost reach the top shelf."

Margaret nods. "Excellent. And?"

Leigh Ann's face scrunches up. She starts to reach for my flashlight but, after noting its lovely spider-webby coating, turns to me. "Um, Sophie, would you shine that over there, on the floor?" she says, pointing to a spot next to the shelves. She bends over to take a closer look.

"What is it?" I ask.

"Footprints. Kind of small—not much bigger than mine—but they're smooth. Definitely not sneakers."

"One more question," says Margaret. "Right- or left-handed?"

"How is she supposed to tell that from the foot-prints?" Rebecca asks.

"Which hand did he use to grab the cleaning supplies?"

I raise my hand, excited because I think I know the answer. "Call on me! Call on me!"

Rebecca clunks me on the head with her flashlight. "Suck-up."

"Go ahead, Sophie, tell them," Margaret says primly.

I point to the shelves where our suspect has stepped with his or her right foot, and then to a shelf at eye level where a right hand has made a clear imprint in the dust. "Based on the angle of the fingers, he was holding on to this shelf with his right hand . . . which means that he grabbed the bottle of cleaning stuff with his left."

Applause from Leigh Ann and Margaret and a hearty Bronx cheer from Becca.

"There's one big problem with all this," she scoffs. "How do you know it wasn't just the janitor coming down here to get cleaning supplies? Isn't that what he does? He's probably down here getting stuff off that shelf every day."

Leigh Ann beams. "I'm starting to get this detective stuff. Think about the janitor for a second, Becca."

' "What about him?"

"How tall is he?"

"I dunno. Pretty tall. Definitely over six feet. So?"

"Soooo, he wouldn't need to stand on this shelf to reach the top one."

"Ohhhhhh," we chorus.

"Now can we get the heck out of here?" pleads Leigh Ann. "It's going to take a gallon of Cleen and Shinee to get these cobwebs out of my hair."

As we backtrack through the basement, I give a secret wave at my whiskered friend and whisper, "We'll be back."

Chapter 3

Brainiac. Prodigy. Rock band manager. Object of clandestine admiration. Margaret's résumé continues its relentless expansion

There is a crowd at Perkatory, the coffee shop just around the corner from St. Veronica's that is also our favorite after-school hangout, so we don't get our usual cool-kids' table. Instead, the four of us squeeze into a love seat covered with fabric that instantly makes me itchy and fidgety—fiditchety.

"Stop wriggling," complains Rebecca, who is halfway on my lap.

"I can't help it," I say. "This couch is gross. Let me up—I'm gonna sit on the arm."

Rebecca claims my abandoned real estate. "And as long as you're up, why don't you go order for us?" She smiles sweetly and flutters her eyelashes at me.

I bow deeply. "Your wish is my command, O Socially Challenged One."

Leigh Ann stands up and takes me by the arm. "Come on, Soph, I'll go with you."

Leigh Ann and I got off to kind of a rocky start, thanks to my irrational, conclusion-jumping alter ego (who looks exactly like me). You see, there's this boy, Raf, who's been my friend, like, forever. But while we were busy chasing down the clues to find the ring, I started having these I-want-to-be-more-than-friends thoughts. Constantly. And then I just happened to see Leigh Ann's cell phone with his number in it, and I basically totally freaked out. Trust me, if you could see the future supermodel that is Leigh Ann, you would understand why I lost it. But everything worked out—for me! (My knees still go a little weak when I think about how well it worked out.) She forgave me for my little journey to jerkdom, and in the weeks since the Unfortunate Misunderstanding, Leigh Ann and I have become great friends. In fact, it feels like she's been part of our group for ages and ages.

"Expect a little something extra in your cup," I say, pantomiming a spit at Rebecca.

The girl behind the counter is new; she has spiky black hair with a streak of orange, and she's wearing a faded purple NYU sweatshirt. Leaning over the counter for a closer look at my blazer, she reads the crest.

"Ah, St. Veronica's. And the green ones are Faircastle. And maroon is Our Lady of Victory. I had no idea there were so many girls' schools around here. It's crazy."

While she goes to work on our order, I ask her how she likes NYU. One of my many dreams is to live in the Village, go to New York University, and play my guitar in all the cool clubs down there, so a girl in an NYU sweatshirt is a source of valuable information.

She gives me kind of a funny look at first, but then she shrugs. "It's okay, I guess. Is that where you wanna go?"

"Yeah, but my parents are pushing for Columbia. We know a guy who—" I stop myself, deciding she probably doesn't really want to hear about Malcolm Chance's promise to help me get in.

She leans over the counter. "Well, don't go telling everyone, but right now my main ambitions are for this place."

I look around at Perkatory's motley collection of furniture, its peeling paint and impressively grungy floor that is only slightly less sticky than a movie theater's. The place is a dump, but it's our dump—know what I mean? I don't know how I feel about somebody new coming in on her first day and talking about making big changes. "They are?"

"Oh yeah. I mean, this is a coffee shop, right? You've got to have music. Live. Real."

Leigh Ann puts her arm around my shoulders. "It just so happens that we have a band."

I elbow her and shake my head. Actually, what we have is an idea for a band. We've never actually played together yet. "We're just getting started," I say, which is only a little total lie.

"Does this band of yours have a name? Gotta have a great name."

Leigh Ann looks at me. "Do we?"

"Um, no."

The girl sets our drinks on the counter. "Well, how about this—the Blazers. Cool, huh? If you like it, it's yours. A gift. You guys let me know when you're ready for your first gig. I'm Jaz, by the way."

The Red Blazer Girls. The Blazers—I like it.

Back on the couch, Leigh Ann tells the others about Jaz's plan to add live music to Perkatory's menu. "And she said we can play whenever we're ready."

I see one eyebrow go up on Margaret's face. "Who is 'we'?"

Leigh Ann looks at me for support.

"Oh, you know, I've been talking about starting a band for a while," I say. "Me on guitar, Becca on bass. And now we have Leigh Ann to sing. You should hear her, Marg. She's awesome."

Leigh Ann tugs on Margaret's sleeve. "What about you?"

Margaret smiles. "Thanks, but I'm not sure a classical violin is a fit. You guys need a drummer or a piano player. Besides, I just don't have time now that I'm in this string quartet."

My mom, who is Margaret's violin teacher, recruited

her to join a youth string quartet. Mom is prepping them for a big competition over at Juilliard in February—very serious stuff—and they have an aggressively ambitious rehearsal schedule.

"Is that, like, short for Jasmine?" Becca asks, completely out of the blue.

Leigh Ann's head tilts to one side, a quizzical look on her face. "Is what short for Jasmine?"

"Her name. Jaz."

Ahhhhh. Jaz-mine.

Speaking of which, there she is, clearing tables and wiping them down. When she gets to us, she points to Margaret and Rebecca and asks me, "So, is this the rest of the band? Did she tell you guys the name I thought of?"

"Noooo," Rebecca says, looking confused.

"Oh yeah," I say. "Jaz came up with a really cool name for the band. The Blazers. What do you think?"

"That depends," Rebecca says. "Am I gonna have to wear my school blazer when I'm playing? Because that is definitely not cool. Art is supposed to be about expressing individuality, not worshipping conformity."

A month of art lessons in SoHo and suddenly she's a rebellious near teen.

"Jeez, Becca. Who peed in your orange juice this morning?"

"Ugh. I really hate that expression, Sophie," Margaret scolds, holding up her bottle of Orangina and grimacing.

My goodness, aren't we a sensitive and delicate bunch.

I look up to see a Greek god towering over me. He is six feet tall, carrying a duffel, and wearing a school blazer with the St. Thomas Aquinas crest, which I recognize because that's where what's-his-name (oh, that's right—Raf!) goes.

"Hey, Leigh Ann," the god says, the glare from his perfect white teeth nearly blinding me.

And that clunking noise you just heard? That was three jaws hitting the floor as Becca, Margaret, and I all spin to stare at Leigh Ann for an explanation.

"Alex! You're back!" She jumps up and hugs him. "How did you find me? Oh my God, you guys—this is my brother, Alejandro, but everyone calls him Alex. He's a senior at Aquinas. He's been up in Cambridge for a week—some kind of math competition. He's a genius."

"Your b-brother?" I stammer. "I guess you did say you had a brother, but you never said he was—"

"Hi, Alex," Margaret says. "I'm Margaret, and these two are Sophie and Rebecca. Math, huh? At Harvard?"

"MIT," Alex says. "There were kids from all over the country. I mean, I guess I thought I was pretty smart, but the competition—"

"Now you're just being modest," Leigh Ann says. "I can't believe how much I missed you! You just can't go away to college next year—unless I can come, too."

Alex takes a look around Perkatory and at the four of us. "Oh, I think you'll survive. So, you about ready to head home? I'm starving, and Mom's making red beans and rice. Nice meeting you guys—Leigh Ann's told me about you all." He takes his duffel and heads for the door.

"Before you go, Leigh Ann," I say, "can everyone make it to my apartment tomorrow for rehearsal? Becca, you don't need to bring your amplifier; you can just plug into mine. This is going to have to be kind of an 'unplugged' rehearsal anyway. I don't think the neighbors would appreciate us blasting the plaster off their walls."

"Just think," Leigh Ann ponders. "One day, when they're interviewing us on MTV after winning our first Grammy, we're going to look back on this as the moment it all started. The Beatles. The Rolling Stones. Nirvana. Coldplay. The Blazers."

As C. Daddy Dickens would say, there's nothing like having great expectations.

Next door to and at the same slightly-below-ground level as Perkatory is Chernofsky's Violins. Anton Chernofsky, the proprietor, grew up in the same town in Poland as Margaret, and the two of them Polish-dish away whenever she stops by. Even though her family left Poland when she was seven, her parents still speak Polish at home, and Margaret tells me that she still dreams in Polish most of the time.

On the way out the door of Perkatory after the historic creation of the Blazers, Margaret pulls me down the steps to the violin shop.

"Yippee," I say with mock enthusiasm.

"Two minutes. I want to tell Mr. Chernofsky about the quartet. He'll be excited. And besides, you love Mr. C. as much as I do."

All too true. Completely guilty as charged. The guy is like everybody's perfect grandpa.

"And there's always the possibility that he'll have another amazing violin he'll let you play, right?"

"You never know," Margaret says, grinning. Two weeks earlier, Margaret had one of those life-changing moments in the violin shop. Mr. Chernofsky came out from the workshop cradling a violin in both hands. "One day," he said, "I hope to make a violin as fine as this."

Margaret's eyes got all buggy when she read the tag hanging from the neck. "Is this really . . ."

Mr. Chernofsky nodded. "He purchased it recently at an auction. He brought it in for a little work."

"Whose is it?" I asked.

"David Childress's," Margaret answered, her voice all whispery.

"Huh." I was painfully aware that I should know who that was.

"He's first violin in the Longfellow String Quartet. He's . . . incredible!"

"Margaret, are you blushing?"

"N-no. That's ridiculous."

"What do you think, Mr. Chernofsky?"

He held his thumb and index finger far enough apart

to slide a single sheet of paper through. "He is very handsome."

"And this old thing is his?" I said. "Gotta tell ya, doesn't look that great to me." The varnish was rubbed off completely in some places, and there were dents and dings all over it.

"Only the sound matters," Margaret reminded me. "And this probably sounds like—Mr. Chernofsky, can I play it? Please? Just for a few seconds. I . . . I just . . . it's so . . ."

She faltered! Margaret! She was so flustered at the idea of playing her idol's violin she couldn't complete her thought.

The wrinkles around Mr. Chernofsky's eyes deepened as a smile slowly curled his lips, and he moved toward the door. After hanging the CLOSED sign in the window and locking the door, he handed Margaret the violin and chose a bow from a rack.

She took a deep breath, played a couple of notes to warm up, and then glided ever so gracefully into Schubert's "Ave Maria."

It is hard to explain just how beautiful the sound was that came pouring out of that dinky chunk of lumber, but I can tell you this: my geese were bumping and I saw actual tears in Mr. Chernofsky's eyes.

When Margaret finished, she just stared at the violin while we applauded.

"So, Mr. C.—what do I have to do to make this my own?" she finally asked, laughing. "Sweep, polish, scrub—you name it. Heck, I'll wipe the dust out of all the violins with a Q-tip. Honestly, I've never heard anything like it. Even your mom's violin, Soph. Hers is nice—I mean, it's a thousand times better than my violin—but this one's in a different universe." Reluctantly she handed it back to Mr. Chernofsky, who hung it on a wire strung across the workshop.

"One day, Margaret Wrobel. One day," he said, eyes twinkling.

As we step inside the shop, the warm, inviting smell of freshly sawn wood greets us even before Mr. Chernofsky ambles out from the back room. With his bushy gray hair and beard, he looks a bit like a skinny Santa Claus. His denim apron is covered in sawdust that is the color of a perfectly poached salmon; a few specks always manage to embed themselves in his beard, and a nub of yellow pencil habitually peeks out from behind one ear. Pumpkin, the shop cat, who is the color of her namesake, rubs her wiry body around my legs vigorously enough to trip me. When I reach down to pet her, my white socks are covered in orange hair.

"Thanks, Pumpkin. Go rub on Margaret now." She does as ordered. The cat loves everybody.

"Ah, Miss Wrobel, Miss St. Pierre! Welcome! So good to see you. Come in the back and have a cup of tea."

"Thanks, but no tea today, Mr. Chernofsky," Margaret replies. "I just dropped by to tell you some news—starting tomorrow, I'm playing in a string quartet!

Sophie's mom is going to be coaching us, and I'm going to be first violin."

Mr. Chernofsky beams. "Wonderful! What does your papa say about this?"

"He thinks we'll be playing at Carnegie Hall by summer."

Mr. Chernofsky laughs so loud the small stained glass window behind him rattles in its frame. "And why not? He is very smart, your papa."

Margaret blushes a little. "Well, I don't know."

"Oh, don't be so modest, Margaret," I say. "You know you're good. Mom didn't pick you because you're my friend. You're her best student. She says so all the time. Really, I have to beg her to stop."

"You see? Your friend knows. Your teacher knows. Your papa knows. I know. I have heard you play," Mr. C. says. "And now a surprise! I have something for you. A package—it arrived this morning."

A deep wrinkle forms on Margaret's forehead. "That's strange. Why would somebody send something to me here?"

From behind the counter, he pulls out a sturdy cardboard tube about three feet long and four inches in diameter and points at the label, printed neatly in all capital letters: MISS MARGARET WROBEL, C/O CHERNOFSKY'S VIOLINS, 158½ EAST 66TH STREET, NEW YORK, NY 10065.

"I think someone sent you a telescope," I say.

"Or perhaps a salami," Mr. Chernofsky suggests.

Margaret turns the salami-telescope tube every which way in her hands, examining it from every angle. She shakes it. She listens to it. She even smells it. "Hmm. Kind of lemony. With no return address. Who would even know I come in here?"

"I'm sure all that is explained inside." Patience is a concept I'm not really fond of.

"Wait, who delivered it?"

"Oh, for crying out loud."

"All right, all right. I'll open it!"

She rips off the tape that holds a wooden plug in one end of the tube, and then uses the smallest blade on Mr. Chernofsky's pocketknife to carefully pry out the plug. That is followed by wadded-up newspaper jammed into the tube to protect whatever is inside. After an eternity, she pulls out a thin object about two feet long, neatly wrapped in heavy brown paper. She tears the paper off, revealing a violin bow with about half of the horsehair missing or broken. A note, typed on stiff white stationery, is curled around the middle of the bow, secured with a perky red ribbon, from which an ordinary house key hangs. Margaret hands the bow to Mr. Chernofsky while she reads aloud:

Dear Miss Wrobel,

The recent story in the *East Sider* that chronicled the exploits of your Red Blazer Girls in the successful recovery of the Ring of Rocamadour was of great interest to me. One day, I should like to congratulate you in person, but for now, and for reasons that will be revealed later, I must limit myself to written communication.

Please consider the enclosed bow a gift, a much-deserved reward for locating the ring and turning it over to its rightful owners. You have proved yourself to be an honorable person, and I firmly believe that honor should—no, must—be rewarded. I apologize for the bow's current condition, but I think you will find it to be worthy of your skill and well worth the expense of new hair. Perhaps your good friend Mr. Chernofsky will see his way toward offering you a discount?

Now, a great bow without a violin on which to play it is like a key without a lock, so I offer you the opportunity to care for the violin that is its longtime companion. Note that I say "care for," because no one truly owns a violin such as this; we are mere guardians, protecting it for a time and then passing it on to another worthy caretaker.

When you are ready to take possession of the violin of your dreams, use the attached key to open the door that awaits you, and it will be yours, with no strings attached, so to speak. Read between the lines, and you will find all the information you need to begin your quest. *Do zobaczenia. Powodzenia.*

> Sincerely,
> A friend

I hold the paper up to my nose. "You're right, it smells lemony—like the dish soap my mom uses. What do these two words mean?" I ask, pointing at the two non-English words at the bottom of the page.

" 'I'll be seeing you' and 'good luck,' " Margaret says. "In Polish." And then, with a knowing smile, she looks up at Mr. Chernofsky. "Ahh. This is from you, isn't it?"

For a second, it looks as if he's going to confess that the letter and the bow are his handiwork, but then he turns his palms up and slowly shakes his head. "I've never seen this bow before, and I swear to you, I did not write this."

Margaret squints at him, still dubious. "Are you sure?"

He continues to deny all knowledge.

"Try the key in the front door," I say. "Betcha ten bucks it fits."

Had anyone taken the bet, I'd be ten bucks poorer: the key doesn't even come close to fitting in the lock.

"There just aren't that many people who know I come here. Even if someone knows I play the violin, there are lots of violin shops around the city."

"And why send it here?" I remark. "Why not send it to the school? The article mentions St. V's."

Mr. Chernofsky's eyeglasses are pushed down his nose, and he is examining the bow with a magnifying glass. "Ahh. This is a very nice bow. Well made, and quite old. I will put new hair on it for you and see what I can learn about it. My assistant will research it for you."

"Your assistant?" asks Margaret.

"Yes, a young man who learned violin making in . . . well, it doesn't matter where he learned his trade. I have taken him on quite recently. He is very skilled, and also clever, much like you girls. He says he will teach me to use a computer! You will leave the bow here with me, and I will have it like new for you on Monday afternoon. As for the letter, I'm afraid I can't help you. Quite unusual, even in America, I think, for someone to offer a gift but not tell you where to find it. What is the meaning of these words 'read between the lines'?"

"It's a figure of speech," Margaret explains. "It doesn't mean to literally read between what is written. It's when the words have one obvious meaning and another, more important meaning that is implied."

"Kind of like a semihidden meaning," I add.

"And this reading between the lines will tell you where to find the door for this key? Well, it is a good thing you are such a bright young woman," Mr. Chernofsky says to Margaret.

"Ahem," I say.

"Excuse me. Young women."

That's better. Not always true. But sometimes . . .

Chapter 4

When life gives you lemons . . . write secret messages?

Maybe this is just a coincidence, but when we get off the train at Eighty-sixth Street, a too-thin-looking man with sunken cheeks and a straggly Abe Lincoln–ish beard is playing one of those done-to-death songs from *The Phantom of the Opera*. Margaret drops some change in his open violin case and smiles at him. He nods once and keeps right on playing. But as we step through the turn-stiles, he plays the opening notes of "Ave Maria," and the hair at the back of my neck stands up. I sneak a peek back at him on my way up the stairs, and he gives me a little wink. What the—

Saturday is a busy day at *la maison de St. Pierre*. Mom has back-to-back-to-back beginning violin students in the morning. Margaret is hanging out with me, waiting for her turn. Dad is in our kitchen, experimenting with some kind of fruit tarts. You'd think someone who spends half his life cooking in one of the best restaurants in town would find something different to do on a day off. When I ask him about this, he glares at me with a wire whisk in his hand and turns on his most outrrrrrraaaaaaaageous French accent.

"Eet ees because I am Frennnnch, you seeellly girl. Any other ridiculous questions?"

"Uh, yeah. Do we get to eat any of this stuff, or is it just for looking?"

"That depends." He dips two spoons into a bowl full of neon yellow custard and holds them in front of Margaret and me. "If you can eat this without smiling, you can have your choice of anything on the counter."

"Piece of cake."

He looks at me like I have two heads. "There is no cake! These are tarts." Even though he's lived in the U.S. for fifteen years and speaks perfect English, expressions like "piece of cake" or "easy as pie" tend to throw him.

"That's just an expression, Dad. Sheesh!"

"Just taste."

I shovel the stuff into my mouth. Must. Maintain. My. Composure. But alas, assaulted by the thermo-nuclear explosion of lemony goodness that is bombarding my tongue, I lose all control over my facial muscles and grin like the happiest idiot. And to Dad's infinite delight, so does Margaret.

"Rohmigosh," she mumbles.

"Not bad, eh?"

"What is this?"

"Un secret."

"If you had enough of this stuff, you could rule the world," I marvel.

Dad puts his index finger to his lips. "Shhh. Perhaps this is my plan."

"More, please," we both chime.

He holds up a tray of minitarts filled with the world-domination lemon custard. We each take two and run back to my room to lick, chomp, gulp, and sigh.

Now, if it were a normal Saturday, I would be getting ready for my guitar lesson, but my guitar teacher is out of town with his own band, which means I have time to spend with some new friends—courtesy of a recent trip to the bookstore with Mom. I lie on my bed, trying to decide between *I Capture the Castle* and *The Princess Bride*. Castles, princesses. Hmm. And the third book is *The Little Prince*. Wonder what all that royalty stuff means?

Meanwhile, Margaret is browsing in my library, her index finger gliding across the spines. She stops on a thin paperback titled *Get Started in Magic!*

"Magic?" she asks.

"Oh, I went through a phase a couple years ago," I explain. "It started after I read a biography of Houdini."

She leafs through the pages, then stops at a chapter entitled "Writing and Reading Secret Messages."

"Hmmm. This is interesting." She stands up, obviously excited. She switches my desk lamp off so that she can look directly at the lightbulb. "This is only sixty watts. Do you have anything brighter?"

"I don't know."

"We need a bulb that's at least a hundred watts. And it has to be the old kind. Compact fluorescents don't get hot enough."

"Well, I don't know how many watts it is, but there's a bulb in my parents' room that gets really hot. It's a halo-something, I think."

"Halogen. That will work. Come on, show me."

We go into Mom and Dad's room and turn on the light. Margaret unfolds the letter and holds it really close to the bulb—so close that a little wisp of smoke comes off the paper.

"It's catching on fire!"

"It'll be okay," she says, examining the paper. "Look, there's writing—between the lines of typing."

"Oh, I see, the heat from the bulb made it appear. Very James Bond, Agent Wrobel. What does it say?"

"There's a date . . . January 17, 1959 . . . and something about a story in the *New York Standard* . . . page three, column five . . . and then . . . 'If you are still interested, visit King Jagiello after school Tuesday. He will have something for you.' Well, that's crazy," she remarks.

"What makes it work—the invisible ink?" I ask.

"Lemon juice. You write the message using a little paintbrush or a toothpick, and it's completely invisible until you heat it up."

"But how on earth did you know it was there?"

"I think it was the combo of your magic book and

your dad's fantabulous lemon tarts," she explains. "Remember how we noticed that the package at Mr. Chernofsky's smelled lemony?"

"Yep."

"And I will never criticize your book-hoarding habit again."

"I am a collector."

Margaret doesn't say a word, but that one raised eyebrow of hers sure does.

I take another look at the letter. "So, what's the *New York Standard,* anyway? I've never heard of it."

"Me neither. But there used to be a lot more newspapers in the city than there are now. We're going to have to make a library run. Somewhere in New York, they have every issue of every paper on microfilm. The hard part is going to be waiting until Monday to go check. Unless . . ."

There's no procrastinating in Margaret's world.

"Unless I go down there now, right?"

"You're not doing anything, are you? Why don't you call Leigh Ann? Her dance class will be over by now. She can meet you there. I already know where to find King Jagiello, so you get to figure out the other half of the message. Just be back here by six for the Blazers' first practice. Come on, Soph! You don't want to wait all weekend to find out, do you?"

The thing is, she's right. And I should probably put some distance between myself and the tarts. I call Leigh Ann and ask her to meet me on the library steps.

"I'll be easy to find," I assure her. "I'll be the one reading . . . between the lions. Get it?"

A long silence, and then, "No."

"There are two big lions outside the library. I'll be between them. Reading. Between the lines."

More silence.

"Never mind."

Is it possible that I'm not as clever as I think I am? Nah!

I tell Leigh Ann all about the letter on the way to the microfilm room. She shakes her head in disbelief. "What is it with you guys and mysterious letters?"

"Well, the package and the letter are actually addressed only to Margaret. And it's not like we went looking for it. We were just minding our own business, and the next thing you know—"

"You're reading microfilm in the library on a beautiful Saturday afternoon with me instead of having a picnic in the park with Raf."

A picnic? Me and Raf? Hmmm.

With a little help from a female library employee who refuses, or is unable, to smile, we locate the January 1959 microfilm for the *New York Standard.* Leigh Ann scrolls through lots of stories about Fidel Castro (how old is that guy?) and the Cuban revolution, and a crazy one about two dogs that survived eleven months in Antarctica after some Japanese explorers abandoned them. When she gets to the seventeenth, we go right to page 3. In the fifth column, there is a story, just a few paragraphs, about an incident from the night before that happened at Carnegie Hall. It seems this German violinist, Horst Wurstmann (hereafter known as Sausage Guy), was appearing as guest soloist with the London Symphony Orchestra. During the intermission, he stepped outside the entrance on Fifty-seventh Street to cool off and have a smoke, leaving his violin unattended in his dressing room. He said he was outside for no more than three or four minutes, and when he returned, his violin, bow, case, and a black cashmere overcoat had all vanished. Although several other musicians were in the area at the time, no one saw anyone entering or leaving the room, and a search of the hall "proved fruitless."

Apparently, Sausage Guy refused to answer any other questions, but the article quoted a violinist who said the violin was made in Italy in the early nineteenth century and was likely worth "twenty to thirty thousand dollars." The police investigated but "admitted to having no solid leads."

Leigh Ann scoffs at the last part. "A guy walks out of the place carrying a violin and wearing a long black coat? You're telling me nobody saw that?"

"True, but whoever it was probably went out a back door," I say. "I wonder why they took the coat?"

"One word: cashmere."

"Ahh. Good point." The girl knows her luxury fabrics.

"I wonder if it was ever found." She scrolls down to

the next day, and the day after that, and then through the films for February, March, and April, but there is no mention of the stolen violin. "This could take all day. Let's look online."

After printing out the page from the newspaper and returning the microfilms, we log on to one of the library computers. Leigh Ann types in "stolen violin Carnegie Hall 1959," and we start going through the results. One site is a collection of information about stolen musical instruments of all kinds, from all over the world. Musicians are supposed to check the site before they buy an instrument—especially an old one—in order to make sure it isn't stolen. There are hundreds of violins listed, everything from cheap student models to a Stradivarius worth an estimated two million dollars. It takes a while, but eventually we find it:

#216 Violin once owned by Horst Wurstmann (Ger., 1918–1967), unknown maker, believed to be Italian, possibly an early-19th-century copy of an earlier instrument

Provenance: Unknown prior to Wurstmann

Description: No photo available. No label displayed inside violin. Dimensions and construction details are typical of those of Italian master violin makers of 17th and 18th centuries. Bow is stamped "JSB" near frog.

Date/Location Stolen: January 16, 1959, New York, New York, USA

Insurer: Uninsured

Estimated Value in 2008: Unknown

Contact: NYPD

"What's 'provenance'?" Leigh Ann asks.

"I think it means its history, like who owned it before. So the police never solved the case."

Leigh Ann smiles as she realizes the significance of that statement. "Wait a minute. Whoever wrote to Margaret and gave her the bow . . . they want us to find out that this is the violin in the letter?"

"Which means they must be the one who stole it," I say. "Or they know who did. Boy, wait until Margaret hears this! Early nineteenth century. If it was good enough for this Wurstmann guy to play at Carnegie Hall, it must be amazing. She is going to freak."

And wouldn't that be something to behold?

Rather than taking the subway back uptown, we decide to walk so that we can go by the sea lions at the Central Park Zoo—something that Leigh Ann, who lives in Queens, doesn't get to do that often. I use the alone time with Leigh Ann to ask about Alex, her disturbingly hot brother.

"So, um, what's the story with Alex? Is he really a genius? And why didn't you ever say anything about him? Does he know Raf?"

"I doubt it. I mean, Aquinas is a big school, and he is a senior. I can't imagine he knows a lot of seventh graders. And I don't know if he's really a genius, but he's pretty smart." Then her eyes get a little watery. "A lot smarter than me. Kind of like everyone else I know."

"Leigh Ann—what's the matter?"

And suddenly her face is like Niagara Falls. I guide her onto a park bench and try to calm her down.

"Gawd, I'm so sorry, Soph. It's just me being stupid. I'm all right. Really," she sobs. She's standing, trying to pull me to my feet.

But I'm not budging. "We're not going anywhere, Ms. Jaimes, until you tell me what's going on." I pull her back down onto the bench and dig through my pockets until I find a napkin from Perkatory so that she can blow her nose.

"You must think I'm crazy," she snuffles.

"Well, no, but you always seem so . . . together. I've just never seen this side of you. So, are you going to tell me what's up? Or am I going to have to tickle it out of you?"

At least that gets me a smile.

"Is it your brother? Are you bummed 'cause he's going away to college next year?"

"I can't believe I'm saying this, but part of me is kind of glad he's going," she admits. "He's always been 'the smart one,' and the older I get, the dumber I feel around him. You don't know how lucky you are, being an only child. But then I feel all guilty about that because he is my brother and I do love him. And when he's gone, I really do miss him like crazy. Man, I sound like a psycho."

"Actually, that sounds relatively normal," I say. "But I don't have any brothers, so I don't really know how you're supposed to feel about them."

"All the way through elementary school, I was never the smartest kid in my class, and all my teachers would always say, 'But you're still a good student'—and I always knew what that meant: 'not anywhere near as good as your brother.' I actually transferred to St. V's to get away from all that. And then I meet you and Margaret and Becca, and once again I'm not even close to being the smartest. You guys, it's like you know something about everything. The only thing I'm good at anymore is dancing. And I'm probably kidding myself about that; maybe I'm not really good enough at that, either. What if I'm just . . . good-average?"

I have to laugh at that one. "Leigh Ann, if you think you're not a good dancer, then you really are crazy. I couldn't do the things you do in a million years. And neither could Margaret. Or Rebecca, for that matter—she stinks! Seriously, Rebecca Chen dancing is like a fish flopping on a pier. You're a great dancer. As far as the smart thing, I've just been around Margaret longer, and some of her brains have maybe just rubbed off. I'll be honest: I don't know if you're smarter than Margaret. She's a freak of nature. But is that really what's bothering you? Because if that's all—"

Leigh Ann blows her nose again. "N-no," she blubbers. "That's not all. It's everything else, too. My life is falling apart."

"What are you talking about? I thought you liked it at St. V's. And now we're getting the band started—"

"No, that's not it. I love St. V's, and you and Margaret and Becca are the best. That's the only part that's normal."

"So, what's the problem?"

"Everything's changing too fast, Sophie. I mean, I'm not even thirteen, and I feel like life is just zooming right past me. First my parents get divorced, and now Alex is going off to college. And he's going to go someplace far away, I just know it. Then, this morning, I found out my dad got a new job—he's moving to Cleveland. I'll hardly ever see him. He'll probably get married again and . . ."

By now she's full-on sobbing, and I'm trying desperately to help her. As I put my arm around her, I remember a conversation we had about the legend of the Ring of Rocamadour—how St. Veronica is supposed to visit you in your dreams and answer your prayers. The night we found the ring, Margaret had asked each of us what we wanted, and Leigh Ann didn't even hesitate before saying she wanted her parents to get back together.

"First of all, your brother won't be leaving for college for almost a year, and second, he could go to NYU. Or Columbia. Or a million other places that are a mere bus ride away. And your dad? That is a bummer—but it doesn't mean you're not gonna see him, or that he's gonna get married again. Cleveland isn't even that far away, and he'll want to stay close with you, right?"

As I say this, I realize I have absolutely no idea how

far away it is. I know it's one of those cities in one of those states in the middle somewhere.

"But why do things always have to change?"

It is a very good question. And I haven't a clue.

"I—I'll have to get back to you on that one."

Chapter 5

In which yet another of my deeper, darker secrets is revealed

Back at our apartment, Mom has pushed all the living-room furniture against the walls so that her neophyte (another visit to my orthodontist, another perusal of *Reader's Digest*'s "Word Power") quartet can sit in a semicircle facing her. They are playing a familiar-sounding piece of music, and considering this is their first time playing together, they sound amazing. (I suspect that the Blazers will not come together quite so quickly.) Their backs are to us as Leigh Ann and I tiptoe past and into my room, where Rebecca is waiting, sprawled across my bed, reading *Seventeen*. She looks up when we come in.

"Hey, loooosers."

"Nice to see you, too, my dearest darling pal," I say.

"Funny, I didn't take you for the *Seventeen* type," says Leigh Ann, who has pulled herself together follow-ing her emotional meltdown in the park.

Rebecca makes a shocked face. "But I just had to

find out which celebrities have 'the look' and which ones have . . . *dun, dun, dun* . . . lost it! Besides, it's Sophie's."

"Where did you find that?"

"Right where you left it. Under your mattress."

I feel myself blushing—a biological response that I am trying desperately to learn to control.

"Back up a second. Why are you hiding *Seventeen*?" a confused Leigh Ann asks. "Won't your parents let you read it?"

Rebecca bounces up and down on my bed like an evil monkey. "She doesn't want Margaret to know she reads it. Isn't that right, Sophie?"

"Yeah, well . . ."

Leigh Ann looks more confused than ever.

"Because Margaret makes fun of her for reading it," Becca reveals.

"But . . . but why?"

Becca shrugs. "Because she's Margaret. If it isn't lit-er-a-tooooor, she won't read it."

"Oh, she's not that bad," I say. "I know it's stupid to hide it from her, but I don't want her to think I'm turning into . . . well, you know."

"Me?" Leigh Ann asks, piling on. "I read *Seventeen*."

"That's not what I meant," I say. "There's nothing wrong with *Seventeen*. I just don't want to—"

Rebecca shakes her head sadly. "You know, you shouldn't let her weirdness—"

"Well, what about you, Becca? Snooping around my room."

"Yeah, I thought I would at least find something with Raf's name or 'Mrs. Sophie Arocho' written out a hundred times."

Phew. So she didn't look everywhere.

"Where were you two, anyway? Your dad said something about the library? On a Saturday." She makes that *tsk-tsk* sound. "And then your dad bet me I couldn't try some lemon goop and not smile—and I lost. I had to wash dishes. Totally worth it."

Leigh Ann, doing a little snooping of her own on Margaret and the kids out in the living room with Mom, says, "Whoa. Who is that?"

"Who is who?" I ask.

"The boy," she answers. "Playing that big violiny thing. He just turned around for a second. He's so cute— in kind of a dorky-preppy way."

Rebecca crowds into the doorway to peek out the crack, so I get up on tippy-toes to look over her shoulder.

His hair is down to his shoulders, and all I can see of him is the back of his head. "Come on, turn around," I urge.

They reach the end of the song they're playing, and I can barely hear Mom talking to them, pointing something out on the sheet music, when Becca gives me a hard shove and we all fall face-first into the hall.

"Sophie!" Mom cries.

"Oh, um, hi," I say, smoothly covering.

"Everyone, meet my delicate daughter, Sophie, who knows she is supposed to be quiet and absent when I'm giving lessons. And these are her friends Rebecca and Leigh Ann. They all know Margaret. Girls, this is Denise, Stephanie, and Andrew."

We ignore the girls. Leigh Ann is all too right—Andrew is cute.

"Hey," we all say, with the same weak, giggly wave.

He smiles and waves back, hitting Margaret in the head with his bow as he does it. Cute, but klutzy.

We run like fools back into my room and slam the door, collapsing on the bed together.

"Yowza."

"Holy smokes."

"Hot-tieeee."

Hey, I never said we were mature.

Margaret joins us in my room a few minutes later. She tries to be mad at us for acting like morons, but she can't hold back a smile when she remembers Andrew whacking her in the head with his bow.

"You should have seen how red he got. Reminds me of you, Sophie."

"So, what's his story?" Leigh Ann asks. "Where does he go to school?"

"Davidson. It's on Ninety-first, over by East End. Very expensive."

"So he's a snobby rich kid," says Rebecca. "Probably has his own chauffeur."

"Just because he goes to Davidson doesn't mean he's rich," I say. "Or snobby. They have scholarships and stuff."

"Actually, I think he might be rich," Margaret says. "He lives on Park Avenue. But he seems okay. Nice."

"And gorgeous?" Leigh Ann adds, giving Margaret a little nudge, seconded by Becca.

For a second, I think I might get to see Margaret Wrobel blush AGAIN, but she recovers just in time to suppress it. "Nice try, Miss Jaimes. But it will never work. For I am a Dashwood and he is a Willoughby."

Rebecca looks puzzled. "You're a dashboard?"

"Dashwood. *Sense and Sensibility*? Jane Austen?"

I nonchalantly kick that *Seventeen* a little farther under my bed.

"I'll bet Andrew knows what she means," Leigh Ann teases.

But Margaret fires right back. "Maybe you all would if you spent your time reading something . . . not glossy." She gives me a knowing smile.

Our stock rises, however, when we show her the printout of the article from the *Standard* and the other information we uncovered on the stolen violin.

"Wow! You did great. What if this really is the same violin? If it was worth twenty or thirty thousand dollars in 1959, do you guys have any idea what it would be worth today? At least ten times that much. We have to find this guy. Tuesday, after school, let's go to the park to visit King Jagiello."

"Who's that?" Rebecca asks.

"Oh, you've seen him a million times," says Margaret. "He's over by Turtle Pond and Belvedere Castle."

"That homeless guy with all the magazines and the dog? Is that his nickname or something?"

"No," Margaret says, laughing. "He's a statue. You know, the man on the horse, with two swords crossed over his head."

"Ohhh! You mean Aragorn!" Rebecca's *Lord of the Rings* obsession is legendary.

"Jagiello was a Polish king. A real king, Becca. Fifteenth century."

"Hey, guys?" I say. "Let's play." I take my guitar out of its case, plug into my amp, and start strumming some chords.

Enough of kings and violins and bows and boys. It's time for the Blazers to rock.

Chapter 6

In which we discover some semistrange things. But believe me, there are stranger things to be discovered in Central Park. Much stranger

"Rock" isn't the most accurate verb for what we did. We sort of, kind of, more or less played two really easy songs. How easy? Let me just say one of them involved a young woman named Mary and her pet *ovis*. (Means "sheep"— just a little Latin I picked up in our last case.) But the whole idea of the first rehearsal was to learn how to play together, and we accomplished that—to some degree. We also figured out that we absolutely need a fourth Blazer. Leigh Ann's singing, my guitar, and Becca's bass are not giving us all the sound we want. Becca says she might have someone to play drums—a girl from her art program—but just to be safe, we post notices on the bulletin boards in the school cafeteria and Perkatory on Monday: WANTED: DRUMMER OR KEYBOARD PLAYER FOR

ALTERNATIVE, SERIOUS BAND. MUST BE WILLING TO RE-
HEARSE AFTER SCHOOL AND ON SATURDAYS.

Within a few hours, I have messages from, oh, Elton
John, Ringo Starr, Chris Martin, all of the Jonas Brothers, Hannah Montana, and SpongeBob SquarePants
(doesn't he play ukulele?).

After school, we make two stops. First, the Nineteenth Precinct, on Sixty-seventh Street, to see what we
can learn about the Carnegie Hall theft. It must be a
slow crime day in New York, because the officer behind
the desk goes out of her way to help us. After six phone
calls, she summons us back to her desk.

"Officially, the case is still open," Officer Grogan announces. "But the guy down in the archives says no one
has pulled the file in at least twenty years. Said there
was about an inch of dust on it. He did have one piece of
information that might be helpful, though. He says
there's a private investigator's card stapled to the file,
along with a note saying to contact him if anything about
the case comes up. Here ya go—I wrote down the poop
on the PI for you. Course, you gotta remember, this is
twenty-five, thirty years ago. The guy's probably retired . . . or dead. Sorry, but them's the facts."

"Why would a private investigator be working on a
case like this?" Rebecca asks. "According to the records
we found, the violin wasn't insured. Isn't it usually the
insurance company that hires them?"

Officer Grogan shrugs, both shoulders reaching past

her ears. "Who knows? Maybe this German guy—what's his name, Wurstmann?—thought the good ol' NYPD wasn't workin' hard enough." She leans over closer to us. "Which, between me an' you, is not the craziest thing I ever heard. Like we have time to go trackin' down a violin belongin' to some fancy-schmancy musician."

Our second stop is the violin shop, where we are introduced to Mr. Chernofsky's new assistant, a Mr. Benjamin Brownlow III, who insists that we call him Ben. (I generally have a problem addressing adults by their first name.) My first impression is that he is warm and friendly like Mr. Chernofsky, but different in practically every other respect. Mr. C. is a big man—six feet, with wide shoulders—his hair and beard always appear to be in need of a good cutting (or at the very least, a combing), and I have yet to see him when he's not completely covered in sawdust or wood shavings. On the other hand, Ben is kinda short, and everything about him is absolutely fastidious ("Word Power"!). If I had to guess his age, I'd say early to mid-thirties; he has perfectly trimmed hair and is—how do you say it?—clean-shaven. Even his shop apron, which he wears over a crisp button-down shirt, looks ironed.

Ben knows about the letter and has already done a very careful inspection of the bow, which he runs back to the workshop to retrieve. On his way in, he stops and wiggles a lever on a wall heating vent, finally pushing it all the way to the right.

"Sorry, it's a little stuffy in here. We had this vent closed because we had a customer in this morning test-driving a violin, and the music was blasting in the coffee shop next door. Sounded like we had the Stones right in here with us. We couldn't provide no customer satisfaction." He smiles at his own joke, but he's the only one.

I place the tips of both index fingers on my temples, close my eyes, and hum loudly, as if in a trance. "I see three letters on this object you are holding. I see a *J* . . . I see an *S* . . . and I see a *B*." I open my eyes to see a dumbfounded look on Ben's face.

"How did you . . ."

"Because I am secretly smart. Something I keep well hidden in order to blend in."

"She read it on some Web site about stolen instruments," Margaret tattles.

"Well. Mr. Chernofsky told me you girls were good, but I am still very impressed. You are exactly right. They're a little worn and hard to read, but if you look right here with this magnifying glass, you can make out the letters *JSB*."

He is vibrating with excitement as he tells us, and I sense his disappointment when we don't respond with instant enthusiasm.

"Is—is that a good thing?" I ask.

He smiles broadly, revealing perfect white teeth. "It's a great thing. The 'JSB' stands for John Simon Berliner, quite a well-respected bow maker in his day.

I'm ninety-nine percent certain that this is the real McCoy. A violinist in the Philharmonic has one, and I'd like to check it against this bow to be absolutely sure." He takes what looks like one of those big English pennies out of his pocket and starts flipping it in the air and catching it, over and over.

We're all thinking it, but Rebecca is the first to blurt it out: "How much is it worth?"

"If—if it's authentic, it's worth eight to ten thousand dollars. Maybe a little more."

Rebecca's mouth drops open. "Shut up! For a bent stick with a little hair glued onto it?"

"Becca! Jeez!" I say.

"Oh, it's all right," he says. "But it is a once-in-a-lifetime find."

Margaret smiles at me and holds up two fingers. Some of us already have one once-in-a-lifetime find under our belts.

"So, what do we do?" Leigh Ann asks.

"Well, how about we make a promise right now not to tell anyone about this, at least until we figure out what is going on with the violin," Margaret says. "If this is a stolen bow, somebody, somewhere, is the rightful owner, not me. But if we turn it over to the police now, we'll never hear from the mysterious, letter-writing possible thief again. So, if it's okay with Mr. Chernofsky, I think we should keep quiet and the bow should stay here. Promise? Everyone?"

"What if they try to stick those bamboo shoots under my fingernails?" Rebecca asks.

"Wear gloves," Margaret says.

Rebecca nods. "I can do that."

Tuesday morning, about ten minutes before the homeroom bell. Margaret and I have our faces buried in her English notebook, studying for a test in Mr. Eliot's class, when we realize Sister Bernadette is hovering over us, arms crossed. She looks—let's go with "not pleased."

"Ladies. My office."

Yikes. Now what?

We take our usual seats and prepare ourselves.

She closes the door and remains hovering. "Two items. One, I have not been able to locate the key to the storage closet you asked me about. The janitor remembers someone borrowing it a while back, but it wasn't returned to him. So we're still looking. And two, something very strange happened in this school building over the weekend. Our . . . mystery man, or woman, has apparently run out of things to clean, so they have turned to making improvements."

"What—what kind of improvements?" I ask.

"Painting. Imagine my surprise yesterday when Mrs. Hoffeldt waltzes in here to thank me for having her room painted. She's been after me for three years to have it done. I, of course, had no idea what she was talking about and looked like someone unaware of the goings-on in her own school. And you know what, girls? I do not enjoy looking like that. So I have brought you in here in the hope that you're going to tell me that you're making progress in your investigation. That you're this close to solving my little mystery. Now, what do you have to tell me?"

In situations like this, I let Margaret do the talking.

"We're definitely getting close," she says. I try not to look too surprised; if what Margaret is saying is true, it's news to me.

"How close?"

"Give us a few more days, and we'll have an answer for you."

"All right, a few days, but then—"

The bell rings, and we are saved—for now.

The four of us enter Central Park at Seventy-second Street, and a few minutes later we are standing before King Jagiello. With his two swords crossed over his head, his armor, and the massive horse, it's not hard to see why he puts Rebecca in mind of *The Lord of the Rings*.

"Let's look for the message," I say. We walk around to the back side of the pedestal, looking up and down the enormous statue, and—spot it! Rebecca pries a small envelope out of the gap between two slabs of marble. It is three inches square, and if there were any doubt about who it was intended for, MARGARET is printed in neat capital letters across the front.

We crowd around her. Inside the envelope are two sheets of matching stationery. One sheet has a grid with six rows of squares drawn on it. Two of the rows contain eight blank squares, while the other four have eleven. Additionally, eleven of the blanks are outlined with much darker lines.

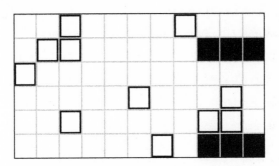

The other sheet has this typed message:

Dear Miss Wrobel,

If you are reading this letter, clearly your aptitude has not been exaggerated. Now that the preliminaries are out of the way, we can get on with uniting you and your violin.

In honor of the many great orphaned characters in literature and our shared love of great books and clever puns, I present your first challenge.

When you complete the grid, fill in the blanks in the following statement with the words formed by the letters in the bold squares:

The _____ player lives on _____ Street,
but not in Apt. 4M
and not at no. 127 or no. 301.

Here are the clues:

Pennies on a baseball diamond
Miss Doe's beneficiary
What the bartender asked the martini drinker
She's certainly Anne
She longs for the coldest season
One fewer than nine filled French pastries

When you have solved it, write the two
words in red chalk on the sidewalk in front of
the violin shop, and await your next clue.
Powodzenia!

Margaret has that nobody's-going-to-outsmart-me
look in her eyes, and I immediately know that she won't
rest until this case is wrapped up tighter than a pair of
size-eight feet in size-six shoes.

Rebecca pounds her head against the marble
pedestal. "NO! NO! I can't take another one of these!"
She shakes a fist at the sky. "Stop torturing us!"

"Calm down, Rebecca," Margaret says. "It's just a
little fun with puns. They're kind of like crossword puzzle clues. And he told us what the category is—all six of
these clues are for the names of literary orphans. We can
probably solve the whole thing in half an hour."

"Tell you what, Becca," I say. "I'll bet you a

macchiato ice cream soda that Margaret can solve number four right now, in under sixty seconds." I choose number four because I already know the answer.

Rebecca slaps my hand. "You're on. No helping."

"What do you think, Margaret?"

"Start the clock."

"Ready?" Becca says. "Go!"

Margaret thinks out loud: " 'She's certainly Anne.' A character named Anne who is an orphan. I'm thinking Anne from *Anne of Green Gables* seems like the obvious choice. She's an orphan. But 'Anne of Green Gables' is way more than eleven letters. Seventeen, actually. Concentrate! What is her last name? Lennox? No, that's Mary from *The Secret Garden*. Nolan? Nope."

"Thirty seconds!" Rebecca shouts.

But I don't think Margaret even registers her.

"Come on, Margaret. Think. 'She's certainly Anne.' Certainly? Definitely? Obviously? That must be part of the clue. Anne Certainly? Anne Definitely? She's Anne for sure. Oh my gosh . . . it's 'surely.' Anne Shirley!"

I pat her on the shoulder. "Seventeen seconds to spare. Thank you, Margaret—I'll think of you as I slurp my delish macchiato."

"Double or nothin' on the first clue—the one with the pennies," Becca counters.

"Ready, Margaret?" I say.

Margaret closes her eyes. "Pennies. Cents. Coins. Abraham Lincoln. Baseball diamond. Bases. What's another name for a baseball diamond? Ballpark? A field. A field of pennies. Penny Field. Wait, what are pennies made of? Copper! A copper field. David Copperfield! Wait, that's too many letters. Maybe just his last name, Copperfield. Is that the right number of letters?"

"Eleven, right on the nose," I say. "Two down, four to go."

"Okay, one more time," Becca says. "But it has to be this one: 'Miss Doe's beneficiary.' "

The Brain That Can't Be Stopped makes the leap into hyperspace. If she were a computer, there would be flashing lights and whirring motors—maybe even some kind of siren blaring—but instead there is absolute silence.

Becca starts a confident countdown. "Ten . . . nine . . . eight, just you wait . . . seven . . . six . . . five, my dream's still alive . . . four . . . three . . . two, and Sophie's through—"

Suddenly Margaret's eyes open wide, and I catch a hint of a smile. "Jane Eyre."

Leigh Ann elbows me. "Is that right?"

I shrug. "Beats me."

Margaret nods. "It's right. Jane's heir. Beneficiary and heir—same thing. And Miss Doe is Jane."

"Wait a second," Rebecca says. "Who is this Jane person?"

"Okay—you know how the police call an unknown man a John Doe, and an unknown woman is a Jane Doe? If a Miss Jane Doe had a beneficiary, that person would also be known as Jane's heir. Jane Eyre, E-y-r-e, is another literary orphan. Charlotte Brontë's, obviously."

"Oh, of course, of course," Rebecca fake-concurs.

On our way back down to Perkatory to collect on my bet with Rebecca, my phone rings. "Now who wants to join the band? Kurt Cobain? Jimmy Page? Hell-o . . . Uh-huh. This is Sophie . . . Uh-huh. You play the drums. I see. And what did you say your name was? . . . Bingo? . . . Uh-huh. Look, you nitwit, it's Ringo, and I've already heard from you. This was only funny the first eighty-seven times. You can just . . . just b-i-n-GO!" I hang up.

"Um, Sophie," Rebecca starts, a strange look on her face. "By any chance, did that person have an unusual accent?"

"Yeah, how'd you guess? Really fake-sounding."

"Her name is Mbingu. M-b-i-n-g-u. She says the *M* is almost silent. It means 'sky' in Swahili."

"Oh."

"Remember, I told you about the girl from my art program? That's her. She just moved here from Africa a couple of years ago. We were talking about music, and I said how we were probably going to be looking for somebody, and she said she thought she could do it. And since, unlike everyone else on the planet, I don't have a cell phone, I gave her your number."

I am scum. "What should I do? She probably hates me."

"Call her back," says Leigh Ann. "Like, right now. Tell her you've been getting all these prank calls."

I call the number and it rings a few times, then goes into voice mail. "Should I leave a message?"

"Yes!" everyone shouts at me.

"Um, hi, uh, Mbingu. This is, um, Sophie, the girl you just called. I am really sorry about, you know, me being, um, a jerkwad. I'm not like that, honest. It's just, um, ever since I put up that sign, I've been getting a million prank calls, and, uh, well, Rebecca forgot to tell me you'd probably be calling. So, like I said, I'm really sorry. Please give me a call back. I definitely want to talk to you about the band. Um, I guess that's it. Call me. Please. Bye." I look at my friends to see what they think.

"You sounded sincere," says Leigh Ann, putting her arm around my shoulders. "If it were me, I would call you back."

"Ladies, I believe the appropriate thing to say right now," Margaret says, "is *hakuna matata.*"

Or maybe—another one bites the dust?

When I get home, I attempt to do my homework, but I just can't stop thinking about Leigh Ann and everything she's going through with her family.

But how to help? How, how, how, how, how . . . hey—Malcolm!

Monsieur Chance and I already have a history of clandestine activity, conceiving and then carrying out a secret mission related to the recovery of the Ring of Rocamadour. I leave him a message, and he calls back a few minutes later.

"Ah, Mademoiselle Sophie! What a nice surprise to see your name pop up! What can I do for you?"

I explain the situation with Leigh Ann's brother. "So, I'm not sure there's anything you can do, but maybe you know a math or engineering professor who could tell Alex how great Columbia is, so he won't go to Harvard or someplace even farther away."

"I think I know just the person for the young man to talk to. She hosts a fantastic math seminar for a few stellar high school students every year—it's four weekends in January and February, I believe. Everyone who goes absolutely raves about it. Life-changing stuff, apparently. Send me an e-mail with his information, and I'll put in a good word."

"That would be awesome."

"Anything else I can do for you?"

"That depends. Know anybody in Cleveland?"

•

Chapter 7

Éclairs for breakfast? *C'est fantastique!*

It's my fault, really.

I made the tragic mistake of falling asleep without turning my phone off, and sure enough: *Brrring! Brrring!* It is precisely six o'clock in the morning.

"Mmmffff. What?"

"I got another one," she says.

"Rruummpphh. Another what?"

"Number six of the orphan puns. After I finished *Great Expectations,* I started reading *Bleak House*— back when we were still trying to find the ring. And remember that clue we had with all the names? Esther Summerson and Mr. Guppy? Sophie, wake up! I can hear you snoring."

"I do not snore."

"Like a buzz saw. So I'm looking at this new clue, 'One fewer than nine filled French pastries.' Obviously, it's eight something, right? But eight what? What is a French pastry with filling? An éclair! Eight éclairs." She tries again, a little louder, as if lack of volume is the problem. "Eight éclairs."

I sit up in bed, trying to get my eyes to focus. "Eight éclairs. Right. Wait a minute. Who has eight éclairs?" Mmm . . . éclairs. Rich, gooey, chocolatey . . . must have them.

"Ada. Ada Clare. She's an orphan character in *Bleak House*. Eight letters."

"That's great, Margaret. Now, do you actually have any éclairs?"

"I'll be over in a few minutes. I want to catch Mr. Eliot at Perkatory first thing so that he can let us into the school. Bring your flashlight."

Exactly eleven minutes later, there is a knock at my door.

I wave off Mom's offer of toast and juice, telling her that Margaret has promised to buy me a breakfast éclair.

"This all seems remarkably familiar," I say to Margaret on the way down in the elevator. "Solving clues, early-morning phone calls, meeting Mr. Eliot at Perk. Will we be staking out a confessional or x-raying any old paintings for hidden messages?"

"No. Well, I don't think so, anyway. But I did talk to our old friend Malcolm last night. We're meeting him at a bar this afternoon."

"A bar?"

"You'll see. It'll be fun."

• • •

Mr. Eliot is at his usual table in Perkatory with his usual copy of the *Times*. When he sees us, he gives us a salute and a sly smile.

In addition to being our English teacher, Mr. Eliot has played an important role in our career as detectives. The whole ring affair got started when I looked out a window in his classroom and screamed (I had my reasons). He has helped us out with clues, smoothed over our troubles with Sister Bernadette, and on one memorable morning, let Margaret stand on his back (we had our reasons).

"The Misses Wrobel and St. Pierre, out on the streets before dawn. What are you two up to? Off to prowl the secret tunnels in Grand Central Station? Interrogate the doorman at the Plaza?"

I shove Margaret up to the counter to buy me a hot chocolate and an éclair.

The new girl, Jaz, takes our order. In contrast to her chipper attitude of a few days earlier, she looks and sounds like she would rather be just about anywhere else on the planet—in the sewers of Rangoon, tied to an anthill in the Australian outback, in that creepy, snake-filled chamber in *Raiders of the Lost Ark*—anyplace other than here.

"Here ya go," she says, setting our food and drinks on the counter, sans smile.

"Thanks, Jaz," I say. "You'll be happy to hear that the Blazers had their first rehearsal the other day."

"That's great," she says with absolutely zero enthusiasm.

"Maybe she's just not a morning person," Margaret whispers as we walk away.

Mr. Eliot folds up his paper when we join him at his table. He raises an eyebrow at my éclair. "In training, St. Pierre?"

"Yep." I take a big, squishy bite, and I am suddenly wishing I had a bagel instead. When I'm an especially good girl, my daddy makes me the real thing; this is nothing more than a tube-shaped doughnut in disguise.

"What brings you two out so early this fine morning?" Mr. Eliot asks.

Margaret squints at him. "Can we trust you?"

"Like Abel trusted Cain."

Margaret tells him about the package, the letter she received at Mr. Chernofsky's, the bow, and what Leigh Ann and I learned about the Carnegie Hall theft.

Mr. Eliot whistles. "Holy mackerel. A hot violin!" He leans over and whispers, "How many people know about this?"

"Mr. C., Ben, the four of us, and you," Margaret says. "And whoever sent the letters."

"What about Malcolm?" I ask Margaret. "What did you tell him?"

"Only that we were working on something new. I didn't give him any details. But I trust him."

"I would think so," Mr. Eliot says. "Now, where do

you go from here? Even if this Wurstmann is dead, and there's no insurance, somebody must have a legal claim to the violin. Have you talked to the private investigator yet?"

"Can't. He died ten years ago," Margaret answers. "But you see, there's also this other case we're working on. It's for Sister Bernadette. And we really need to get into the school before it's open. Can you let us in, pretty please?"

"We wouldn't ask if you weren't the bestest English teacher who ever learned me," I add.

Behold the power of mostly sincere flattery.

The basement door is unlocked, and I push it open, cringing as the hinges creak. I shine my light down the stairs so that anything scampering, skittering, or skedaddling can get the heck out of my way. Then I tiptoe into the abyss.

When I get to the bottom step, Margaret whispers in my ear, "Do you hear that?"

At the far end of the basement, behind several stacks of cartons and old chairs, I hear what sounds like a chair being dragged across the floor, followed by a few sharp raps, as if someone is hammering on something metal. And now—he's whistling. ("Beethoven," Margaret whispers.) Still, we creep forward, flashlights clicked off. Our view of the area is obstructed, but as we get closer, the glow from a candle or a small lantern throws a flickering shadow of what looks like some horribly deformed giant on the back wall. In fact, the room itself seems to be alive as Margaret, with one hand on the small of my back, pushes me gently but persistently. "Just a little closer. We're—"

CRASH! Just behind us, a stack of metal chairs falls over. Margaret's fingernails dig into my arm as the noise goes on and on, seems to pause for a breath, and then continues for a few more seconds, till—*poof!*—the light is gone, along with our giant.

I exhale.

Gone where? I wonder as my breathing and heartbeat resume.

"There's no way he slipped past us to go up the stairs. Either there's another way out, or he's still down here," Margaret says, blazing a trail with her flashlight. "Hel-lo! Is anybody there?"

I squelch the urge to shush her—a person who breaks in and upgrades just doesn't seem that scary (just weird). We go to the workbench, covered with paint cans and old rollers and brushes, some of which are still wet after being rinsed out.

"Boy, is Sister Bernadette gonna be ticked off," I say.

"Which means we're going to be in for it. We have to catch this guy." Margaret walks toward the back corner of the room, shining her light on the wall, the ceiling, the floor. Stopping next to the shelves where I stepped in the paint, she kneels down to get a close look at the floor.

"What?" I ask.

"Somebody cleaned up that spilled paint, even your

footprints. But see these marks on the floor? These shelves have been moved. Here, give me a hand."

Despite its size, the shelf unit is surprisingly easy to move when we put our shoulders into it and pivot the thing on one corner. I shine my light at the wall behind it, and—voilà!—one mystery is solved. At about waist height is a metal door about two feet square. I recognize it because Margaret's dad, who is the super in their apartment building, once showed us an identical door in his basement office. It is an old coal chute, from the days when the school had a coal furnace. Margaret grasps the handle and gives it a twist, and—a blast of fresh air hits us in the face, and we realize we are looking out into the alley behind the school. From my vantage point, I can see the back of the school, the church, the convent, Elizabeth Harriman's house, a row of four more townhouses, and the building where Perkatory and Chernofsky's Violins are located.

"What's this for?" I ask, tugging on a rope tied to a metal strap that is screwed into the back of the shelf unit.

Margaret nods with admiration. "Oh, he's a clever one, isn't he? After he climbs out, he reaches back in and pulls on this so that the shelves cover up the door."

"But where did he go?"

"It looks like the only way out of the alley without going through another building is that narrow space between Mr. Chernofsky's and that townhouse with the nice garden." She pulls the door shut, and then we push the shelf unit back into place. "There. You can't even tell we found the door."

"Unless he's hiding somewhere out there, watching us right now," I say, creeping myself out. "We need to get out of here—first bell is in a few minutes," I warn.

Margaret grunts in agreement. "Well, we may not know who or why, but at least we know how he's doing it."

Personally, I'm in favor of telling Sister Bernadette so that she can just weld the door shut and be done with it, but Margaret just has to know the who and the why—so we'll sit on this, for now.

And in the meantime, if another room or two get painted, let's hope he picks a nice color.

On our way to Spanish class, I duck into the bathroom to check my phone for messages. (Yes, I'm aware that using my phone on school property is against the rules. Confession is next week.) Still nothing from Mbingu, but I do have a really sweet text from Raf, who wants to know if we're actually going to see each other in person ever again. See, we have a very modern-modem relationship: we talk on our cell phones, and we text. Beyond that, our relationship is still . . . becoming.

I mean, Raf is definitely more than a friend. But a boyfriend? That sounds so . . . not yet. And my dad has absolutely forbidden me even to say that word. The fact is, with Central Park being the geographical obstacle it is, our actual personal contact is pretty minimal, which is probably the reason my parents haven't objected too much—so far. When I tell Margaret about Raf's text message and sigh woefully about the complications that go along with a long-distance relationship, she bops me a good one on the forehead.

"Soph, he lives a mile away."

"Technically, that's true, but in Manhattan, a mile across town is like fifty miles anywhere else. The Upper West Side might as well be in Albany. And you know how I hate crosstown buses."

"Still, if you want to see him . . ."

"I'll see him Saturday, after guitar. We're going to a movie. I have to pick this time, and I'm actually kinda nervous. When it's his turn, he always finds these amazing old movies that I would never watch if it weren't for him. Last week, we saw *The Ghost and Mrs. Muir*—I went through, like, a box of Kleenex. It was soooo good."

"I can do a little research if you want," Margaret offers. "We'll find a movie without any beheadings. Hey, why don't you have him meet us after school today—down at the St. Regis Hotel on Fifty-fifth? We're seeing Malcolm there, remember?"

"Actually, you didn't tell me exactly where. I've never actually met anyone at a bar."

"It's the King Cole Bar. The back wall has a mural painted by Maxfield Parrish in 1906. I've always wanted to see it, so this is the perfect chance."

"Are you sure they're going to let us in?"

"Malcolm said he'd take care of that. Becca has to go home right after school, but I'll check with Leigh Ann to see if she can come—if that's all right with you."

"Why wouldn't it be?"

"Oh, I just kinda remember how you were when you thought Leigh Ann liked Raf. It cost me a fortune in ice cream."

I wave off the very idea. Me? Jealous? *C'est impossible!*

(But the ice cream part is undeniable.)

Chapter 8

Bartender, another round for my friends!

Raf is waiting for us outside the entrance to the St. Regis Hotel, leaning against the wall in his khakis, navy blazer, and green and gold striped tie. Oy. I'm not exaggerating—I literally have to hold on to Margaret when I first see him.

For Margaret's sake, and because the entrance to the St. Regis is kind of intimidating, we keep the PDA to an absolute minimum. A hug. A quick hand squeeze. Inside my red wool blazer, my heart is ker-thumpin' and I suddenly feel a little . . . sweaty.

A few seconds later, we spot Malcolm and Leigh Ann strolling down the sidewalk. Together they're wearing enough plaid to outfit a Scottish wedding party. With plenty left over for napkins.

"Hey, isn't that—" Raf starts.

"Malcolm Chance," I say.

"And Leigh Ann," Margaret adds. "You remember Leigh Ann, don't you, Raf?"

I dig a pointy elbow into her ribs.

Malcolm gives Margaret and me grandfatherly hugs, and shakes Raf's hand. "My, you're all looking well. A veritable vision in vermilion. Elizabeth will be jealous when I tell her I've seen you." He winks at me. "Leigh Ann and I have been having a nice chat about her brother, Alejandro. Apparently, sharp minds run in the Jaimes family."

A uniformed doorman holds the door open for us as we enter the hotel lobby, which is beautiful in that don't-touch-it-it's-too-too-perfect kind of way.

"How is Elizabeth?" Margaret asks. "Any news for us?" Since the conclusion of the ring case, Malcolm and his ex-wife, Elizabeth Harriman, have been "seeing one another" again, a development that I find quite ironic. After all, the first time we met him, I thought he was a total creep, and Elizabeth gave him a hearty Bronx cheer as she practically kicked him out the door of her townhouse.

Margaret's inquiry puts a cryptic little smile on Malcolm's face. "Always the detective, eh?" he says, not answering the question. At all.

Hmmm.

He leads us to the entrance of the famed King Cole Bar. There are only a couple of people in the bar, so he motions for us to come in for a better look at the mural on the wall behind the bartender.

"Now, what can I get everyone to drink? Then we can sit and you can tell me what you are all up to."

"I would like a martini," Margaret announces, straight-faced.

Malcolm laughs out loud. "Oh, would you, now? How about something that won't get me thrown in jail?"

"Okay, I don't really want a martini; I just want to hear what the bartender says when someone orders one."

"And I'm sure you have a very good reason for wanting to know that."

"An excellent reason."

"It's settled, then. I'll have a martini. Purely for the sake of research."

"Of course," says Margaret.

Raf, Leigh Ann, and I sit at a table and listen while Malcolm and Margaret get the bartender's attention.

"Yes, sir. And miss. What can I get for you?"

"Four piña kid-ladas," Margaret says.

"And for you, sir?"

"A martini."

We all swivel our heads to catch what comes next. What does the bartender say to the martini drinker?

"Olive or twist?"

Malcolm asks for two olives and then looks over at Margaret, whose head is tilted back, staring off into space.

Across the table from me, I watch Leigh Ann. First comes a smile, then her mouth opens in an oh-my-God-I-know-this expression. "Of course. Charles Dickens. Again. It's always Dickens!"

"Is anybody else confused?" I ask.

Raf and Malcolm raise their hands.

Leigh Ann explains. "Don't you get it? The question he asked was 'Olive or twist?' Now say it faster."

"Oliveortwist. Ohhhh! Oliver Twist!" I shout. Dickens, he loved his orphans.

Margaret hugs Leigh Ann, who looks like she might just spontaneously combust with pride.

"I love that story," Leigh Ann gushes. "Last year, I was Nancy in the musical *Oliver!*"

Rebecca, who has sneaked up behind me, whispers in my ear, "What did I miss?"

"Becca! You made it! I thought you had to babysit," I say.

"Eh. They're fine on their own. No—I'm kidding. My mom came home early and said I could come. Course, I didn't tell her I was going to a bar."

"Well, Miss Jaimes here just solved another clue," I say. "The bartender said 'Oliver Twist.' "

"Of course he did."

Margaret then turns to Malcolm. "I guess you deserve an explanation."

Over two rounds of sticky-sweet piña kid-ladas and one martini, she fills him in.

"The story about a violin being stolen from Carnegie Hall sounds vaguely familiar," Malcolm says. "Sounds like you girls have stumbled your way into another quest for lost treasure."

I have to agree—it all seems a very strange coincidence. Is someone playing a game with us?

"What's the next step?" Raf asks.

"There's still one more of these rows to fill in," Margaret replies, unfolding the paper with the grid drawn on it. She reads the final clue: "She longs for the coldest season." Then she says, "When we get that, we'll have the two words that go in the blanks. Then we write those on the sidewalk in the park and wait for the next clue."

Raf takes the paper from Margaret. "So you have everything except number five? I'm guessing 'she longs for' means 'she misses,' and the coldest season seems pretty simple: winter. The problem is that 'Mrs. Winter' and 'Miss Winter' are both too short. You need eleven letters."

All of a sudden, Becca puts on her sassy face and says, "Last night I dreamt I went to Manderley again"—with an accent straight out of Bensonhurst (a neighborhood in Brooklyn, for you non-Gothamites).

Raf's face brightens. "I think you're right, Becca. Mrs. de Winter. Like 'misses the winter,' but with a Brooklyn accent. She misses da winter."

"Who is this Mrs. de Winter?" Leigh Ann asks.

"She's in a book called *Rebecca*," Becca says. "I saw it in the Strand Book Store one day and just had to have it because of the title. I never finished reading it, but I did watch the movie."

"I didn't even know there was a book," Raf says. "I've seen the movie a few times. It was one of my grandfather's favorites. Laurence Olivier and Joan Fontaine. Grandpa was hot for her."

I smile inwardly, knowing that it's only a matter of

time before Raf and I will be sharing a tub of popcorn and holding hands as the opening credits for *Rebecca* roll.

"The girl in the story doesn't even have a first name," Becca adds. "She's just Mrs. de Winter."

"And she is the second Mrs. de Winter, as I recall," Malcolm adds.

"If the girl in the story doesn't have a name, then who the heck is Rebecca?" I ask.

"Rebecca is the guy's first wife," Raf says. "The first Mrs. de Winter. She's dead."

"She's dead? Then why is the book called *Rebecca*? Shouldn't it be *What's-Her-Name*? And where is Manderley?"

"I'll explain it later," Raf promises.

Good enough.

Meanwhile, Margaret fills in the remaining blanks on the grid, which now looks like this:

"The letters in the outlined boxes are P-I-A-N-O-H-E-S-T-E-R. 'Piano' and 'Hester.' The piano player lives on Hester Street." Margaret looks up, smiling proudly.

"And that means something to you?" I say.

"Is that even a real street?" Leigh Ann asks.

"Hester Street is on the Lower East Side. As for what this all means, however, you're on your own. Your young brains are far sharper than mine, I'm afraid." Malcolm gulps down the last of his martini. "Ahhh. But age does have its advantages."

I'm skeptical of Mr. Columbia Professor for Thirty Years' modesty. His brain is plenty sharp.

"This is just one clue," Margaret begins. "If someone really has this violin, they're going to make us jump through many hoops before they hand it over. We're supposed to prove we're worthy of it. I can respect that."

Rebecca corrects her. "I think what you mean to say is that *you're* going to have to jump through some hoops to prove that *you're* worthy."

"Well, I still think there's something fishy about the whole thing," I say. "It's kind of creepy. Either someone's spying on us, or they have someone else doing it for them."

"Suspicious much?" Raf says.

"It's not suspicion if people really are spying on you."

Malcolm roars with laughter at that. "Sophie, I do like your perspective on life. You are truly one of a kind."

"Why, thank you, Malcolm."

I've always thought that one of me is more than enough.

Chapter 9

We have met the enemy, and she is part of our group project

Margaret and I are on the stairs Thursday morning, on our way to Mr. Eliot's class, when we're almost run down by Sister Bernadette barging through the doors from the fourth-floor classrooms. Her face is—well, if she were wearing a red blazer, you wouldn't be able to tell where blazer ended and head began.

"Sister Bernadette! What's the matter?" Margaret asks. I cower behind her skirt. "Don't tell me. He struck again. What was it this time?"

Too stunned to speak, she motions for us to follow her into the fourth-floor library.

Oh my gosh. This place has been transformed into something out of a Jane Austen novel. The cracked, peeling drab green walls have been expertly covered with a pale blue striped wallpaper, all the wood trim around the windows and doors has been repainted in a tasteful soft cream, and here and there on the walls are wallpaper decorations that look like sculptures and paintings. There's even a nice-size matching rug in the center of the room. It's all really quite stunning. And we're stunned.

"Wow," I finally manage to say. "This is beautiful."

Sister Bernadette, she harrumphs.

"No way one person did this in one night," Margaret says, examining the workmanship. "Look at it. It's perfect."

And then she sees it. There's a new bookcase against the wall near the door, filled with the Harvard Classics—salvaged from our moldy basement. For a second, I think Margaret is going to . . . cry? She was heartbroken back in September when Mrs. Overmeyer, the librarian, told her those books were in storage. Slowly, lovingly, she runs her hand over the spines of the books, stopping only when she gets to a gap near the end of the fiction volumes.

"Volume eighteen is missing." She thinks for a moment. "Dostoyevsky. *Crime and Punishment.*"

I knew that. Of course. Really. You dare to doubt me?

"Girls, I want answers!" Sister Bernadette says, and storms out.

A few minutes later, Mr. Eliot stands before his podium and utters the two words that strike a note of dread into our hearts: "group project." Teachers love them; we hate them. Yes, I know, I know: there are going to be times in life when I'm going to have to work with other people, and I'm going to have to be collaborative and flexible and learn to delegate responsibility, yadda, yadda, yadda.

Mr. E. loves to use open-heart surgery as an example of a group working together toward a common goal—you know, everyone is responsible for some part of the procedure, and if somebody screws up, the patient kicks it. Well, my argument is, if the anesthesiologist (let's call her Bridget O'Malley) decides the night before surgery that she absolutely must spend six hours online instead of preparing for the operation, it's not the patient who suffers. It's me.

Though Mr. Eliot is unmoved by our howls of protest, he's at least letting us choose our own groups. Rebecca's not in our section of English, so Margaret, Leigh Ann, and I quickly size up the rest of the class, looking for our fourth. Miss O'Malley, thank God, has found three other unfortunate victims, and strangely enough, everyone seems to be already in groups of four. Fine by us. We are more than happy to divide the work three ways; the extra 8⅓ percent of the labor each is fine by us.

Our joy is short-lived, however, as Mr. Eliot reminds us that there is one girl absent. Olivia "Livvy" Klack. He declares himself to be certain we will be thrilled to have her as our fourth. Here's everything you need to know about Livvy:

Before Leigh Ann showed up, she was the prettiest girl in our grade. Ergo, she hates Leigh Ann.

She hates Margaret with a deep and irrational passion.

She would sell her soul to the devil to be at one of those real Upper East Side private schools instead of having to slum it with us nonrich, unfabulous peons at St. Veronica's.

I open my mouth to protest, but Mr. E. cuts me off. "Don't waste your energy, Miss St. Pierre. Ah, speaking of which . . ."

Livvy strolls into the room and hands a late pass to him with a dramatic flourish. "I couldn't get a cab. It's raining, you know."

We all roll our eyes at each other. A cab. She lives, like, three blocks from the school, for crying out loud.

"Well, I just assigned a little project for next week, and you are going to be joining these girls. They'll fill you in on the details."

"Su-per," she says with the fakest smile.

The project: each group is assigned a punctuation mark and is responsible for teaching the rest of the class everything about it—the rules, the exceptions, and of course, some examples. Mr. Eliot walks around the room with folded pieces of paper in his hand, passing them out. On each paper are two critical pieces of information: the punctuation mark and the date the group must be prepared to present. Livvy unfolds our paper and reads it. "Apostrophe," she says. "Awesome. We're presenting on Tuesday." She sticks the paper in her bag.

"Well, the apostrophe is much better than the comma," I reply. "Those rules are impossible."

"Then I suppose you three just have all kinds of wonderful ideas, being the famous Red Blazer Girls and all. Maybe somebody will write another story about you in the paper—you know, how you girls made learning about the apostrophe just so interesting."

I resist every urge and instead go with: "Jeez, Livvy. All we have to do is make a PowerPoint presentation with all the rules and some kind of handout to give to the whole class."

"Don't forget the 'creative' element," Leigh Ann adds. "Mr. Eliot said we can do anything we want as long as it is creative in some way."

"We have to get creative using apostrophes?" Livvy whines. "This is stupid."

"How about a poem?" I suggest, ignoring her. "Or even better, a song. We could sing it. What do you think, Margaret?"

She sets her mouth into a grim line. "I think it's going to be a long week."

I receive a text from my mom saying Mr. Chernofsky would like Margaret and me to stop by his shop after school (they know each other from violin stuff).

"Welcome, ladies. This was on the floor when I came in this morning," Mr. C. says when we enter, handing an envelope to Margaret. "Someone must have slipped it under the door. No postage, no address, just your name."

This time the envelope is plain, white, and very

businesslike in appearance. Margaret gives it a good sniff, tears it open, and then unfolds a sheet of paper with this message:

> To hear each beat,
> Amid sounds she omits,
> Only names please leave,
> And yearn each return.
>
> Love is valued ever,
> Silence is never tempered,
> While ordered justice begs
> Untold times, nearer obstacles.
>
> Thrilling ovations, newborn games,
> Random analogies, naturally denied,
> Occupied recently, easily silenced,
> Such excesses, xylophone.

To which I can only add: Huh?

And penciled in the margin are the words "Leave your answer on the underside of the park's biggest mushroom."

The lines on Margaret's forehead grow deeper and deeper, and her lips pucker and twist as she reads it and then rereads it. She takes another good whiff of the paper, shakes her head, and hands it to me.

"Do you smell anything?"

"Paper."

"Yep," she says, retrieving the letter from my hands.

"Happy to help," I say. "I do know where the biggest mushroom in the park is, though. You know the statue from *Alice's Adventures in Wonderland*? Alice is sitting right in the middle of a huge mushroom."

"Thanks, Soph. At least if we ever solve the clue, we'll know where to leave the answer," Margaret says.

Ben comes out from the workshop, and even though it is late afternoon and we presume he's been hard at work all day, his apron is still spotless. His shirtsleeves are rolled to his elbows—the first sign of casualness I've seen in him—but further investigation reveals that they are perfectly rolled. I find myself wondering how he accomplished this.

"Hi, girls," he says, tossing a coin high in the air and catching it. "What's new?"

Margaret holds out the letter to him. "Can you do me a favor? Read this, and tell me if it means anything to you."

He scans it once quickly, makes a similar confused face, and then reads it slowly out loud, as if hearing the words will help make sense of them.

"Is this supposed to be a poem?" he asks.

"Allegedly," Margaret says, "this is a clue to help locate the person who has the violin that goes with the Berliner bow. We already solved the first one—something about a piano player living on Hester Street, but not at certain addresses or apartment numbers. But what all that has to do with the violin, I got nada."

Ben hands the letter back to her with a shrug. "Sorry I can't help. Try looking online—type it in and see what turns up."

"He used lemon juice for invisible ink in the first let-ter," Margaret explains. "Well, I guess it was too much to ask that he use the same method twice. Still, there must be other things you can use for invisible ink." She holds the letter up to the light and looks at it from the back and at every angle imaginable.

"You see anything?" I ask.

"Not yet. But let's go to your apartment and take another look at that magic book of yours. And then I sup-pose we should do some work on this goofy project for Mr. Eliot. I can't believe we have to work with that Livvy. I would almost rather have Bridget."

"At least Livvy cares about getting a decent grade. That's about the last thing on Bridget's mind."

"True, but at least we now know that Bridget is com-pletely undependable. We don't know what to expect from Livvy."

Over the next two hours, my bedroom is transformed into a forensics lab as we subject the letter to all sorts of tests. My beginner's magic book had only one more pos-sible invisible ink to check, but a quick online search came up with a few more. First we rubbed the dust from pencil lead over a small section to see if a secret mes-sage had been written in milk. Nothing.

Then we tried a cotton ball dipped in ammonia. Phe-nolphthalein, the active ingredient in Ex-Lax, of all things, makes another great invisible ink. You grind up a tablet with some rubbing alcohol and write your message. Later, when you touch it with ammonia, it turns red. Pretty cool, and worth remembering for the future, but our letter remained stubbornly black and white.

Another good candidate for the ink is laundry detergent, which glows brightly under black light, but the only place we can think of with a black light is the shop on St. Marks Place where I bought my mood ring. It's packed with clothes (polyester!) and albums (vinyl!) from the seventies, along with a collection of those wacky psychedelic black-light posters. However, it's almost time for dinner, and there's no way my mom is going to let me go downtown to some sketchy psychedelia shop on a school night.

"So, tomorrow?" I ask, completely out of ideas. "Maybe something will come to you tonight. It's probably right in front of our eyes. Between the ring and this case, just think of all the clues you've deciphered. You'll get this one, too. And just imagine, an Italian violin—yours."

I thought that would bring a smile to Margaret's face, but she is frowning stubbornly. "I don't know. The more I think about the whole thing with the violin, the more I doubt I'm ever going to get it. And I feel bad dragging you all over town when you're not going to get anything out of it in the end. It's not like the ring—at least there we were doing something really good. We were even bringing a family together. This time it's all for me." She turns away so that I won't see her eyes watering up.

"If it will make you feel better, we'll sell the violin

and split the money, and I'll spend mine on something you'd never approve of."

"Growf."

While I'm trying to translate that, she reads the new text message on her phone. Wait a second—is that a smile I see just before she turns her back on me?

"Whoa, whoa, WHOA!" I say. "No secrets. Hand it over, or ve vill be forced to find other vays to make you talk."

She holds it up, and this is what I see:

Measure 44, affrettando??? A

"Is this another kind of code?" I ask. "And why are you smiling? Fifteen seconds ago, you looked like you got a B on a test."

"I'm not smiling," she says.

I drag her over to the mirror on my wall. "That, my dear friend, is a smile. And you have some 'splainin' to do. Oh my God. 'A' is Andrew."

She nods, still grinning.

"And 'affrettando'?"

"It means 'hurrying' in Italian. Musical term."

"Okay, now explain that," I say, pointing at her mouth. "I've seen these symptoms before. Googly eyes. Perma-smile. Now, where was that? Let me think. Oh yeah—ME! You looooove Andrew."

"That's ridiculous. I hardly know him."

"I can't believe you didn't tell me!"

"Tell you what?"

"That you two had a text-lationship."

"This is, like, our third text."

"How did he get your number? Did he ask you for it? Tellmetellme."

"Actually, that was your mom's idea—in case we had questions for each other between rehearsals."

"Way to go, Mom!"

At that moment, Mom knocks on my door and sticks her head in. "Way to go, me! What did I do?"

"Nothing," Margaret says before I have a chance to leak the legumes.

"Well, it's time for dinner. Margaret, do you want to stay? There's plenty. It's just us girls tonight. Nothing special, hamburgers."

"C'mon, Marg. Stay," I say. "Burgers and ice cream."

Seriously, who could say no to that?

Besides a lactose-intolerant vegan, that is.

"Okay, okay. Thanks, Kate." She recently started to call my mom Kate, which kills me.

"We'll be there in a minute, Kate," I say. "Margaret was just helping me understand something really complicated. Weren't you, Margaret?"

"You two," Mom says, closing the door.

I block the only exit. "So, are you going to go out with him?"

"Let's not get carried away. Three text messages. That's all. And even if I wanted to—and I'm not saying I do—my dad is not quite as open-minded as yours when it comes to boys."

Hmm. "Open-minded" seems like a generous-to-the-point-of-completely-inaccurate description of my dad's attitude on the topic.

"It's not like he's a gangster."

"Let me put it this way, Soph—if Andrew were one hundred percent Polish and Catholic, played for the Philharmonic, and owned Carnegie Hall, I could possibly go out with him when I turned sixteen."

"Eek. Then you need to have a talk with your dad."

The look on her face tells me that's probably not going to occur.

"Two questions. One, do you like Andrew?"

The grin reappears.

"I'll take that as a yes. Two, would you go out with him if you could?"

"It doesn't matter what—"

"Yes or no?"

"Yes."

"There. That wasn't so bad, was it? Now let's eat. I'm going to need lots of energy to figure out how to bring the dashing young Romeo/Andy and his stunningly beautiful Juliet/Margaret together."

"Um, Soph? Could you maybe use a different literary allusion? Things didn't exactly work out for those two."

"Gotcha. Ixnay on the Omeoray and Ulietjay." See, I can code stuff.

Chapter 10

In which a less glamorous use for nail polish is discovered

Two smile-inducing events occur in the cafeteria just before the first bell. First, Leigh Ann breaks the seal of the Tupperware container full of chocolate cupcakes her mom sent in for a Drama Club bake sale, and we help ourselves to another gorgeously unhealthy breakfast. Second, Becca puts her arm around Margaret's shoulders, jangles an enormous set of keys, and says, "Guess what I found."

"Are those the janitor's?" I ask.

"Even better. Sister Eugenia's. Word is that she has a key to every lock in the building."

"Where did you get those? You have to take them back," I say quickly. "You really don't want to mess with Sister Eu."

"Sophie, are you afraid of Sister Eugenia?" Rebecca teases. "She's, like, ninety years old."

"I—I'm not afraid of her. I just don't want her mad at me. Please take her keys back to her." I stand up, because when Sister Eugenia sneaks up on us—which is going to happen—I don't want to be anywhere near those keys.

"Relax, she's at Mass. Guess she must be getting forgetful; she left these in the door to her office. Look at it this way: I'm doing her a favor. If I hadn't taken them, somebody else, someone not nearly as—ahem—trustworthy, would have grabbed them."

"But now that you have them," Margaret says, "you're thinking that you might as well use them, especially if it is to help solve a mystery for Sister Bernadette."

"Exaaactly. Let's hurry."

We gather our book bags and follow Margaret to the basement door. The only flashlight we have is the tiny one on Margaret's key chain, so we go down the stairs in conga-line fashion, hands on the shoulders of the person in front.

"Tell me again why there are no lights down here," Leigh Ann says. "I mean, I know it's the basement, but isn't there electricity?"

"Sister B. says they started rewiring it a few years ago," Margaret explains, "but the electrician disappeared before he finished the job, and they haven't gotten around to replacing him yet."

After quietly winding our way past the junk piles, we come to a stop in front of Mount Textbook, which seems to have grown since our last visit. Margaret tries the door, but it is still locked.

"Maybe you should knock, just in case," Leigh Ann says.

In case what? I wonder.

Margaret raps twice, then puts her ear to the door and shakes her head. "Can I have a look at those keys, Becca?"

I get a second look at Sister's key ring, and a glance at my watch, and start to panic. The ring is about three inches in diameter, so the circumference is a little over nine inches. (That's pi times the diameter, if you're keeping score—I love math.) If there are eight or nine keys per inch of key ring, that means we might have to try seventy or eighty keys before we find the one we need. And in five minutes, we have to be out of the basement, up four flights of stairs, and ready for a Spanish quiz. Numbers don't lie.

Margaret, in the meantime, has yet to try a single key in the lock. She is taking her good old time flipping through them.

"Ah, here we are," she says. "This is it."

I'm dying to know how she knows, but I don't want to slow her down in case she's right. Which, of course, she is.

The key turns easily in the lock, but when she pulls on the door, it doesn't budge.

"Ohhh, I almost forgot. The first lock. Becca, can you take care of it?"

Rebecca holds up her library card. "See, Sophie, I

do use this thing." She then slides it into the space between the door and the frame, and turns the knob. "Ta-da."

Becca pulls the door open a few inches and peeks inside. After determining that it's safe, she throws it open the rest of the way so that we can all see. It's a storage closet, about eight feet long and six feet wide, lined with shelves crammed with more old textbooks—and an army cot with a pillow at the head and a blanket, neatly folded, at the foot. Next to the cot is a low table with a battery-powered lantern, a portable radio, a windup alarm clock, and, Margaret solemnly points out, Dostoyevsky's *Crime and Punishment*—the missing volume 18 of the Harvard Classics.

A suitcase covered with stickers and looking like a prop from a 1950s movie is shoved under the cot, but otherwise, the room is uncluttered and spotless. The shelves have been dusted and the floor scrubbed clean.

"This is cleaner than your room, Sophie," Margaret says.

All too true. "You think whoever sleeps in here is the person doing all the cleaning and painting?"

"Yep. They can use the coal chute to get in and out of the building without being noticed."

"Um, Soph, we really need to get upstairs," Leigh Ann reminds me with a tug on my blazer. "Remember the quiz?"

"She's right," Margaret says, pushing us out the door and locking it with the key. "Here you go, Becca. You'd better get these back to Sister Eugenia. We need to digest all this. *Crime and Punishment.* Not your typical bedtime story. Yet another mystery."

"The mystery I'm most interested in right now," I say as we trudge up the stairs, "is how, with a choice of, like, a hundred keys, you chose the right one on the first try."

"A tiny dot of nail polish on the key. Exactly like the one on the lock. It's a super's trick—and I am a super's daughter. Except my father uses paint."

"Excellent work, Sherlock."

"Why, thank you, Watson."

"Feeling better today?"

"Thanks to you—and the magical healing power of ice cream—I'm ready for anything."

Perkatory is strangely quiet as we order our after-school libations. (I may be developing a piña kid-lada problem. Is pineapple juice habit-forming?) Jaz is in a much better mood than the last time we saw her. A few minutes later, she throws four bags of chips in front of us and pulls up a fifth chair.

"These are on the house. Mind if I join you for a while? It's dead in here today."

"If only you had some live music," I say with a snap of my fingers.

Jaz's face lights up. "Exactly. You are so right. How are the Blazers coming along, anyway? You guys almost ready?"

Becca nearly chokes on her Dr. Brown's. "Um, that would be a no."

"Oh, come on, Rebecca," Leigh Ann says. "We just need a little more practice. We're starting to come together."

"We are?" I say. "I mean, we are."

"Did you ever hear back from that Mbingu girl?" Leigh Ann asks.

"No, and I've left a couple more messages. I must have really ticked her off."

"She's real, I swear," Rebecca says. "I'll call her."

"Well, let me know when you're ready," Jaz says.

Margaret, who is ready for clue business, unfolds the letter that has been tormenting her since yesterday and sets it on the table.

"Okay, we are usually four intelligent girls. No one leaves until we solve this thing. Agreed?"

"What is that?" Jaz asks.

Margaret avoids giving the details about the violin, instead saying only that it is some kind of puzzle we are trying to solve.

Jaz reads the letter and makes the same face everyone else has made. "I'm definitely not smart enough for your school."

"I don't know," Rebecca says. "I've been taking Spanish for two years now, and I just pray I never get lost in Spain or Mexico—or Washington Heights. And they won't even let me into the same English class with these three."

"Oh, please," says Leigh Ann. "What about me? Most of the time when Margaret was explaining all that graphing stuff, trying to figure out where the ring was, I got so lost I started thinking about what color to paint my nails."

I tap Jaz on her arm. "Don't listen to either of them. They're both really smart. And, Becca, I don't know why you're not in our section of English. I mean, jeez, Bridget O'Malley is in there."

Margaret has been ignoring our conversation completely, focused instead on the paper in front of her. "I've looked between the lines. I've read it backward. Every other word. Every third word. If it's a code, it's not like any code I can find anywhere."

"We should take another look at that first letter," I say. "You know, maybe you have to put them together or something."

"Ohmigosh," Margaret says, her eyes racing back and forth over the letter. "That's it." Her head snaps around to face me. "Sophie, you're a genius."

"I am? I mean, yeah, I know. So you think they are connected somehow?"

"What? No, just the first thing you said—about looking at the first letter."

"I am one confused genius."

"Shhh! Listen!" Becca says. She points at the

heating vent next to her on the wall. "I can hear some-one talking through this."

We all lean toward the vent, straining to listen.

"It's coming from Mr. Chernofsky's shop," Margaret whispers. "Remember, Ben said they could hear the music coming from over here. There's probably one furnace in the building, and these air vents go everywhere."

"I think that's Ben's voice," I say.

Becca and Margaret each have an ear pressed against the vent, and Jaz is right between them. Leigh Ann and I give each other the what's-the-big-deal shrug.

"And I'm telling you, this is huge," the voice says. "No, he's gone for the day. Got the place to myself. Remember, I told . . . fiddle in the shop, belongs to . . . that's right . . . the Longfellow Quartet . . . at auction . . . a little digging around . . . nothing about the sale in . . . Childress doesn't know . . . but he likes . . . thinks it might be worth . . . so he has us checking it out . . . [*long pause*] . . . doesn't look . . . special . . . no label inside, but I . . . flexible camera that I can stick in through the f holes . . . nosing around . . . I see it, plain as day . . . by the neck . . . three letters carved . . . *NAF*, Niccolo Antonio Frischetti . . . yeah . . . positive . . . all his instruments . . . front has never been off, so it's not a fake—no one could have done it later . . . bottom line is, with the paper label missing, the only way to . . . be sure it's a Frischetti is to take the front off . . . until my little camera . . . yeah . . . that's the sixty-four-thousand-dollar question . . . quick online search . . . Frischettis sold at auction . . . past ten years . . . to guess, I'd say it's worth—"

A barrage of boisterous boys bangs into Perkatory, making so much noise that we miss the punch line. Ben must have heard the boys, too, because the next thing we hear is the sound of him rattling the handle of the vent control over in the violin shop. And then nothing.

"Well, that was interesting," Jaz says. "And I'd love to sit and chat, but I suppose I ought to take care of my other customers."

We all stare at each other for a few moments after she leaves.

"Too bad that's not the violin we're trying to find," I say. "Sounds like it could be worth a fortune."

"Yeah, Margaret, what would you do if you knew all these goofy clues were leading to something like that?" Rebecca asks.

"Well, I don't think I'd be sitting here with you three drinking sodas and eating chips—"

Leigh Ann interrupts her. "Hey, what was that about Sophie being a genius—right before you heard the voice from next door?"

"That's right! Thanks, Leigh Ann. See, Sophie, I told you I'm losing it. I'm forgetting things from thirty seconds ago." She sets the letter on the table in front of us, smoothing it out with her hands. "Look at the first letter."

I make a face at her. "Uh, Margaret, this is the second letter."

"No, no," Margaret says. "Look at the first letter of each word."

I read the first part:

> To hear each beat,
> Amid sounds she omits,
> Only names please leave,
> And yearn each return.

She copies the first letter from each word of the nonsensical verse across the top of the page:

THE BASSOON PLAYER

"You see it?"

Okay, so maybe I'm not technically a genius, but anyone can see that it reads "the bassoon player."

She copies the rest of the letters:

LIVES IN TWO J BUT NOT ON GRAND OR ESSEX

All of which breaks down into "The bassoon player lives in 2J, but not on Grand or Essex."

"Right in front of my nose all this time," Margaret remarks. "All those experiments. Honestly, Sherlock would rightfully sneer at me."

"*C'est vrai, mademoiselle*, but now we're experts on writing invisible messages. And you just never know when that will come in handy," I say.

On our way home, we walk past the small boat pond and over to the bronze sculpture of Alice, the Mad

Hatter, the Cheshire Cat, and other characters from *Alice's Adventures in Wonderland*, where Margaret tapes our solution under the biggest of the mushrooms.

She crawls out from beneath the colossal fungus and spreads her arms wide. "Bring it on, Mr. Violin-Stealing Tricky-Clue-Writing Weirdo!" she shouts.

Chapter 11

Help! I'm being held captive by a knife-wielding Frenchman. And he's trying to serve me!

The weather on Saturday morning is just about perfect. It's one of those Winnie-the-Pooh-style blustery days with big, dramatic clouds chasing one another across a preposterously blue sky. Margaret is busy practicing scales and getting ready for quartet rehearsal. Rebecca is painting or sculpting something incredible at her art class. And Leigh Ann is singing and dancing her heart out at a studio over on Broadway. Which leaves me with a beautiful morning, a good book, and not a care in the world. I'm up and out of the apartment at a full gallop, ready to soak it all in.

And now, a confession. (No, not that kind—although, come to think of it, I'm probably overdue.) The fact is, I'm glad everybody except me has something to do. I'm ready for a little "me time," something that can be hard to find in a city of eight million potential friends and acquaintances. Within minutes of my mad dash out the door, I am stretched out like a lizard on a sun-warmed rock in the park's Cedar Hill area and diving headfirst into "The Red-Headed League," the second story in the collection of Sherlock Holmes stories that Margaret has loaned me. It's the one where the naive redheaded shop-keeper hires a new assistant, who tells him about this in-credible opportunity for anybody with red hair. But it's all a scam, because—well, I'll stop there. Don't want to spoil it for you.

Two hours later, the sun is behind the clouds, my rock has cooled off considerably, and I begin to wish for a surprise visit from the blanket fairy or for a heavy sweater. I'm gathering my stuff when I see something unexpected. It's Ben and Sister Eugenia (!?) walking to-gether on the path a hundred feet or so down the hill from where I'm sitting. Sister Eu is one of the few nuns at St. Veronica's who still wears the full habit—and I mean the whole enchilada, including the hat—so she is kind of hard to miss, even in New York, where noting tragic fashion choices is a blood sport. Even stranger, she is smiling, no, laughing! I am dead certain I have never even seen her smile before now. I always have a hard time talking to her face to face—I swear she could win a stare-down with a hoot owl. And she's a better lie de-tector than any machine they're ever going to invent. Criminals would be begging for mercy after five minutes in a room with her.

The Dubious Duo sit on a bench with their backs to me, chatting away and drinking coffee from paper cups with the Perkatory logo. Dying of nosiness, I do my best to eavesdrop, but I can't hear them above the constant rustling of the leaves above me. So I wait until their heads are turned enough to identify them both, and do what we modern spies always seem to do. I take their picture with my phone. At least this way I have some proof for Becca, who will never believe it. She is convinced that Sister Eugenia is a nun-bot (think the Terminator) created by a supersecret Vatican organization dedicated to tormenting young girls who roll up their uniform skirts (to make 'em shorter) and wear their blouses untucked.

When I get home, I send the picture, without a word of explanation, to Margaret, who calls me within seconds. She stopped by Mr. Chernofsky's shop after quartet rehearsal to have a buzzing in her violin checked out, and walked in just as Ben was leaving for the day.

"He did seem like he was in kind of a hurry. Just rushed past me and jogged around the corner. I figured he was trying to make a train. Walking in the park with Sister Eugenia, though? I have to admit, I didn't see that coming."

"What's wrong with your violin?" I ask.

"Nothing big. It's an okay violin, but it's not great. Mr. C. is taking a look at it, but he says that for now, I'm probably going to have to live with the buzzing whenever I play an F-sharp."

"Can't you just buy a better violin?"

"Good violins cost a lot of money."

"Then just don't play F-sharp."

"Excellent solution, Beavis."

"Or, I know where we can steal a really nice violin. A Frenchetti."

"Frischetti. Oh, sure, I don't think Mr. Chernofsky would mind. Or David Childress."

"Well, unless Ben told them what he found, neither one of them knows it's a Fren—a Frischetti. So they wouldn't really miss it, right?"

"Your logic, Soph, is almost Rebecca-like. I suspect they'd both mind. I'm sure Ben has told Mr. C. by now and he has told Childress. And besides, I would mind playing a stolen violin."

"Hey, wait a minute. What about the one in the letters? That's a stolen violin. Will you be able to play that?"

"I'll cross that bridge when I get to it."

"So, what do you think about that picture? I mean, who knew Sister Eu was a real person? I was actually starting to believe Becca's Vatican nun-bot conspiracy theory."

Margaret laughs at that. "Becca kills me. She has a theory for everything, usually involving the Vatican or the CIA or Gollum or Voldemort—or all four."

"Which means that Ben must be CIA," I say. "Think about it. It's the perfect cover. Violin shop. Nun friendship. Who would ever put it all together?"

"Well, you, for one."

"Yeah! I mean, indeed I did, my dear Holmes."

My guitar lesson actually gives me hope for the Blazers. At first, I hesitate to tell my teacher, Gerry, about the band because I'm afraid he'll say I'm not ready, but when I finally work up the courage, I get this:

"Go for it, dude. You are totally ready! Get out there in front of some people and play. There's nothing like it. What are you guys gonna play? You writing your own stuff?"

I laugh at that. "We're gonna cover some other bands' stuff for now. Some Ramones. Some Beatles. I've never even tried any songwriting."

"Wait, you telling me you never wrote any poetry? C'mon, who's the guy you were on the phone with when you came in?"

I feel myself blushing. "That's Raf."

"So, write a song about him."

"Seems kind of cheesy."

"It doesn't have to be. I'm not saying it has to be 'You Light Up My Life.' Please, please, don't make it like that. Just write about what's going on in your life. How you feel, what you want, who you want. Give it a shot and bring something in next week. I'll help you with the music part. And bring the rest of the band along. We'll get you guys rockin' before you know it."

I make a promise to try to write something, but deep inside, I have my doubts. It's one thing to play somebody else's songs; spilling my guts about my love life—or any other part of my life—is a whole different story.

Raf is supposed to meet me outside Gerry's apartment after my lesson so that we can hop on the crosstown bus and head for the East Side. When I get out there, he is nowhere in sight. I dig out my cell phone and call him.

"Where are you?" I scold.

"I'm right where I said I'd be."

"I'm right where you said you'd be, and you're not here."

"You're cute when you get mad and put your hand on your left hip like that."

"Say what?" I scan the sidewalk on both sides of the street, but there's no sign of a too-cute-for-his-own-good boy talking on his phone. As I'm standing on the edge of the curb, a scooter almost runs into me as it pulls in to park.

"Watch it!" I shout.

The scooter driver revs his engine, and I turn away, annoyed. "Jerk."

"What did you call me?" Raf says in my ear.

"Oh, not you. Some idiot on a scooter almost ran me over."

"I am that idiot."

I turn around again and find myself staring

openmouthed at Raf, who has taken off his helmet and is aiming that knee-buckling smile of his at me from the seat of the scooter.

"What the—who—how did you—what are you doing on that thing? Oh my God, Raf. Did you steal it?"

"It's my uncle's. He's out of town, and he told me I can use it whenever I want."

"Um, isn't that . . . illegal? Don't you need a license or something? You're twelve!"

"Yeah, but with the helmet on, you really can't tell. C'mon, get on. I have another helmet for you."

"Do you even know how to drive it?"

"How do you think I got here? Uncle Luis taught me. There's nothing to it. Like riding a bike. Except you don't have to pedal, and you actually have to stop at red lights."

"Rafael . . . ," I start, which gets his attention.

"Uh-oh. She's serious. It's 'Rafael.' "

"Do you have any idea what would happen to me if my parents found out that I had been on a scooter with you? For one thing, you would never see me again. They would pack me and my stuff up and send me to a boarding school someplace in another galaxy, like New Hampshire."

"Well then, I guess we'd better be careful," he says. "Just put the helmet on. You don't want to miss the movie, do you?"

"You'll be careful? And park far away from my building?"

"Cross my heart."

I am putting on the helmet, I am throwing a leg over the scooter. "Um, what am I supposed to hold on to?"

"Um, me," he says, pulling my arms around his waist. (If you're keeping score, that makes it Scooter 273, Bus 0.)

And off we scoot!

What a blast! When we get to the East Side, I'm having so much fun that I beg Raf to take one more lap around the park. When the ride is over, I make him park eight blocks from my building, on a street where my parents, or anyone who knows them or me, is unlikely to see us. Thanks to the scooter, we're ahead of schedule. But that's about to change.

Mom greets us at the door. "Hi, honey. You just missed Margaret. Rafael, nice to see you again. Are you hungry?"

I jump in before he has a chance to say anything I'm going to regret. "No, we're going to grab a slice before the movie."

"All right, but I think I should warn you, your father made macaroni and cheese. I'll bet Rafael has never had anything like it. Remember the first time Leigh Ann tried it? She was ready to move in."

Dad comes out of the kitchen waving his favorite knife. "Did I just hear someone turn down my *macaroni au fromage*?" Dad's mac and cheese is nothing like "the orange horror," as he refers to the stuff that comes in a box with powdered (*sacrebleu!*) cheese.

Raf takes a good long look at that knife. The glint of razor-sharp steel and the incredible smell wafting from the kitchen convince him. "Sure, I'll try some."

Dad points the knife my way, squinting menacingly. "Mademoiselle Sophie?"

"*Oui, mon père.* Bring it on." I plunk myself into a chair next to Raf at the kitchen table.

"You will be thrilled you succumbed," Dad says.

Mom sets a plate in front of me. "Oh, Margaret said to call her as soon as you can. Said it's important. And to be sure to tell you that she 'got another one.' "

"Agrnother wab?" Raf asks through a mouthful of macaroni. "Mmm."

"Just eat." After a struggle to dig my phone out of my slightly tight jeans, I call her. "Hey, Marg."

"Where are you? Aren't you supposed to be out with Raf?"

In a loud voice, I say, "At the moment, I'm being held captive by a demented Frenchman with a gnarly-looking knife and an enormous tray of mac and cheese."

"Where's Raf?"

"Oh, he's here, too."

"You know, Sophie, after he tastes your dad's macaroni and cheese, he's going to want to marry you."

Oh, reeeaaallly. Hmm . . . mmm.

"Speaking of that—boy, do I have a story to tell you!" I say. "But I can't tell you now. So, what's your big news? You got another letter?"

"Yep. When I stopped by Mr. C.'s this morning,

there was another note waiting for me. Same as before—no return address, no postage. Just dropped through the mail slot."

"And what challenge have the clue gods chosen for us this time?"

"It's in some kind of code. All symbols, no letters or numbers."

"Weird. I just read that Sherlock Holmes story with the code. 'The Adventure of the Dancing Men.' Is it like that?"

"It doesn't look like that one, but I assume it's the same basic idea—a substitution code. You substitute a symbol for a letter. I just have to figure out which symbols equal which letters. In fact, I may need the book back to see how Sherlock did it. But you'd better get back to Raf and your engagement entrée. Have fun at the movie. I'll talk to you tomorrow."

"Wait a second—just out of curiosity, did Mr. C. say anything about that violin? You know, the one that Ben was talking about, being so valuable and all."

"No, he didn't mention it. That is interesting. I saw it hanging in the back. It still has the tag with David Childress's name on it. I wonder if he knows about the Frischetti initials."

"It seems like the sort of thing he'd know you'd be interested in," I say. "Oh well. I'd better go before my dad decides to invite himself to the movie."

"Eek," Margaret says. "Run, Sophie, run!"

Chapter 12

Where's Vanna White when you really need her?

My movie pick stinks, but I don't really care. The weird part of the evening—okay, the other weird part, after an illegal scooter ride across town, and after having dinner with my parents and Raf—is when we're standing in line waiting to go in the theater and we run into Livvy Klack. She's with a group that includes three other girls from St. Veronica's and some boys I don't know—except for one. That one is Andrew.

"Hey, it's Andrew, right? I'm Sophie. My mom is your—"

"Oh yeah, hi."

"You two know each other?" Livvy asks, incredulous.

"We just met," I say. "He's in this quartet with Marg—" I try to pull the name back into my mouth, but it's too late.

Livvy turns the sarcasm knob all the way up to ten. "You know the great Margaret Wrobel? Gosh, Andrew, what's she really like? Please tell us. Is she as perfect as everyone says? Where is she, by the way? Off feeding the homeless, or reading to the blind, I'll bet. She's just so super."

I know Andrew just met Margaret and all, but it kind of ticks me off that he doesn't do or say anything. He just lets Livvy yammer on and on about Margaret. I suppose it's not fair of me to expect him to defend her, but I can. I get right in Livvy's grille and say, "Margaret Wrobel is a better person and a better friend than you'll ever be, Livvy. You're just jealous because she has about sixty IQ points on you and you know you can't beat her at anything. She'll be first in our class at St. Veronica's, and then she's going to go to Harvard or Juilliard and she'll be first in her class there. And you'll be at Cheap and Mean University, still trying to figure out how to beat her." I take a deep breath. "And at least everything about her is real," I add, staring right at her chest, which seems to have grown a cup size or three in the last twenty-four hours.

I take a shell-shocked Raf by the hand and storm inside to watch the stupid movie.

He doesn't say anything until we are in our seats, sharing a box of Junior Mints. Finally he looks over at me and smiles. "You just make friends wherever you go, don't you?"

I bury my head in my hands. "What have I done? Margaret is going to kill me. Why didn't you stop me?"

"Stop you? I was trying to figure out a way to applaud you."

"What do you think of Andrew?"

"The guy that was with Livvy? I don't know. Who is he again? And what's up with that hair?"

"He's one of my mom's students. I like his hair, but now I'm not sure how I feel about him. Tell me that you would stick up for me if somebody said stuff like that about me."

"Of course. But I've known you for a long time. Didn't this Andrew kid just meet Margaret?"

"Well, yeah. But it just seems—"

"Look, Soph, I think you're thinkin' too much about this."

"You don't get it. Livvy has powerful friends. She can make my life—and Margaret's—miserable if she wants."

"Powerful friends? Has the Mafia taken over St. Veronica's?"

"Trust me, she will get even. The girl can be evil."

I wait until early Sunday afternoon to give Margaret the icky update on Livvy. But other than the immediate impact on Mr. Eliot's ill-conceived punctuation project, she doesn't seem too concerned.

"I wouldn't worry about it," she says.

"But see, she's hated you for years," I say. "She didn't hate me until last night."

"Livvy is all squawk."

Frankly, that's what scares me. God only knows what kind of damage that big mouth of Livvy's can do.

"Anyway, I think I might have a good lead on this new letter," she adds. "I saw Malcolm and Elizabeth at Mass this morning, and we had a chance to chat for a while. Malcolm suggested I talk to Caroline about the newest code. In addition to all the puzzles and math problems her grandfather used to give her, they also used to make up codes and send messages back and forth. She even thought about majoring in cryptography. Since she's going to be at Elizabeth's this afternoon, he said I should drop by with the letter. You want to come?"

"Sure, as long as it's not going to be late. I've been goofing off all weekend, and I need to do some work."

"All right, I'll call Becca and Leigh Ann, too. So turn off your computer and your phone, put your guitar away, and get to work."

"Yeeesssss, Sis-ter Mar-ga-ret."

Elizabeth greets us at the familiar red door of her townhouse with big hugs, followed by more squeezing, gushing, and questioning. (After we recovered the ring and became practically family, I agreed to start calling Elizabeth by her first name, but part of me still struggles with it.) It has been only a few weeks since that amazing night we handed over the Ring of Rocamadour to Malcolm and Elizabeth's daughter, Caroline, but this already feels like a reunion.

And even though I met Caroline just that one time, I feel like I know her. After all, it was her birthday card that got the "treasure hunt" for the Ring of Rocamadour started. Caroline's grandfather—Elizabeth's father—had set up all the clues and hidden the ring as a gift for her fourteenth birthday, but then he died before he ever had a chance to even give her the card. When Elizabeth accidentally discovered the birthday card twenty years later, she turned to us for help, because by then, she and Malcolm were divorced and she hadn't spoken to Caroline in years.

"We simply must have some tea," Elizabeth says. "Malcolm, dear, make a big pot of tea. Flower Power is their favorite."

Malcolm grins at us as he heads for the kitchen. "You see what's happened to me? I'm the new Winnie!"

"Are you going to spy on us like she did?" Leigh Ann calls out after him. Elizabeth's former housekeeper, Winifred Winterbottom—wife of the church deacon that we butted heads with—was always spying on us every time we visited Elizabeth.

"You can count on it," he shouts from the kitchen.

"Oh, that Malcolm," Elizabeth says. "He thinks he is so clever."

"Is he at least a better housekeeper than Winnie?" I ask. On more than one occasion, Elizabeth told us of Winnie's failures as a housekeeper, especially her unwillingness to vacuum under furniture. The horror!

Rebecca is her usual nosy, sassy self and starts her interrogation of Elizabeth. "So, what's going on with you and Malcolm, anyway? Are you going to get back together or what?"

"Becca!" Margaret puts her hand over Rebecca's mouth. "Sorry. She still hasn't completed her obedience training."

"No, no. Don't shush her," says Caroline, laughing. "Actually, Mother, that's a very good question. We're all dying to hear the answer, aren't we, girls?"

Elizabeth maintains her dignity—well, as much dignity as you can maintain when you're wearing lime green riding pants with knee-high boots and a paisley blazer (a typically daring fashion choice for her). "I have no idea what you're talking about," she says, her chin jutting forward.

"Maybe I should ask Dad."

"Don't you dare. Things are just fine the way they are, thank you very much. And let's leave it at that. I've been living on my own for a long time now, and I'm not sure I'm ready for a change. Believe me, I've lived with your father; he can be difficult."

"Unlike you," Caroline says with a teasing smile. "You're always so easygoing. But fair enough—you don't want to talk about it. The children are always the last to know anyway. Now, Margaret, tell me about this letter. Dad told me a little about the new case you're working on."

Margaret sits next to her on the sofa and takes out the envelope containing the letter. "Each clue has been in a different kind of code. The first one was invisible ink that turned out to be simply lemon juice. When you heat it up, it turns brown and you can read it. Then we had a series of riddles, kind of like crossword puzzle clues. All the answers were names of orphans from literature. David Copperfield, Anne Shirley, Jane Eyre. Your dad actually helped with that letter. He took us to a bar—"

"He WHAT?" Elizabeth shrieks. "Malcolm! Come in here!"

Malcolm appears in the kitchen doorway, looking, as my dad would say, like foie gras wouldn't melt in his mouth. "Yes, my precious?"

"Don't you 'yes, precious' me. Did you take these sweet girls to a bar?"

"Not just a bar. The King Cole Bar. I figure if I'm going to corrupt them, it might as well be someplace with a little class."

"It's not like it sounds," I say. "We had mocktails."

"And what about you, Malcolm? What did you have to drink?" Elizabeth asks.

"Now you've got me dead to rights, but it was all in the name of research. I'm afraid the girls made me drink a martini."

Elizabeth snorts. "Ha! Made you. I'll bet."

"Actually, he's sort of telling the truth, Elizabeth," Margaret admits. "I needed to know what the bartender would say when somebody ordered a martini. By the way, the answer is 'Olive or twist?' which was the answer to one of the puns."

"Humph," Elizabeth says.

"And the letter just before this one was in a code so simple I'm ashamed I didn't figure it out sooner. It looked like a twelve-line poem, and I kept looking for something between the lines like the first letter. The poem itself was really just gibberish, but the first letter of each word gave us the clue. That brings us to this next one, which is all symbols. Ever seen anything like it?"

Caroline looks at the letter and smiles knowingly. "Pigpen."

"I beg your pardon," Margaret replies.

"It's what they call a substitution cipher. I think this is the first code my grandfather taught me. It has been around for a long time. They call it the pigpen cipher because each letter is put into its own compartment, kind of like pigs in a pen, I suppose. Here, I'll show you."

On the back of the envelope she draws two tic-tac-toe grids and two large X's. In one of the grids and one of the X's, she makes a dot in each section. Then she adds the alphabet, printing one letter in each of the twenty-six "pens."

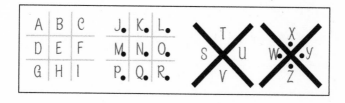

"To write a message, you simply substitute the lines surrounding your letter and the dot, if there is one, for the letter itself." She writes Margaret's name on the envelope and then adds a symbol beneath each letter.

"Pretty cool, huh?"

"That's it? This is easy," Margaret says.

"Well, there is one catch," Caroline says. "Whoever wrote the letter probably didn't arrange the letters in the pens exactly like this. There are lots of different ways to personalize this code, so even if the message is intercepted by someone who understands the basic idea of the code, it will be hard to break.

"Here, I'll show you another example, and this time we'll start with an X. For the X's, you have to decide where to start and which direction to go. The trick is to be consistent—always start in the same place so that you'll remember the sequence. Same thing with the grids—start in a corner and then follow a set pattern. For example, you might do something like this."

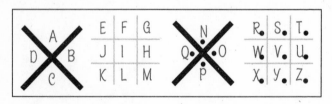

"Now your name would look like this," she continues.

Margaret twists her lips as she ponders the new version. "Hmmm. I see what you mean about the different possibilities."

"When you're setting up the pigpens, do you always have to start in a corner?" I ask.

Caroline thinks for a second. "Well, you don't *have* to, but it's a lot easier to remember that way."

"Let's take a look at the first part of the clue," Margaret suggests.

Elizabeth leans in closer. "Now what?" She looks at me, I look at Leigh Ann, and we all do a unishrug.

Caroline puts her arm around Margaret's shoulders. "Now comes the fun part. First, you try the easy option and hope they used that one."

Margaret starts decoding. "That would make the first word . . . J . . . B . . . E. Somehow, I don't think that's right."

"Ah, but it's more helpful than you think. The most common three-letter word in English is 'the,' which is also commonly used to start sentences. And the letter *E* is the fifth letter in the alphabet, so it usually ends up in the center square of the grid, no matter where the *A* is—

as long as there's a grid in the first position and not one of the X's."

"Well, so far both clues have started with 'the,' " Margaret says.

"Great. So for now, let's just assume that first three-letter word is 'the.' "

"Which means we can also find all the other *T*'s, *H*'s, and *E*'s, right?" Margaret asks.

"Wow, you are good," Caroline says.

After Margaret fills in those letters, Leigh Ann says, "It looks like something from *Wheel of Fortune*."

"I agree," Elizabeth adds. "And the seventh word must be 'street.' "

"Nice work, Mother. I think you're right," Caroline says.

"Makes sense," says Margaret. "The other clues also referred to streets. And that gives us the *S* and the *R*."

With those letters filled in, it looks like this:

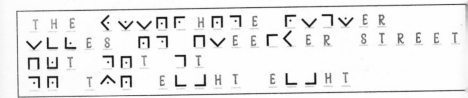

Elizabeth is jumping up and down. "I know another one! The word right before 'street.' If it's in New York, the only thing it can be is 'Bleecker.' "

Caroline and Margaret consider it for a second and nod.

"Way to go, Mother."

Elizabeth sticks her tongue out at Malcolm. "See, Mr. Smarty-Pants? And you're always saying that game show is for simpletons." Under her breath, she adds, "Old coot."

Leigh Ann elbows me; we are both about two milliseconds away from totally cracking up.

With those letters, Margaret now has:

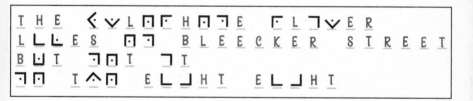

"And now I think you have enough to solve the puzzle," Caroline says. "Start filling in the pens that you know, and you'll see the pattern. Then you just fill in the rest and you're done."

Margaret draws the first grid and neatly prints the *B, C, E,* and *H* in the correct spaces. Her fingers move to her temples, and after some extra-deep thinking, she draws a big X and fills in the *K* and *L.* Then she adds a second grid—with the dots—and adds the *R, S,* and *T.*

"And now, the X with dots," she says. "It has to be *W,*

X, Y, Z, but we don't have any of those letters, so we don't know where to start—unless it follows the same pattern as the first X, right?"

"But you can fill in all these other letters, can't you?" I ask. "The *A* has to go in the bottom left corner."

"The bottom row in the second grid must be *N, O, P,* with *Q* above the *P*," Leigh Ann says. "And that means the *D* goes above the *C,* because it's the same pattern."

Margaret adds those letters and then fills in everything except the final four letters.

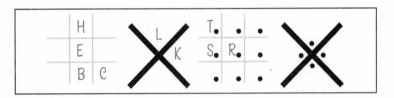

"And now for the final test," she says, starting on the remaining blanks in the clue.

```
T H E   ⟨∨L O P H O N E     P L A ∨E R
L I V E S     O N     B L E E C K E R     S T R E E T
B U T     N O T     A T
N O     T ∧O     E I G H T     E I G H T
```

The rest of us watch in silence as her eyes go back and forth and she copies the letters into the empty spaces. Within seconds, the clue looks like this:

"Voilà!" Margaret looks at the grids one more time and smiles. "That second word has to be 'xylophone'—

the _X_ and _Y_ fit the pattern perfectly. The third word is 'player,' and that must be 'two' in the last line."

Leigh Ann, Rebecca, and I slap her on the back. "All right, Margaret!"

She waves us off and looks at Caroline. "They should be thanking you. It would have taken me years to get this without your help."

"I just pointed you in the right direction," Caroline says. "You did the work."

"Well, before we go, let me check out the second part of this just to be sure it's the same."

"Good idea. Set it up."

And now, dear reader, it's your turn. My good friend Margaret already did all the hard work. All you have to do is substitute the right letters for the symbols. Piece o' muffin for somebody as smart as you, right?

Here you go:

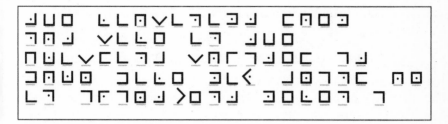

Chapter 13

You'd better not be starting this chapter if you don't know where the violinist does not live. I'm not kidding. Go back right now and do it

When we leave Elizabeth's, we have four clues in hand and seem well on our way to tracking down a violin, stolen in 1959 by someone who now wants Margaret to have it. Go figure—wait, you did, right?

And here's what you know:

- ✓ *The piano player lives on Hester Street, but not in Apt. 4M and not at no. 127 or no. 301 (the orphan clue).*
- ✓ *The bassoon player lives in 2J, but not on Grand or Essex (the first-letter clue).*
- ✓ *The xylophone player lives on Bleecker Street, but not at no. 288 (the first pigpen clue).*
- ✓ *The violinist does not live in the building located at 456 Grand or in Apt. 7A (the second pigpen clue—the one you were supposed to solve on your own).*

"You do see where this is going, don't you?" Margaret asks.

"Um, I think so," I lie.

"It's a logic problem. These clues are like lights on an airport runway. Except he's turning them on one at a time instead of all at once. Right now we're in a holding pattern, metaphorically speaking, but at some point we're going to have enough information to know where this goes." She holds up the key that was taped to the back of that very first message wrapped around the bow, and that now hangs from a black cord around her neck. "We just have to figure out how to put it all together. I assume we're looking for the violinist's address, but we definitely don't have enough information to find it yet. There must be at least one more clue."

"I kind of like that pigpen code," Leigh Ann says. "We could use something like that to send each other secret messages."

"Um, Leigh Ann," Rebecca says, "you can send text messages. Why do you need a secret code? Do you really think anybody wants to snoop on anything we have to say?"

"All right, so maybe we don't need it. But it seems cool."

"I'm with Leigh Ann," I say. "If we're serious about being detectives, we need our own code. No pigpens, though. Our code will be based on ice cream. Twenty-six flavors."

"What flavor is *A*?" Leigh Ann asks.

"Fudge swirl?" I suggest.

"I don't know—fudge swirl has more of a consonant feel to it," says Margaret. "How about mint chocolate chip?"

"Yuck!" Becca shouts. "Mint chocolate chip is, like, *X*. Or *Q*. Definitely not a vowel."

This could take a while. So I'll get back to you. Someday.

Monday. Hoo boy, what a day.

Here's how it starts for me: I'm already late as I scuttle out of the building and toward the subway stop at Eighty-sixth Street. Halfway there, it starts to drizzle. I don't have an umbrella, but no worries, right? Here in New York, the trains run underground. *C'est fantastique!*

Except when I get there, the station is closed. I hear something about a police investigation as I start the trek down Lexington to the stop at Seventy-seventh, and just to make things special, it starts to pour. Luckily, a few doors down Lex there's a shoe repair shop advertising umbrellas for sale for five bucks, and I duck in the door and out of the rain. Which is when I realize my wallet and all my cash are on the corner of my dresser and not in my book bag. *Zut alors!* Deep breaths, Sophie.

The Seventy-seventh Street station is open, but there's a cop in an orange poncho announcing that the 6 train isn't running, and if we head back up to Eighty-sixth, the 4 and the 5 are moving. Thanks, Officer!

By this time, I'm mega-soaked, so I schlep the remaining twelve blocks down to the school at Sixty-fifth Street, swearing and shivering every step of the way. I walk in the door two seconds after the first-period bell rings, and—*bingo!*—Sister Eugenia stands before me.

"Just a moment, young lady. You're tardy. You'll be needing a late pass."

Seven years without a tardy or an absence. And just like that, my perfect record is kapowed.

"Oh, please, Sister. I know I'm late, but it was only a couple of seconds." I feel tears welling up in my eyes. "The trains weren't running [*sniff*] and it's raining [*sniff*] and I'm soaked because I forgot my umbrella [*sniff, sniff*] and my wallet—"

"All right, all right. I get the picture. Just get a move on."

I feel kinda like hugging her, but I wisely pass. "Thank you so much, Sister. I really appreciate this."

A barely perceptible smile and shake of the head. "Move it!"

Because we have a school Mass later in the day, the class schedule has been changed and I have English first period. I run all the way up to the fifth floor. The door to Mr. Eliot's class is already closed, and he is writing on the board with his back to the door. I try to tiptoe in without making too much commotion, but my shoes are squishing and squeaking like mad, and the whole class busts out laughing.

"Ah, Miss St. Pierre. Good of you to join us."

"Sorry, Mr. Eliot. Please don't make me go back downstairs for a late pass."

He takes pity on me, no doubt because I am so pathetic standing there in a puddle growing bigger by the second as my hair and uniform continue to drip. "Well, you can't stay in here like that, for crying out loud. Go down to Sister Eugenia's office and see if you can find some dry clothes. And take the elevator; we don't need you spreading Lake St. Pierre on the stairs."

Although I am totally skeeved out at the idea of wearing somebody else's clothes, I find a blouse, a skirt, and a sweater that fit and feel a heck of a lot better than my own sopping uniform.

But stay tuned. There's more.

Back to class, and the first group is just finishing its presentation on the semicolon (which I'm truly sorry I missed; I happen to love the semicolon). They are followed by the period people, who are surprisingly entertaining. Everyone applauds, then Mr. Eliot thanks them and turns to Margaret.

"And that brings us to the apostrophe. Miss Wrobel, is your group ready to go?"

You can practically hear the blood rushing out of Margaret's face; she turns absolutely white. Leigh Ann looks at me, those big brown eyes of hers opened wide, and I spin around to see Livvy already moving toward the front of the room, carrying a poster board and a handful of index cards.

"I'm ready, Mr. Eliot," she announces, glancing over her shoulder at me, a grin of pure malice contorting her stupid face.

"What about the rest of your group?" he asks.

"We're not supposed to go until tomorrow," I protest. "It was on that paper you gave us. We're not prepared—we all agreed that we would work on it after school today."

Mr. Eliot consults his notes. "Nope, I have semicolons, periods, and apostrophes today, and everyone else tomorrow. Do you still have that paper with the assignment?"

"I have it right here," Livvy says. (My goodness, isn't that convenient?) "Let's see. Gee, it looks like you're right, Mr. Eliot. Apostrophe, Monday."

The wheels of the bus she has just thrown us under roll over our stunned bodies. *Ka-thump. Ka-thump. Ka-thwomp.*

"You told us it was Tuesday," Margaret hisses at Livvy. "Mr. Eliot, this isn't fair. She did this on purpose."

He looks at Livvy, who shrugs innocently. "I don't think so. It says Monday right here. Why would I tell you Tuesday?"

"Because you hate us," I say. "You totally sabotaged us."

Accusations. Denials. Screams. Smirks. Tears.

Finally, mercifully, Mr. Eliot holds up his hand to

silence us. "Stop. Everyone. We're not going to waste time arguing about who said what and why in the middle of this class. I'll see you all after school today. We'll deal with this then."

More time with Livvy Iscariot. So I have that to look forward to.

Although Rebecca says she knows some people who could "take care of our Livvy problem," we agree to take our punishment silently. For now. Mr. Eliot knocks ten points off our project grade for being unprepared, even though I get the feeling he believes that Livvy deliberately misled us. And we still have to finish the project— with Livvy.

The hardest part, however, is when he drops the d-word bomb on us.

"I'm very disappointed in you girls. The whole point of group projects is for you to work together. To delegate and share responsibility. I don't know whose fault it is that you got the date wrong, but I can't help thinking that if you had just tried to get along well enough for one little project, this wouldn't have happened. Not to mention that you chose to wait till the last minute to do the work. So I want you to get together right now and finish up what you need for tomorrow."

Margaret, Leigh Ann, and I stare glum-faced and glassy-eyed at our desks.

While Klack Butt files her nails, totally ob-Livvy-ous.

• • •

If ever there has been a day the Red Blazer Girls need ice cream, this is it. We consider splurging and going to Serendipity, but decide to go with the more geographically and economically desirable choice, Perkatory. Four mocha floats later, Rebecca finally gets us to smile when she performs a pitch-perfect dramatic re-creation of me sobbing to Sister Eugenia in my dripping-wet uniform.

Jaz stops by our table to ask if we want anything else.

"Tempting, but no," I say.

"At least you're all smiling again. I thought somebody had died when you came in. Hey, have you heard the big news about next door? That little violin shop?"

Margaret perks up. "What news?"

"The cops have been over there all day. I don't have any details, but I heard some stuff through the vent about a stolen violin. And one of the employees has disappeared. I'm, like, dying to know what's going on."

"Oh my gosh," Margaret says. "Poor Mr. Chernofsky. Let's go."

Leigh Ann and I slurp up the last of our floats and run after Margaret and Becca, who are already out the door.

We walk in as two cops in nearly identical gray suits are leaving. Mr. Chernofsky, leaning against the wall and rubbing his beard, looks like he's had a day he would like to forget, too.

"Ah, girls. You know."

"We just heard," Margaret says, giving him a hug.

"What happened?" I ask.

Mr. Chernofsky looks at me with sad, tired eyes. "It's gone." He then turns to Margaret. "That violin you liked so much. Gone. Disappeared. With Ben. I'm so sorry."

Her hand goes over her mouth in surprise. "David Childress's violin? But how? When?"

"Sometime yesterday. Maybe late Saturday night. I was here until eleven p.m. on Saturday. I locked the doors and set the alarm like I always do. When I come in this morning, the door is still locked and the alarm is still on. But the violin, it is gone. This is where I left it." He points to an empty space between two new, unvarnished violins.

"What's this about Ben? Where is he?" I remember the overheard conversation from the vent in Perkatory. "Maybe he just took it somewhere to have it looked at?"

"Benjamin has vanished," Mr. Chernofsky says. "I have not seen him since Saturday, about noon. I think I made a big mistake. A young man comes to me, tells me about his past, tells me that those days are behind him. That he's changed. And I believe him, I put my trust in him. This is what happens when a foolish old man trusts someone new."

"What do you mean, about his past and those days being over?" Margaret asks.

"Before he comes to me, Ben worked down on Wall Street and got mixed up in some dishonest business with stocks and bonds. Many good people lost all their savings, and the company he worked for was to blame. He testified for the government, but they still sent him to prison for three years. This is where he learns about violins. In the prison, they have a workshop and he teaches himself how to repair, even how to build, violins."

I can't get the image of him and Sister Eugenia sitting on that park bench on Saturday morning, drinking coffee and sharing laughs, out of my mind. There must be another explanation. I want to think that it's a long way from a little stock fraud to breaking and entering and grand theft fiddle.

"What did the police say?" Margaret asks.

"Once I told them about Benjamin, and that he is the only other employee, they seem to make up their minds. He has keys and the code for the alarm. They are looking only for him. But the officers who just left tell me that the phone number I have for him is no good, and I only have a post office box, no address. He could be anywhere by now. South America. Japan. It will be a difficult item to sell here. I have given the police pictures and a description."

Margaret rubs her temples for a few seconds, deep in thought. Then she tells Mr. C. about the half conversation we overheard through the vents. "And he said he is positive it is a Frischetti. Just when he was saying how much it might be worth, we couldn't hear because there was so much noise around us. But I got the sense that it was a lot. Is . . . it true? That it's really a Frischetti?"

Mr. Chernofsky nods. "I believe Ben was correct. But I am not one hundred percent certain, because I did not have the opportunity to fully examine it. Now we will never know."

"But he did tell you," I say. "Don't you see? Why would he tell you what he discovered if he was planning to steal it? It doesn't make sense. I'll bet he took it to someone else for a second opinion, and something happened that kept him from calling you or coming in to work."

Rebecca chimes in with her opinion. "Or he didn't decide to steal it until yesterday, and now he's long gone."

"There is one more thing," Mr. Chernofsky says quietly, reaching into his apron pocket. He holds out a perfectly ordinary button, walnut brown and about one inch in diameter; it's the size and color you might find on a barn jacket from L.L. Bean. "Have you seen this before?"

Margaret takes a close look and nods. "Sure. That's the button Ben's always tossing and catching."

"I always thought that was a coin," I say. "Are you sure?"

"Positive. The other side of it has something written on it."

Mr. Chernofsky turns the button over in his hand. The number 33 has been scratched deeply into its surface.

"How did you know?" Leigh Ann asks.

"I observed," Margaret answers.

"Margaret is right, it is Ben's. And this morning, I

found it right here." Mr. C. points to a spot on the hard-wood floor directly below the gap where the violin used to be.

I suggest another possible conclusion for people to jump to. "Maybe he lost it there on Saturday morning. Or even Friday afternoon. It could have been there all weekend."

Mr. Chernofsky shakes his head sadly. "Impossible. I swept the floor in here before leaving Saturday night. My broom and dustpan are right where I left them. I would have seen it."

It doesn't look good for Ben. But in my gut, this con-clusion doesn't feel right to me, and I always trust my instincts. After all, they've let me down only . . . fifty or sixty times.

Chapter 14

An alibi uncovered. Literally

We help Mr. Chernofsky retrace his steps from Saturday afternoon, hoping that he has simply misplaced the violin, or that Ben moved it to another location inside the shop for safekeeping. By my count, there are nineteen empty violin cases, twenty-three cases containing violins—most of which belong to customers—and twenty-eight violins not in cases, including partially completed ones. We check every one.

"Rule number one of detective work: eliminate the obvious. Violins all look pretty much the same. Once we determine it's definitely not in the building, then we can expand our search," says Miss Marple.

Twenty minutes later, Rebecca perfectly sums up our progress: "I'm stumped."

We huddle up while Mr. Chernofsky is back in the workshop. "Look, I know we're all busy with school and music and everything," Margaret says, "but remember what that cop told us. They aren't going to kill themselves over one violin that may or may not be valuable.

And we already know one thing about this Ben Brownlow guy that the police department doesn't. We know he has at least one friend in New York."

"That's right!" I say. "Sister Eugenia could lead us to him."

"Hoo-yah! I knew the Vatican was mixed up in this!" Becca cries triumphantly.

"Becca, just because the guy knows a nun doesn't mean the Vatican is involved. It doesn't even mean the nun is involved," Margaret says.

Becca scoffs. "You're so naive, Margaret. They only control everything."

"Well, all right, then. You're officially in charge of the Vatican connection in this investigation."

"Eggggs-cellent," Becca says, rubbing her hands furiously.

"Let's put our brains together," says Margaret. "Our suspect had means and opportunity, and a really obvious motive: money."

Leigh Ann looks puzzled. "But how are we supposed to find him? Mr. Chernofsky said his phone number and address are fakes."

I put my arm around her shoulders. "Ah, that's where Sister Eugenia comes in. She must know how to contact him. Tomorrow, you and I are going to become Sister Eugenia's new BFFs."

Margaret grins at that image. "And I'll see what else I can learn about our Mr. Benjamin Brownlow. Maybe someone saw him coming or going on Sunday."

"You know what?" Rebecca starts. "I was wrong. It's not the Vatican. I think a supersecret anti-Vatican organization has infiltrated the school, and now they're branching out. Think about it. That room in the basement, all that cleaning and painting—it's all part of their grand plan to confuse us. That's how they work, you know. I'll bet there are secret messages—coded messages—all over the school. We're being brainwashed and don't even know it."

"That's a really, um, interesting theory, Becca," Leigh Ann says.

"So why steal the violin?" I ask.

"The conspiracy business ain't cheap, honey."

Indeed it ain't.

Tuesday. St. V's cafeteria. Last period. Me. Leigh Ann.

Normally, we have PE, but the roof over the gym is leaking, so we have a rare free period. Margaret uses the opportunity to go to the computer lab to work on an essay, leaving me with a chance to talk to Leigh Ann alone.

"So, what's the latest with your dad and Alex?"

"You know, it's funny—Alex told me yesterday that he got invited to take part in this thing at Columbia. Some kind of math program for geniuses. He's really excited about it—said it just came out of the blue."

"Maybe one of his teachers recommended him," I say.

"Yeah, that's what he thinks, too."

"Well, it's good news, anyway—right? Maybe he'll love it there. And then, who knows?"

"Now if I could just change my dad's mind."

"Cleveland, huh?"

"Yeah."

"You know, I was looking online, and Cleveland isn't so bad. The Rock and Roll Hall of Fame is there. And Lake Erie!" I take a paper from a folder in my book bag. "Look! Fifty fun things for kids to do in Cleveland!"

She takes the paper from me, smiling. "Sophie, you are the best."

"Is any of this helping?"

"Yeah. And what about you? What's going on with you and Raf?"

"I have to tell you something," I whisper, afraid that girls at the other tables can hear me. "I haven't told anyone, even Margaret, and I'm gonna bust if I don't tell somebody."

"Oh my gosh. Tell me now!"

I tell her about my little scooter adventure.

"That is so awesome. Were you scared?"

"A little at first. But then—no! I wanted to keep going and going. But I was afraid somebody would recognize me. My parents will kill me."

"And Raf. I've seen your dad's knife. So, does Raf still have the scooter? I mean, are you guys going to—"

"I don't know," I say. "It was so much fun. But it's too . . . I don't know. So many people out there know my parents. That's why I can't tell Margaret. It's kind of like the thing with the *Seventeen* magazines; I can't face the look she would give me if she knew. Plus, she sees my mom all the time, and I don't want her to have to lie for me."

"Well, I'm glad you told me. And don't worry, I'll take it to the grave."

"Thanks. Let's hope it doesn't come to that!"

"Well, I suppose we ought to get to work. You ready?"

"Ready."

"You have the stuff?"

"Check." I hold up a sturdy plastic grocery bag from Eli's Market containing the St. Veronica's uniform skirt, blouse, and sweater I borrowed on my wet 'n' weird Monday, all freshly cleaned and folded.

Operation Sister Shakedown is under way.

We walk with terrified determination toward Sister Eugenia's office. I knock twice on the door. She opens it and says nothing. Just stares at us. Oh, she's a cool customer, this suspicious sister.

I am cheerful. I am friendly. I am oh-so-grateful for what she did for me yesterday, letting me slide in two seconds late without a tardy slip, and then finding me warm, dry clothes to wear. I am so flippin' sincere I'm making myself sick.

"Anyway, thank you again, again," I say, handing her the plastic bag. "I washed everything."

Wait, is that a raised eyebrow I see?

"And you're welcome, welcome," she says. "I trust

that with all this sincerity and sorriness, there will be no repeat performances." And so our little bonding moment has come and gone. She turns crisply away and starts to head back toward her desk.

"Uh, Sister?"

"Yes?"

"Just one more thing. You know my friend Margaret Wrobel, right? Well, she's friends with Mr. Chernofsky, who runs that little violin shop over on Sixty-sixth Street, and he's kind of worried because he has this guy who works for him, Benjamin Brownlow, who hasn't shown up for work for a couple of days and hasn't called, and Mr. Chernofsky doesn't know how to get in touch with him—"

"And how does this concern me?"

Wait, is that a bead of sweat on her forehead?

"Well, first off, I have to tell you, I swear I wasn't snooping. I was just minding my own business reading in the park the other day, and I saw you and Ben together, so I know you know him, and thought you would know how to get in touch with him."

"Because, you know, Mr. Chernofsky is really worried," Leigh Ann adds. "He's afraid something terrible or tragic might have happened."

I watch her closely, waiting for her to reveal . . . something, but this sister, she is a rock. I'm talking igneous.

"I do know the young man you're speaking of, and yes, we spoke the other day in the park. He happens to be a former student, from my days at a boys' school, if you must know. But even if I knew where to find him, I would not tell you girls. Mr. Brownlow has the right to be left alone if he wishes. Now, on your way, please." She shoos us out of her office and closes the door. Decisively.

Leigh Ann and I smile at each other. Sister Eu knows exactly where to find him. I press my ear to her door, hoping to hear her call him, but instead I hear her chair scraping on the floor and the unmistakable sound of sensible sister shoes coming right for me.

"Run!"

We duck around a corner and wait and listen. The door opens, followed by the jangle of keys as she locks up behind her. Leigh Ann peeks around the edge of the wall.

"Well?" I whisper.

"Come on!" She waves me forward, and we creep down the hallway, jumping into a doorway whenever she stops or slows down. When she strides through a set of swinging doors, we stop to peer through one of the small rectangular windows.

"She's headed for the basement."

Leigh Ann's shoulders sag at the thought of a return to Ratland. "Do we have to follow her down there?"

"You don't have to go."

"But you're going, right?"

I shrug. I nod. I shnod.

"If you're going, I'm going."

Behold the power of peer pressure.

We pause at the basement door, opening it a crack to look down into the void. "If she falls on these stairs, she'll be dead," I say.

"Maybe she has a light."

"Good point." And right on the money, as it happens. I stick my entire head through the doorway and see shadows flickering on the wall as Sister Eugenia makes her way toward the back of the room. "Stay close."

This last request is entirely unnecessary; Leigh Ann is absolutely glued to my back as we descend the stairs. With her flashlight, Sister Eugenia is able to move much faster and reaches the far end of the basement well ahead of us.

"Oh dear," Sister Eu says. "Oh, no, no. This isn't supposed to be here."

I turn around to face Leigh Ann, whose eyes are WIDE open.

"What isn't supposed to be there?" she whispers.

"Not sure. Keep moving." Like a very small herd of very large turtles, we trudge ahead. Finally we're close enough to take advantage of the dim glow from the nun's flashlight, and we see the problem.

A pile of construction materials is leaning against the door to the secret hideaway we discovered. There must be ten or twelve sheets of heavy plywood and even more plasterboard, and a stack of those ginormous buckets of paint. Only the top two feet of the door is visible.

"Benjamin!" she says in the loudest voice she can manage. "Can you hear me? Are you in there?"

A muffled "Yes!" comes from behind the door. "I'm trapped!"

"Oh my goodness," she says, sounding distinctly panicked. "What should I do?"

"Sister, you have to get me out of here!" Ben shouts. "Just get me out. Please." He sounds desperate.

"Sister Eugenia," I shout. "We can help. Shine your light over here for a second so that we can see."

"Girls! Did you follow me?"

"Well, yeah, kinda, but please let us help. We know about the room, but we didn't know who was staying in it."

Leigh Ann and I start dragging the plywood and the rest of the stuff out of the way. It takes about ten minutes, and we are sweating like a couple of fat men in a sauna when we get to the last sheet of plasterboard.

As we slide it out of the way, Ben pushes the door open. "Ohmigosh! Thank you, thank you, thank you. Thank God you found me, Sister. I have been trapped in there since Saturday afternoon."

Sister Eugenia crosses herself. "Saturday! Gracious. This is Tuesday! You poor thing. What happened?"

"Sister, I promise to tell you everything, but right now I really need to use the bathroom!" He skitters away to the janitor's closet-size bathroom, leaving Leigh Ann and me stranded with Sister Eu for a few uncomfortable minutes.

When he returns, Sister Eu shines the light on him and I get a look at his scruffy, pasty-white face and the circles—dark enough to do a raccoon proud—around his eyes. And either his clothes grew, or he shrank a couple of sizes. The poor guy looks awful.

"Whew. That's better," he says. "What happened was, I came back here after our walk in the park and was inside reading when I heard people coming down the stairs. They were making a lot of noise moving things around, and I thought they were going to open the door and find me for sure, so I just kept quiet. When they left, I tried to open the door, but it wouldn't budge. I ran out of food and water yesterday, and I'm starving."

I hand him the full water bottle from my book bag, and he drinks it all without even stopping to breathe.

"You're not going to believe what's happened," I tell him. "Somebody stole a violin from Mr. Chernofsky over the weekend, and he thinks it's you. And so do the police."

"What violin?"

"The Frick, er, the Frischetti."

"But . . . how? Who even knows about it?"

"We'll explain everything we know in a little while. Right now we have to get you out of here."

But how? Where? I feel as if my brain is under enemy attack. Lame ideas are whizzing past, and I'm blasting them out of the sky. Normally, I would just turn to Margaret for a brilliant solution, but this time it's up to me. I can do this!

Right?

Of course!

Chapter 15

In which Quasimodo and some of our other old friends reappear

And then it hits me. "Sanctuaryyyyyyyyy," I say in my best Quasimodo voice.

"You're taking me to a bell tower?" Ben asks.

"Close," I say. "But not the church itself—someplace connected to it."

"Elizabeth's?" Leigh Ann asks.

"Exactly. We can sneak him up the back stairs." Elizabeth Harriman's townhouse used to be owned by the church and is connected to it by a staircase and a long hallway that we discovered when fate led Ms. Harriman into our lives.

"But wait," Leigh Ann says, pulling me aside for a private confab. "Shouldn't we ask her first? It is the teensiest bit possible that she might not want a confirmed felon—who's a suspect in another crime—in her house."

"Hmm. You may be right," I say, remembering Elizabeth's art collection. "I'd better call her."

Following a quick explanation, in which I leave out every single important detail, Elizabeth insists that we bring our friend up immediately.

Leigh Ann bites her bottom lip. "We can't get in trouble for this, can we?"

"I . . . er . . . well—" I stammer, not at all sure how to answer that question.

"If anyone sees us, I'll explain everything," Ben says. "Just get me out of this godforsaken basement. I want to see the sun again."

"And we'll bring Sister Eugenia along as a character witness," I say.

"Bring me where?"

Yipes! In the dark of the basement, I forgot she was so close.

"We have a plan to get Ben out of here so that he can get cleaned up and tell us what is going on. But if we're going to help him—"

"What do you mean 'help him'?" Sister Eugenia says, shining her light right in my face. "You girls shouldn't be mixing yourselves up in this."

"Sister, we know what we're doing," I state with un-questionable confidence. Then I take a Red Blazer Girls Detective Agency card from my wallet and hand it to her. "We're used to stuff like this."

With a weirdly chastened Sister Eugenia leading the way, elbows swinging dangerously from side to side, and the rest of us struggling to keep up, we scamper up the back staircase that leads from the school to the church foyer, where our old friend Robert, the ancient security guard, sits at his post reading this month's *Vogue*. I smile and wave as I pass, praying he doesn't recognize me as the girl he once busted for church-snooping.

He seems none too concerned. Or maybe the sneak preview of next summer's fashions ("Shorts, Shorter, Shortest!") is simply too fabulous to look away from?

When we get to that very familiar door with the stained glass chalice, the very one that leads to the "secret" staircase to Elizabeth's, I know exactly what to do—thanks to Becca. I bend a bobby pin just so, wiggle it around in the lock, and then turn the knob with a satisfying click. Sister Eugenia gapes, her hand clapped on her heart.

"I do have a key, Miss St. Pierre."

I shrug. "Sorry. Old habit, Sister. Hey, get it? Habit? Sister?"

"Keep moving," Leigh Ann whispers.

As we wind our way up the dark, twisting stone stairs, Ben jokes nervously about us locking him away in another secret room. Then, at the final turn, he stops dead in his tracks. "Holy Catzilla! Look at the size of that thing!"

"Teazle!" I shout. "Come here, big fella." I hoist up all twenty-five pounds of him. "He belongs to Ms. Harriman—Elizabeth."

"Who is going to be your new temporary landlady," Leigh Ann says, patting him on the shoulder. "You're gonna love her."

"Some questionable fashion choices, maybe, but she's cool," I add.

Elizabeth is waiting at the door, and after quick introductions, she directs Ben to the old servants' quarters on the top floor. "He can stay in Winnie's old room. I'm afraid it still smells like stale cigarettes. I'll open a window to air it out. P.U.!"

Both Winnie and her husband, Gordon, were chainsmokers, and it is going to take about three years to purge the room of the ashtray stink.

"I set some of Malcolm's old things on the bed, but now that I see you, I'm afraid they're going to be a bit large on you."

Malcolm has a good ten inches on Ben. But at least he'll be warm and nattily attired. Malcolm is the Earl of Tweed. The Count of Cashmere. The, uh, Minister of Merino?

Meanwhile, Teazle leads the rest of us down to the living room, on the ground floor. Seeing Elizabeth's art collection makes me hope and pray that we haven't misjudged Ben. That nice little Matisse at the bottom of the stairs is worth a lot more than the violin—even if it really is a Frischetti.

Sister Eugenia tells us half of Ben's story, and when he emerges from Winnie's old domain, we get the other half straight from the horse's mouth. Yes, it's true he spent time in prison. No, he didn't kill anyone. ("Not yet, anyway," he adds with a smile.) Yes, he has been living in the school basement for a few weeks.

And finally, he admits that he is responsible for the cleaning, the painting, the decorating, etc.

"It's part of my penance," he says quite seriously. "When I got released, I came back to New York. I wanted to start my life over again. You know, the whole clean-slate thing. But I didn't have any place to stay. Fortunately for me, I ran into Sister Eugenia in the park one day. She was my eighth-grade math teacher, and I guess I must not have been such a rotten kid, because she wanted to help me out. She knew about the coal door and the storage room. Said it would be our little secret. A place to crash for free, just for a few weeks, until I got back on my feet."

Sister Eugenia looks at him like a proud mother. "But he wouldn't agree to it unless he could do something in return. So he started cleaning. And when he ran out of things to clean, he started painting."

"We know," I say. "Sister Bernadette hired us to find you. You're driving her crazy, you know. That was Margaret and me the other day—we almost caught you, and then all those chairs fell, and you disappeared."

"Well, after what you did to the library," Leigh Ann says, "I'm not sure we should ever tell her. St. V's should hire you."

"I'm sorry I'm making Sister Bernadette nuts—that wasn't my intention. I suppose I did get a little carried away. The wallpaper was a little much, huh? Maybe when this is all over, I can apologize to her. If I don't end up back in prison, that is."

"Impossible," I say. "You're innocent, and we can prove it."

"Well, I'm not so sure you can," Ben says. "You're taking my word that I was in that room since Saturday. I could be lying to all of you. Believe me, that's the way the police will see things. My alibi has a big hole in it because no one saw me between Saturday and today. And then there's the sticky issue of my button. How did that end up on the floor? It's always in my pocket. That little piece of plastic is very special to me."

"What is it from?" Leigh Ann asks. "I'm sorry, is that too personal?"

"No, it's all right. That button is from the winter coat they gave me in prison. I got it on the first day of my incarceration."

"Why did you scratch the number thirty-three in it?" I ask.

"Thirty-three months. Nine hundred ninety-nine days, to be exact. That's how long I knew I would spend in prison. I carry the button to remind me of every day."

Just then I see my reflection in the mirror. The girl I see has a familiar, full-throttle look about her—the very one I'm used to seeing in Margaret. And I like what I see.

"Well, even if we can't prove you didn't do it, we can prove somebody else did. We will find that violin."

Won't we?

Chapter 16

In which the significance of sushi and Seventeen is debated

With Ben safely tucked away upstairs and Sister Eugenia on her way back to school, Leigh Ann and I thank
Elizabeth once more. I'm still a little nervous about the
situation, but Elizabeth doesn't seem the least bit concerned about what the police just might see as inter-
fering with an investigation. Which we are. Definitely.
Gulp.

"After everything you girls have done for me, it's
the least I can do. After all, I hardly knew you when I
trusted you with that letter from my father, and that
certainly turned out well. If you say he's innocent, and
you bring Sister Eugenia along to vouch for him, who
am I to argue? I spoke to Malcolm and he's firmly opposed, but I'll unruffle his feathers. He can be such a
ninny."

"Just don't be surprised if you hear Ben vacuuming
at two in the morning," I say. "And let him know if

you want your kitchen remodeled or if Teazle needs a manicure."

Elizabeth smiles at that possibility. "I certainly won't stop him if he decides to do any of those things."

Leigh Ann gives her a kiss on the cheek. "We'll be in touch."

As the red door closes behind us, I check my phone and see that I have missed four calls from Margaret and one from Rebecca. I call Margaret.

"Where are you?" she asks.

I look at my watch. Oy squared. School has been out for forty-five minutes!

"I'm with Leigh Ann. We're just leaving Elizabeth's. Boy, do we have news!"

"Well, Becca and I are leaving Perk right now, on our way to the violin shop. Meet us there?"

"Ten-four."

Outside Mr. Chernofsky's shop, Leigh Ann and I spend ten minutes explaining the events of the past hour and a half to the envious-but-impressed Margaret and Rebecca.

"That was quick thinking, taking him to Elizabeth's," Margaret says. "You two rock. But we're back to square one in our investigation. Since you two found him, you get the last word, but I vote we keep Ben's location secret for now."

"Sounds good to me," I say. Becca and Leigh Ann chime in, agreeing to keep mum.

"But if it's not Ben, who?" Becca asks.

"And how?" I add. "We need to get a good look at the outside of the building. There's gotta be another way in."

The two front windows have iron security grates bolted right into the brick. Rebecca reaches up and gives each one a good shake and then hangs from them while screeching like a monkey; thus we confirm that they are solidly attached. Scribbling in a small spiral notebook, Margaret notes that the front door has three levels of security. It has double locks, both with serious-looking dead bolts, plus a hinged iron grate with a padlock that Mr. C. closes every night. Next to the door is the alarm system keypad, where the word "Ready" flashes off and on.

Mr. Chernofsky welcomes us with a tired smile. "Hello, ladies."

"Anything new from the police?" Margaret asks.

He shakes his head. "Afraid not. And still no word from Benjamin. I'm afraid he is long gone by now."

"You know, Mr. C.," Margaret begins, "we were thinking. What if it wasn't Ben?"

"Yeah, there could be a perfectly reasonable explanation for why he hasn't shown up for work. Like, he could be in the hospital," I say.

"Or maybe he has amnesia?" Leigh Ann offers. "Like those people on soap operas."

Mr. Chernofsky rubs his beard. "I know you girls are fond of Benjamin. You don't want to believe something bad about him. But there is no one else, no other explanation. The doors were locked. He has keys. The alarm was set. He knows the code. He discovered the violin is valuable, and now the violin is gone. He carries around a button, and where do I find that button? Right here. Ach. My insurance company is not happy with me right now."

"Well, if it really was Ben, then the police will be all over that evidence, and I'm sure they'll catch him," Margaret says. "But if it was somebody else, and the crime was committed in some other way, then how about giving us a chance to suss out that possibility?"

He sighs and smiles. "Okay, girls. You want to investigate, go ahead. What's the harm?"

No doubt humoring us, he allows us to poke around the shop for a bit while he sands and saws away in the back.

As the artistic one, Rebecca is given the job of making a scale drawing of the interior layout of the shop, to which she'll add outside details. Margaret and I measure the rooms with a tape measure from the workshop. Rebecca's drawing shows the size and exact location of the windows and doors, the furniture, the heating vents, virtually anything and everything.

From the inside, we notice the metal tapes for the alarm attached to the two large front windows. We call in Mr. Chernofsky to demonstrate how a broken or opened window will trigger the alarm.

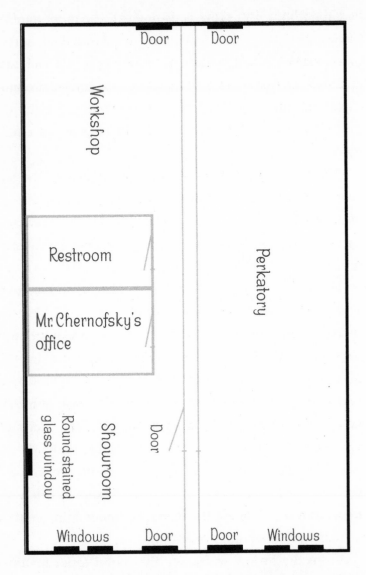

"Are there motion detectors?" Margaret asks, flashing newly acquired security system expertise.

Mr. C. explains that they are not practical because of Pumpkin, the cat, who would set them off constantly.

Some might find this irresponsible. I think it's sweet. So there.

A heavy, solidly built wooden door with three industrial-strength dead bolts separates the violin shop from Perkatory.

"How about this door? Can you open it for us?" I ask.

He turns the tarnished brass knobs of the bolts with satisfying *ker-chunks* and pulls the door open, revealing the back side of an identical door.

"Where does this go?" Rebecca asks, trying the knob of the second door.

"Think about it, Becca," I say. "You know that door in the wall of Perkatory? The one with all the coat hooks on it and the table right up against it? This has to be that same door."

Becca examines the edge of the door frame. "There's no alarm on this door. Maybe someone picked the locks—" She stops midthought as a slight grin curls the right side of her mouth.

"What? Do you see something?" I demand.

"It's what I don't see. Look at the back side of the door into the violin shop. What do you see?"

"Umm. Nothing?"

"Exactly. No one could pick the locks, because there are no locks to pick! These bolts are accessible only from inside the shop. Same thing with the door to Perk. No place to put a key from the outside. I guess that's why it doesn't need an alarm. These doors are as good as a wall."

The door is closed and the bolts turned again.

Leigh Ann raises her hand. "Um, I have a question."

"Go ahead, Miss Jaimes," Becca says with a smile.

"The violin was stolen on Saturday or Sunday, right? Well, what if the thief knew about this door, and what if he came in here, you know, pretending to be a customer, and turned those three locks while nobody was looking? Then he could come right through the door from Perkatory, right?"

We all look at Leigh Ann in openmouthed awe.

"Behold the Dancer Detective!" I shout.

"Way to play, L.A.!" Becca raps.

"It is a great idea, Leigh Ann," Margaret says, "but there's one problem. Mr. C., were the bolts locked when you came in this morning?"

He scratches his head. "Yes. I remember. I am positive. The police asked me to open the door. I had to unlock all three for them."

Leigh Ann slaps a palm to her forehead. "Ohhhh! Duh. The only way to relock the locks is from the inside. And there's no other way out, except for the front and back doors."

"Which were locked and alarmed," Margaret finishes.

"The only other opening big enough for a person to get through is this," Rebecca says. She crosses the room to a circular stained glass window located just above her eye level. It is beautiful; dozens of small triangles of different colors are pieced together to form a geometric pattern that creates the illusion of being three-dimensional.

The shadow of the iron grate outside is barely visible through the glass, and Becca points out the unbroken metal tape of the alarm system around the outside edge.

"What about the floor? The ceiling? The vents?" I ask, ask, ask.

Margaret, who is down the hall in Mr. Chernofsky's office, calls out to Becca. "Did you draw that?" she asks, pointing out a rectangle of wood trim in the corner of the office ceiling.

Becca nods. "Got it, boss. What is it?"

Margaret climbs up on Mr. C.'s desk, but she still can't reach it. "It's like a trapdoor. It must go to the second floor."

Mr. Chernofsky comes into his office looking for us, and smiles at the sight of Margaret up on his desk in her stocking feet. "Find anything good?"

"I don't know. Where does this door lead?"

"It doesn't really lead anywhere. It's there so the plumbers and electricians can get to the pipes and wires in the ceiling."

"But isn't there an apartment above you?" Rebecca asks. "I'll bet I could crawl through to there."

"There is about a foot of space between the ceiling here and the floor of the upstairs apartment," Mr. C. says. "It has been a long time since I looked in there, but I don't think you could fit. As I said, there are pipes and wires; it's very crowded. And even if you could squeeze yourself in, there would have to be an opening in the apartment floor, and I don't think there is one."

Margaret hops down from the desk. "So, who lives up there? Any suspicious characters?"

Mr. Chernofsky chuckles. "I think you should meet them for yourself. That will satisfy your suspicions."

Our suspicions are going to have to wait, though. Mom calls just as we're leaving Mr. Chernofsky's shop and tells me I need to come home. Dad has the night off from the restaurant, and we're going out for sushi.

"Where are you, anyway?" she inquires in a Mom-like way. "Who are you with?"

"We're, like, just leaving Chernofsky's. Something big happened. I'll tell you about it later. Right now it's, like, just me and Margaret. Becca and Leigh Ann left, like, a minute ago."

"Well, that's, like, good. Now get, like, home. And, like, tell Margaret she's, like, welcome to, like, come with us."

Mom has apparently been attending the Mr. Eliot School of "Humor."

"You made, like, your point, Mom. Twice. I'll ask her. Bye."

"Ask me what?"

"Sushi?"

She wrinkles her nose. "Me and sushi—not so much."

"You don't know what you're missing."

"Raw fish?"

"Well, yeah. But when you call it that, it sounds

gross. 'Sushi' and 'sashimi' sound so much better. Come on. You're always telling me that colleges like students with lots of life experiences, and how you have this 'insatiable thirst for knowledge'—and all that yakkety-yak-yak. How are you gonna get into Harvard if you won't even try a spicy tuna roll?"

"I don't think that's what they mean," she says.

"Oh, I think you're wrong, Miss I'm Too Too Clever to Read *Seventeen*. I think it's exactly what they mean. And don't look at me like that. I know that you know that I read it, and I don't care. In fact, I may read it out loud to you . . . on the train. In front of strangers. You might just like it if you gave it a chance. I think you're afraid to try it." I take a much-needed breath.

"Sushi or *Seventeen*?"

"Either! Both!"

She stares at me with that raised eyebrow of hers. "Why are you getting so mad?"

"I'm not mad. I—I'm—never mind."

In silence, we start walking up Lexington. When we get to the Sixty-eighth Street station, Margaret asks, "Subway or sidewalk?"

"Subway," I grumble, and we take the stairs down to the platform. Across the tracks, on the downtown side, the old violinist with the Abe Lincoln beard we saw at Eighty-sixth Street is playing "Master of the House" from *Les Misérables,* a song that could make an undertaker smile. So I'm grinning like a chimp when suddenly he spots us—and stops in midsong to stare. I'm not exactly scared, but I am creeped out enough to be glad the dreaded third rail is between us.

Without taking my eyes off him, I whisper to Margaret, "Why is he staring at us?"

Before she can answer, a train pulls up and we squeeze into the steamy, crowded car, thankful that we're going only two stops. While we're standing there waiting for the doors to close, our fine fiddling friend starts to play "Ave Maria."

We finally start moving, and I relax. "That guy did exactly the same thing the last time we saw him. He's wiggin' me out."

"Last time he was playing songs from *Phantom*."

"I mean the staring. And the other song. 'Ave Maria.' "

"It's probably the blazers," she says. "He sees our Catholic-school uniforms. What if that's the person sending me the letters? What if that's the violin? Wouldn't that be an amazing coincidence?"

Can't argue with that.

"Shoot! That reminds me—I forgot to go over to the park to leave the message that we solved that pigpen code. I guess I've been preoccupied with that other violin."

"So, how's your plan coming along?"

"My plan?"

"Your plan for getting inside Mr. Chernofsky's upstairs neighbors' apartment."

Margaret grins. "You know me too well, Sophie St.

Pierre. As a matter of fact, I was just starting to think about that. You have any ideas?"

"Girl Scout cookies?"

"We don't even know any Girl Scouts."

"Suspiciously underage census takers? Jehovah's Witnesses?"

"Actually, I'm thinking we could be reporters for the school newspaper, doing a story about people in the neighborhood. They'll let us in; people automatically trust kids in parochial-school uniforms. They shouldn't, but they do. We ask them a few questions: how long they've lived here, what they remember about the old days, that kind of thing. We take a few pictures. And while we're there, one of us asks to use the bathroom and does a little snooping."

"Aren't you jumping to a little bit of a conclusion? I got the impression that Mr. C. thinks it's funny that you might even consider them. It's probably a ninety-year-old lady."

"I bet there are ninety-year-old thieves. Right now everyone is a suspect. I just saw this guy on the news pulling a tugboat out in the harbor, holding the rope in his teeth. He's eighty-five."

"His teeth?" My jaw tightens up just thinking about it.

His orthodontist must be very disappointed.

Chapter 17

Personally, I like my revenge served with a glass of ice-cold milk—and cookies

"You know, I've been stewing about this for two days," Leigh Ann says between bites of dry, slightly burned cafeteria toast. "I know that you guys want to help out Ben and Mr. Chernofsky, and, Margaret, I know you're busy trying to figure out all these clues to find this guy who wants to give you that violin . . . BUT I think we're forgetting something important."

The rest of us look at each other, confused. "We are?"

Leigh Ann has a diabolical look in her eyes—a look I've never seen before. "It's a little thing I like to call revenge," she says. "Guys, Livvy Klack totally burned us. Well, not you, Becca, but the rest of us."

"No, count me in. I love revenge."

"My, this is an interesting development," Margaret notes. "Leigh Ann, I had no idea you were so devious. I like it."

"I just think we have to get her back somehow."

Margaret chews on her thumbnail. "You know what

they say about revenge, don't you? It is a dish best served cold."

"I've heard that but never understood it," Becca admits.

"It means that it is most satisfying when some time has passed after the reason for the revenge. When it's completely unexpected."

"So, you agree we should do something really heinous to her, but not quite yet," Leigh Ann says.

"Precisely," says Margaret.

"Public humiliation," I suggest.

"She's a witch! Burn her!" Becca shouts a little too loudly, earning a shhh-and-scowl from Sister Eugenia, seated two tables away.

"Nah," Margaret says firmly. "There are sprinkler systems and fire extinguishers all over the school. We need to get her back in a way that shows exactly how much smarter we are. Sophie, remember how you felt the moment when you knew you just had your old buddy Mr. Winterbutt? That perfect instant when you snapped his picture? That's the kind of revenge I'm talking about."

Leigh Ann nods enthusiastically. "I have an idea, but I need a day to think it through. We will make Livvy Klack regret even thinking about messing with us."

She used to be such a nice girl.

Margaret is waiting for me to cram my coat into our locker before English class when she leans in close and whispers, "Guess who I heard from last night."

By the smile on her face, I figure it out. "No way. Andrew?"

She nods. "We texted back and forth for about twenty minutes. He's coming today."

"Coming where? Here?"

"Remember? Basketball?"

One of Sister Bernadette's latest brainstorms is to invite kids—boys included—from other schools for "some fun, coed, no-pressure basketball." She is generally opposed to school dances, so this is her compromise with the student council. Today, seventh and eighth graders from three schools will invade St. Veronica's smelly gymnatorium.

"What else did he say?"

"He wanted to know if we were going to play."

"We are, aren't we? And I'd better text Raf and remind him. He probably forgot."

"Kind of like you did?"

"I didn't forget. And stop trying to change the subject. I want to hear more about Andrew."

"Come to think of it, he did mention that he's quite curious about something you said the other night."

"Me?" Gulp.

"Uh-huh. He said to ask you if you really think they're fake."

Because the four of us and Raf are standing there in our gym clothes at 3:01, Sister Bernadette picks us to play the first game against some girls from Faircastle

Academy. The FAs have recruited LaShawn Taylor, a kid from Raf's school, St. Thomas Aquinas. He is a year older and a full head taller than Raf, and he looks as if he's a minute away from playing for the Knicks.

Raf is our best player, followed by Becca, who can at least dribble without constantly losing the ball to the other team. Margaret, Leigh Ann, and I occasionally rise to so-so-ness.

The game starts, and Becca spends most of it yelling at us to move or to pass the ball or to shoot. Raf is stuck with the impossible task of guarding LaShawn. And though the four girls on his team honestly stink, LaShawn single-handedly destroys us, 21–9.

Andrew, who's with a few friends from Davidson, is waiting for us as we walk off the court.

"Already?" he asks. "What happened?"

Raf, whose tongue is hanging out like a golden retriever's, points at LaShawn. "He happened."

"So, it did not go well."

Leigh Ann elbows me and jerks her head toward the door. "Uh-oh. Incoming."

It's Livvy, and she is aiming right for us. Well, right for Andrew, anyway.

"Anybody got a match?" I say.

"I'm so glad you came! God, can you believe how many losers are here? It's like some kind of convention for geeks from Queens." Livvy says "Queens" like it's a leper colony.

While Margaret is stuck standing there next to

Andrew, Leigh Ann pulls Rebecca, Raf, and me together. "Did she just call us losers?"

"And she called you a Queens geek," Rebecca says. "Jeez, what would she say if she knew I live in Chinatown?"

Leigh Ann fumes. She starts making a move toward Livvy. "I'm going to slug her."

Rebecca and I grab her by the arms and pull her away. "No, no, no, you're not," I say. "You'll just get in trouble, and Livvy will come out on top. Remember what we talked about this morning? Wait till it's colder."

"Just one punch," Leigh Ann says. "I promise I'll make it count. I've never punched anybody, but man, she really needs one." She finally calms down enough to be safe to herself and others, and then tells us with a straight face, "You know, I'll bet your first punch is way more memorable than your first kiss."

Becca and I both burst out laughing at the absolute sincerity she says it with and at the thought of our graceful, stunning friend punching anybody.

"Maybe," Becca says. "But we're not gonna find out about either today."

Me? I'm not so sure Leigh Ann is right. In order to beat out my first kiss, it would have to be one heck of a punch.

Margaret escapes Livvy's laser beam and leaves Andrew with her to be led around the gym like a prize bull.

"Do I appear solid?" she asks. "Because just now I

was invisible. Livvy stood there talking to Andrew for five minutes and never once so much as flicked a fake eyelash at me."

"What did Andrew do?" I ask.

"He kept looking at me, and I think he rolled his eyes at her once when she wasn't looking. Do you think he knows what she's really like? I gave him the text-me sign when I left. I'm dying to know what he thinks about her."

I don't say anything, but for me, that's two strikes against this guy. I mean, how could he just leave Margaret standing there like that?

"There's no way he likes her," Leigh Ann says. "He looks too smart to fall for her."

"Maybe. But what was going on over here with you guys?" Margaret asks. "What did I miss?"

"Remember that sweet, innocent girl named Leigh Ann?" I say. "Well, she's gone. This girl, who took her place, was ready to clobber Livvy right here in the gym, in front of Sister Bernadette and everybody."

After we tell her about Leigh Ann's first-punch theory, Margaret puts her arm around our friend's shoulders. "I had a feeling that crack about Queens would get to you."

"Well, it's no wonder Livvy hates you," I say. "I mean, look at you. Even in sweaty gym clothes you look like a model. Come to think of it, I hate you," I say, looking down at my gawky own self.

Sister Bernadette, who is making the rounds of the

gym, stops in front of us. "Well, girls? I think it's a big success, don't you?"

Margaret at least tries to be enthusiastic. "It was fun, Sister."

Sister Bernadette looks at Raf, then at me. "Aren't you going to introduce your friend, Miss St. Pierre?"

"Oh. Um, sorry, Sister. This is Raf, er, Rafael Arocho. He goes to Aquinas."

"Ah, I remember this young man. You were a St. Andrew's student, am I correct?" St. Andrew's is the boys' school right next to St. Veronica's. Raf attended through sixth grade.

Raf nods. "Uh-huh. I moved over to the West Side last summer."

"Well, I'm happy that you could make it today, Mr. Arocho." She starts to turn away but stops midturn. "Before I go—any news to report, girls? Regarding our little investigation?"

"I think it's safe to say we've solved the case, Sister," Margaret says.

"Well, that is good news. You can tell me all about it later. Looks like I need to get the next game organized."

Across the gym floor but directly in our line of sight, Livvy continues to flirt shamelessly with Andrew. First she laughs a little too much at something he says, and then she touches him on the arm, and finally, with a look over her shoulder to make sure we're watching, she flips her hair for the forty-seventh time and drags the poor guy off to meet more of her friends.

"I'm telling you," says Leigh Ann after witnessing this sorry spectacle. "One good punch."

"Who feels like getting something to eat?" Raf asks. "I'm starving."

I stick him with my elbow. "When aren't you hungry?" It's true. The kid has the metabolism of a hummingbird and the digestive system of a goat. He's a humminggoat.

Margaret pulls me away from Raf and through the doorway. "We don't have time. We need to stop by Mr. C.'s to see if there's anything new from my violin guy. I left the message about the last clue in the park this morning."

"Weren't we going to try to meet the people upstairs today?" I remind her. "You know, the 'interview' for the school paper."

"Right. We're going to have to put that off until tomorrow, right after school. Can everybody come?"

Rebecca tugs on my blazer. "Um, Sophie, weren't we supposed to be rehearsing after school tomorrow? We missed yesterday, and I think Tuesdays and Thursdays are the only days we can use the back room at Perkatory. If we're going to play anytime in the next century, we need to practice."

"I need my days to be a few hours longer," I say. "Twenty-seven or -eight would be just right."

"Well, if you're not going to eat, I'm heading home," Raf announces.

I stick out my lower lip in a fake pout. "Call me later?"

He gives me his own version of the shnod.

Rebecca, Margaret, and Leigh Ann begin to chant, "Byyeee, Raaaafffff!" as he turns and ambles away for the distant lands of the Upper West Side. What they don't know, but I do, is that he's not headed for the bus stop on Seventy-second Street—he is much too cool for the bus now that he has experienced the wind in his face and the taste of bugs in his teeth. He is Scooter Man, and his trusty mechanical steed is parked a block away.

"Be careful!" I shout after him, which earns me a what-the-hell? look from Becca.

"At least we didn't have to witness any PDA this time," she teases.

"What? We barely touch in front of you guys."

"She's teasing you, Soph," Leigh Ann says. "You guys are so cute together."

We are?

Her words are still hanging in midair when Malcolm and Elizabeth, both carrying those "green" reusable bags packed with groceries, turn the corner and practically run into us.

"Ahem. I assume you are referring to us as being cute," Malcolm says, puffing up his chest and straightening his bow tie.

"I, um . . . yeah, definitely," Leigh Ann says, unable to hold back a smile.

Malcolm chuckles. "You can't even say it with a straight face, Miss Jaimes. Elizabeth, I think we should be insulted."

"Nonsense," she replies. "What a nice surprise running into you all. Everyone heading home?"

"Eventually," Margaret says. "How are things working out with Ben?"

Please, please, please don't say he has disappeared with his new friends Pablo Picasso and Henri Matisse.

Elizabeth leans close to Margaret. "Can I keep him? He's so adorable! And he's a wonderful cook, too. Last night, he made a seafood risotto that was absolutely to die for. It was the best thing I've ever tasted."

Malcolm clears his throat again, and she gives him a good-boy pat on the back. "Malcolm, dear, I'm sorry. Your grilled cheese sandwiches are still the best. Girls, you see how men are? You need an extra room just to hold their ego!"

"That's a relief," I say. "I mean, that it's working out with Ben."

"And I didn't even tell you about the furniture," Elizabeth gushes, causing Malcolm to raise his eyebrows dramatically. "He completely rearranged my living room! I've been trying for years to make that room cozier, and he walks in and does it in a day. Like magic!"

"As long as we're on the topic of cozy rooms," Rebecca

begins, "I have a question. Your house has a basement, right?"

Elizabeth nods. "Oh yes. I don't go down there much. There's a Ping-Pong table and an old couch. Not much else. Why do you ask?"

"Well, me and Soph and Leigh Ann are starting a band, and we're having a hard time finding a place to practice. And I was just wondering . . ."

"Anytime you want. You won't bother us at all. If you close the door, we won't hear a thing. But I can't imagine the three of you make that much noise anyway."

"Oh, you'd be surprised," I say. "But thank you. That would be awesome."

"We'll definitely be stopping by one day this week," Rebecca promises. "Won't we, Sophie?"

"Yes, Becca."

Malcolm gives Elizabeth a nudge. "We'd better keep moving. We don't want to keep the kitchen magician waiting for these groceries."

"Tell him we might have a break in the case," Margaret says. "We should know more tomorrow."

Elizabeth winks at me. "You girls take all the time you need. And I'll take good care of Benjamin."

We're just starting to walk away when Elizabeth calls out to me. "Sophie, this might seem odd, and I'm probably mistaken, but I could swear I saw you the other day on the back of a scooter with a boy that looked like your friend Raf. You had a helmet on, but I caught a glimpse of your beautiful smile—or at least I thought it was yours."

Gulp. "On a scooter? Me? Where?" I'm sure the look on my face is a mixture of confusion and terror, but lucky for me, Elizabeth seems to notice only the confusion.

"Oh, it must have been somebody else. I have to admit, it did seem a little strange. Toodle-oo, girls."

As Malcolm and Elizabeth continue on their (mostly) merry way, and I try to do the same, Margaret and Becca, arms crossed, block my path.

"Sophie Jeanette St. Pierre. Have you been scooting?"

Trapped. Exposed. Betrayed yet again by my tomato red face.

"A scooter? With Raf? What were you thinking?" Whoa, this is a Margaret who is really mad at me.

"I dunno. I wasn't going to, and then—"

"Sophie, do you know how dangerous that was? How stupid? Raf doesn't know what he's doing."

Sucker punched, I fight back the tears that are coming because of the overload in my emotional fuse box. Why can't I tell her how much fun it was?

"He does, too! His uncle taught him. He was careful. And it was only the one time. It's no big deal. And at least Raf is the kind of boy who would stick up for me."

It's an Andrew slap, and I regret it the second it hits her, but . . .

I have to cry. And so, I run.

Chapter 18

In which the blazers do get us in the door

Leigh Ann calls me at nine-thirty, late for her.

"You okay?" she says.

"Yeah."

"Have you, um, talked to, um, Margaret?"

"No. She might have tried to call, but I had my phone off."

"Sophie, when you ran off, she was crying, too. You're her best friend, and she's afraid something bad might happen to you. That's all. She's not mad at you."

"She called me stupid."

"She said riding the scooter with Raf was stupid."

"Was she mad about what I said about Andrew?"

There's a long pause on Leigh Ann's end of the conversation. "Um, what did you say about Andrew?"

"That at least Raf would stick up for me."

"That was about Andrew? I'll admit, we were all kind of confused when you said it, but we just figured you were upset and not making sense. What did you mean?"

"See, I can tell Margaret likes him, and sorry to put

it this way, but I think he's kind of a jerk. Twice I've seen him with Livvy when she was either talking about Margaret or being rude to her, and he didn't do anything."

"Soph, you need to call her about this—right now. Call me later if you want."

I'm still debating the pros and cons of calling Margaret when the phone rings.

"I just thought of how to get Livvy back!" Leigh Ann exclaims. "It's a beautiful plan, if I do say so myself."

I'm immediately interested, and besides, I really don't want to deal with my Margaret situation right now. All recent evidence to the contrary, I am not a big fan of confrontation. "Okay. Does it involve anything illegal, immoral, or unethical?"

"Um, no, no, and probably not."

Revenge without guilt? Seems unlikely. "Okay, let's hear it."

"See, it's all about appearance. Livvy just has to believe that we—well, Rebecca, actually—did something illegal. I think we've proved that we can act, right? It's time for another performance by the Red Blazer Players. Okay, you know that big science test we have next week? Multiple choice, on everything we've covered so far this year? We're going to convince Livvy that Becca hacked into Ms. Lonneman's computer and stole the test and the answer key."

"But why would we tell Livvy? She'll never believe we'd help her."

"This is the beautiful part. Livvy is going to intercept

a note from Becca to me, talking about what she did, and how we have to keep it a secret from you and Margaret because you guys are such goody-goodies that not only would you not cheat, you'd probably tell Ms. Lonneman what was going on and ruin it for the rest of us. Livvy will believe that."

"Are you kidding? I believe that."

"Then, at the end of Becca's note, she'll say that the copy of the answer key will be under the books in the top of our locker, which everyone knows we never lock."

"And you think Livvy will steal it?"

"I guarantee it. She's a sneaky one."

"Ohhh. Then she will totally bomb the test. And it's not like she can complain. An answer key supposedly hacked from a teacher's computer, which she stole from a locker. Good plan, Leigh Ann! Hey, I'm writing a song that's kind of inspired by Livvy."

"Ewww."

"Well, not so much by her. More the dreaded apostrophe project."

"Your song is about apostrophes?"

"You'll see. I'm done with the lyrics, and I think I've got the music figured out. Gerry is going to help with that part when I see him for my lesson Saturday. But I promise, I'll bring what I have to our next rehearsal. You know, I'm going to be really happy when we find this violin, so we can all get back to our normal crazy schedules."

• • •

Leigh Ann hangs up again, and this time I don't hesitate; I speed-dial Margaret. As I listen to the phone ring once, twice, three times, I realize my heart is pounding. I'm calling my best friend in the world for, like, the gazillionth time, and I'm nervous. The fact is, I know she's right, essentially. Getting on a motor scooter to ride across the city with a twelve-year-old boy, even a reasonably responsible one like Raf—I shouldn't do that. The fact that I was discovered proves—yet again—that I am the world's worst criminal. I have been caught every single time I have broken the law. First, there was that incident with the St. Christopher medal at the St. Patrick's gift shop, then getting busted in the church by a half-blind, hearing-impaired security guard, and now the scooter. I wasn't on that stupid thing ten minutes, and Elizabeth Harriman spots me. Some people just aren't cut out for the shady side of the street.

Margaret answers on the fourth ring. "Hi."

"Hey."

"I tried calling."

I grunt. "I turned off my phone so I could think."

"Oh."

"Margaret—"

"Wait. Let me go first. Look, I'm—I just freaked out a little when I thought of you and Raf zooming across town on a motorcycle—"

"Scooter."

"Fine. A scooter. Sophie, what if something had happened to you?"

"But nothing did."

"This time."

"Look, Margaret, I know the scooter thing was dumb—but it was also a-MAZ-ing! And don't you have to do something crazy once in a while? I mean, sailing across the Atlantic Ocean in 1492 was dumb, too, but look where it got Columbus."

"You're comparing yourself to Columbus?"

"I'm trying to make a point—that you have to try new things. Sometimes you have to take chances. Even if I never get on another scooter—"

"Which you won't, if I have anything to say about it."

"I have that experience to carry with me. Forever. And you don't have to say anything about it."

"Hmmm. I understand what you're trying to say. You're wrong, but I understand."

"So, should I call Raf? He can take you for a ride, too."

"How 'bout we start with some not-too-exotic sushi?"

"Deal. And for your thirteenth birthday—a subscription to *Teen Vogue*?"

"Don't push it, Magellan."

All that day-before drama is mostly forgotten as four girls in red blazers and plaid skirts climb the stairs to the apartment directly above Chernofsky's Violins. No matter what perils await us on the other side of the door, we're ready.

Margaret pauses before knocking. "Remember, we're reporters for the school paper. Sophie, you have the camera? Leigh Ann, a notebook?"

"Check."

"Got it."

She knocks firmly, and to our surprise, the door opens almost instantly. Two women, both about four and a half feet tall, with short gray hair and trim, athletic-looking builds, stand side by side. They're not quite identical, but the resemblance is close enough that I blink a couple of times to make sure I'm not seeing double.

"Hello," says the one on the left. "Can we help you?" Classical music is playing on the radio in the background, and the smell of just-baked cookies perfumes the air.

Margaret introduces us and explains the "purpose" of our visit, and we are invited into a comfortable, simply furnished room. Margaret is right about the power of the school uniform. It's the equivalent of top-secret security clearance. Could I walk into a bank vault simply because I'm wearing a blazer and a plaid skirt?

The two women are Natalia and Anna Mendlikova, and it turns out they are cousins—not sisters—from Romania. Anna is the talkative one, while Natalia is a little skittish; she smiles and nods, but rarely makes eye contact with any of us. Every few seconds, she looks nervously at the door as if she's waiting for the KGB to come crashing through and arrest them.

"Everyone thinks we are sisters," Anna says. She moves her face even closer to Natalia's to emphasize the similarity. "We grow up together in Romania. We leave Romania together. Now we live together in America."

"How long have you lived in the United States?" Rebecca asks, taking notes like the good little reporter she isn't.

"We defect in 1976, but we spend almost one year in Canada before coming here."

"You defected?" I ask. I start to regret that I don't actually write for the school paper. Even if they have nothing to do with the violin, this might make a great story.

They nod in unison, and then Anna begins to speak very deliberately. "From the Olympics, in Montreal. Natalia and I were gymnasts, on the Romanian national team. You have, of course, heard of Nadia Comaneci, winner of many gold medals? She was our teammate. After the final events, Natalia and I disappear. Everyone pays so much attention to Nadia, so it is not so hard to do."

Leigh Ann leans forward in her chair, captivated. "And then what happened?"

"We are lucky. We have friends in Canada who help us. It was difficult time. We tell our families what we plan to do before we go to Olympics, but still, it is very painful. We do not see them for many years."

"But now you can see them, right?" Margaret asks.

"Yes, yes. Some come to America, too. My nephew Sergei lives here in New York. This is picture of him." Anna takes a double frame from the table behind the sofa and hands it to me. "Now we make some tea for you girls and bring out some cookies. Then we will answer all your questions."

As they disappear into the kitchen, I get my first look at the photographs. And guess what? Sergei is a gymnast, too. The first picture shows him hanging from the rings in a position that seems humanly impossible—well, at least for this human. In the second, he is in a suit and tie, standing between Anna and Natalia, both in floral-print dresses; he is only slightly taller than the two women. Making sure that they are out of hearing range, I whisper to Margaret, "I'll bet he could climb through a trapdoor."

Her eyes widen when she sees his picture, and she grins as she shows Becca and Leigh Ann. "We need to find that door and make sure it's possible to get through it and into the violin shop."

"I'll ask to use the bathroom," I say. "I think I can find the spot that's right over Mr. C.'s office. It will only take a second."

Did you just hear me? I really should know better than to say things like that.

"Just be careful," Margaret says. "Don't leave anything behind."

One time I left my stupid book bag with my ID under

a table in the middle of a secret mission, and I'll never hear the end of it.

"We need a code word," I say. "If someone's coming my way, just say, um, 'book bag' really loud."

"That's not a code word," Rebecca says. " 'Enigma.' Now, that's a code word."

"Just say 'book bag' if someone's coming."

"Are you sure you don't want to make it—"

"Becca!"

"All right. 'Book bag.' Jeez."

Do you see what I have to put up with?

After asking for permission to use the bathroom, I go down the hall and peek in the first bedroom. My quick calculations tell me that the trapdoor should be about where the closet is, so I step inside. I open the louvered closet door and get down on my hands and knees. Naturally, it's one of those New York closets that extend beyond the door in both directions. The good news is that the floor is clear, and I can see the outline of the trapdoor; the bad news is I can't open it. I can't tell if it's jammed or if it has been nailed shut. I'm lying on my stomach, with only my feet sticking out through the closet door, and wishing I had a screwdriver—when someone grabs my ankle and pulls.

I go into immediate cardiac arrest and then struggle to turn around to get a look at my captor.

"What was that code word again? I forgot," Rebecca whispers.

"Becca, I am going to kill you," I hiss. "What are you doing here?"

"I'm helping you with your contact lenses."

"I don't wear contact lenses."

"Yeah, well, if anyone asks, just go along with it. Did you find it?"

"Uh-huh, but I can't open it. We need something to pry with."

"How about a key?" She gets down next to me and starts digging around the edge of the trapdoor. We are both completely inside the closet, and just as we get a good grip on one edge of the trapdoor, the closet door closes with a click. We're too absorbed in the trapdoor to care, though, finally pushing it up far enough for her to stick her head through.

"Well? Whaddya think?"

"Oh yeah," she says. "I could do it. I think. It would be really tight, but it's possible. The opening to the ceiling in the violin shop is not exactly right under this one. It's over about a foot, so you'd have to go in at kind of an angle. And there are a couple of big pipes in the way. It would have to be somebody who can bend like a pretzel."

"Like a world-class gymnast? Good enough for me. Let's get out of here."

Becca reaches for the doorknob and tries to turn it, but nothing happens. "Uh-oh."

"Stop fooling around, Becca," I say. "Open the door."

"Fine. You try."

Annoyed, I grab for it, quickly realizing that she's telling the truth. We're locked in a closet in the apartment of two nearly identical, retired Romanian gymnasts. What are the odds?

Oh, I'd say about even.

Chapter 19

This one is for all those people who think a cell phone is not an absolute necessity

"Now what?" Becca asks.

"I'm thinking, I'm thinking," I say. "And get off my foot."

"I'm not on your foot."

"Yes you are. Move!"

"Maybe I can pick the lock," she says, kneeling on my hand.

"Oww!"

"Well, get outta my way."

She takes out her library card and tries to slide it between the door and the frame, but because the door opens out, there is no room for it. "It won't work in this direction. From the outside it would be easy."

"Oh, that's helpful."

"Hey, don't get all biffy with me. It's not my fault."

"Oh, I suppose it's mine? I was doing just fine until you came in here, Becca."

I gasp.

"What?"

"I just felt something—alive!—buzzing right next to my leg. Arrgghhh! There it is ag—oh! It's just my phone. Sorry." I dig the phone out of my blazer pocket and check the screen. Margaret.

"Um, hello. What are you guys doing in there?" she asks.

"We're locked in the closet."

"No way."

"Get us out of here before we kill each other."

Ten seconds later, the closet door opens. Margaret looks down at us with a goofy smile and mercifully doesn't say a word until we're almost back in the living room.

"Just out of curiosity, before I called, did you two have a plan to get out of the closet?"

Becca and I glare at her and each other.

"Now, please tell me you didn't leave anything behind this time, Sophie."

Grrrr. Grrrr.

"I'll take that as a no," Margaret says. She then reminds me of the problem I'm having with my contact lenses. We return to the living room with me rubbing my eyes dramatically, and Anna asks if everything is okay.

I reassure her that I'm fine; I'm still adjusting to my new lenses and I got something in one eye. (That one's going to cost me a couple extra Hail Marys.)

"Anna was just telling us that Sergei comes and visits

every Saturday and stays the night," Margaret says. "Isn't that nice?"

"He is good boy," says Natalia, obviously proud of him. "He helps us."

"You know, he looks kind of familiar," Leigh Ann says. "I think I've seen him in Perkatory."

Anna beams. "Ah yes, Sergei always stops for coffee on Saturdays. Sometimes I think he comes first for the coffee, second for the girl who works in the coffee shop, and third for us." She laughs. "No, not really. I make a joke. Natalia is right. He is good boy."

Margaret stands up and motions for the two women to move closer to each other. "Do you mind if we take some pictures? Sophie, maybe you can get one of them holding up the picture of Sergei. Maybe even take a close-up of him, too."

Okay, on three, everybody smile and say "Sergei!"

Mad rush back to the violin shop, where we find Mr. C. in the workshop varnishing a violin that he made. He listens to our story without taking his eyes off his brush or saying a word. When he finishes, he hangs the violin on the wire that's stretched across the shop, and then sits in the only seat in the room, a simple wood stool that he also made.

"So, you believe that this young man—"

"Sergei," I say, as if the name itself implies a certain degree of guilt.

"Yes, that this young man named Sergei, who you have never met, climbed down through the hole in my ceiling, stole a violin that only a few people in the world know is valuable, and then crawled back through the ceiling without a ladder. And while he's down here, he drops a certain special button on the floor so that I will think that my assistant is guilty. Tell me why he does this?"

Ah, that pesky button again.

"There must be an explanation," says Margaret. "I just haven't figured it out yet. Give me a little time. But in the meantime, don't you think you should ask the police about the hole in your ceiling? They could at least look into it, ask a few questions of their own. Maybe Sergei has a criminal record that he's hiding from his aunt."

"Here is what I will do. When the police come back tomorrow, I promise you I will point out the opening in the ceiling so that they can investigate. I think it's best if I don't tell them that you girls were in the closet up there without permission of the two very nice ladies. That might be hard for you to explain."

Oh yeah. Hadn't thought of that.

"Any, um, new letters for me?" Margaret inquires.

"Nothing today. I hope he has not changed his mind."

"Don't worry. It's only been one day," I say. "Those clues and codes and things must take some time to figure out. Or maybe he didn't find your answer. Maybe he's in the hospital. Or in prison. Or—"

Margaret pats me on the back. "Easy, Soph. I'm not giving up. We're going to find both of these violins. Let's start by talking to your friend Jaz, to find out if she was working last Saturday."

Jaz worked all day Saturday, and provides us with what might be the missing piece of the puzzle: the link between Sergei the gymnast and Ben's button. We show her the picture of Sergei and she smiles, recognizing him instantly.

"Oh, the little guy with the accent. He's a sweetheart; kinda has a crush on me. Saturday, let's see. Yep. Twice. The first time was right after I opened at seven. Had his usual extra-large coffee with a double shot of espresso thrown in."

Rebecca whistles in admiration. "Wow. A total java junkie."

"Yeah, he always leaves wired."

While we're talking, I note that Jaz is fiddling with a long, expandable aluminum pole. It has a rubber suction cup on one end, which she wets with a little spit. Then she reaches up over our table, sticking it to a burned-out lightbulb. "Sorry, guys, I'll be done in a second. This thing is easier than dragging out a ladder."

"I've never seen one of those before," I say. "Pretty handy."

She twists the handle slowly, unscrewing the old bulb, and then lowers it to the table with the pole. She then sticks a new one onto the suction cup and screws it in. "There. All done. Why are you guys looking for my little buddy? Wait a minute. Don't tell me he had something to do with that break-in."

"We're not sure," Margaret says. "Maybe. We've been sort of, um, unofficially working on the case. Mr. Chernofsky is a good friend, and we're just checking out all the possibilities. You say Sergei came in twice on Saturday?"

"Yeah, the second time was probably a little before noon. He was sitting over there." She points the lightbulb changer at the very table where we were sitting the day we overheard Ben talking on the phone.

"You thinking what I'm thinking?" I say to Margaret.

"That he heard Ben and Mr. Chernofsky talking about the violin through the vents? That's about the time I saw Ben leaving the shop on Saturday," Margaret says. "That would explain how he knew. But we still need a connection between those two."

"Who's Ben?" Jaz asks.

"Mr. C.'s assistant."

"Ohhh, I know who you mean. He's the other little guy. Kinda preppy-looking?"

"That sounds like him," Leigh Ann says.

"The cops are lookin' for him right now," Rebecca blurts out. "He's a fugitive from justice."

Margaret sends her a pointy look. "Becca, that's a little overdramatic, don't you think? As far as we know, the police just want to ask him some questions. They simply don't know where he is."

"And neither do we," I add, in case anyone has forgotten that it's supposed to be a secret.

"Well, he comes in here every once in a while—a small decaf and a hazelnut biscotti. But not since . . . hey, you know what? He was here Saturday, too. Same time, a little after noon. He was sitting on that couch over there, right behind double-espresso guy, reading the *Times*. They even talked a little bit. I remember now because I was thinking how much alike they seemed. Both sorta small, both sorta cute, and—oops, customer! Gotta go."

When Jaz is out of range, I lean over the table and motion for everyone to huddle closer together. "Maybe Sergei and Ben know each other. They could have set this whole thing up."

"Maybe they met in prison," Becca says.

"Think about it, Margaret," I say. "It's kind of like that Sherlock Holmes story 'The Red-Headed League.' Maybe the only reason Ben went to work for Mr. C. was to steal stuff, and that whole story about being locked in the basement for three days is just a convenient alibi. Or—"

Margaret cuts me off. "Slow down, Soph. That doesn't make any sense."

"I hope you're right." I'm picturing Elizabeth tied to a chair in her house, and her entire art collection packed up and on its way to Romania.

Margaret motions for us to follow her to the places where Ben and Sergei sat on Saturday, according to Jaz.

"Here's what I'll bet happened. Ben is sitting here, drinking his coffee, minding his own business, and reading his paper. Sophie, let me ask you a question. What happens every time your dad sits down on the couch?"

"He falls asleep?"

"Okay, but what happens to the stuff in his pants pockets?"

"Ohhh. All his change falls out! That drives my mom crazy. Why does that happen?"

"I don't know why, but it happens with my dad, too. Something about the way men's pants are made. And I'm willing to bet that when Ben sat here on Saturday, all his change—and the button—fell out of his pockets."

"And ol' Sergei picked it up when he left," Leigh Ann finishes.

"When they talked, Sergei probably found out that Ben worked in the violin shop," Margaret continues.

"So now what?" Rebecca asks. "Are we gonna tell the cops?"

"It wouldn't do any good," Margaret says matter-of-factly. "Even if we could prove that Sergei picked up Ben's button, it wouldn't prove a thing."

We all stare down at the table, chins in our hands and fresh out of ideas.

But gradually our collective craniumachine comes to life. With a screech and a puff of steam, the gears begin to whir. Wheels spin. Lights flash. Synapses fire. Eyes meet. Knowing nods are exchanged.

A plan is born.

• • •

Margaret and I make a quick stop at Elizabeth's to talk to Ben, who confirms Jaz's version of events from last Saturday. He was at Perkatory and did talk to someone who was sitting at a nearby table. And he is positive that the button was in his pocket when he reached into it to pay for his coffee. When I show him the picture of Sergei, his eyes light up.

"That's the guy I talked to in the coffee shop. He's Romanian. A gymnast."

"Well, you're gonna love this," I say. "He's also the nephew of one of the two ladies who live right over the violin shop."

He is impressed but a wee bit disturbed by our little snooping adventure. "You can't be doing stuff like this for me. You hardly know me. What I mean to say is, I'm really grateful for everything you and Elizabeth and Malcolm are doing, but it's just not right. I should just turn myself in now and take my chances with the police."

Is he bluffing? I wish I knew!

"No, no, please don't do that—not yet," Margaret pleads. "Give us a few more days. I have a plan to catch Sergei in the act, but we can't put it into action until Saturday."

Ben sighs and looks us in the eyes. "All right. Saturday. But after that—"

"Make it Sunday. Morning. I promise. We'll know by then. Now, tell me about the computer you installed at Mr. Chernofsky's."

"What do you need to know?"

"Its capabilities. It's part of the plan. The Red Blazer Girls Detective Agency is going high-tech."

You'll see.

I call Raf later that night to give him an update on the case. His favorite part is when Becca and I were locked in the closet together.

"You really do stink at being the bad seed," he says.

"Tell me about it. I'm just going to have to accept that it's my lot in life to be a good girl—I mean, I even have 'Saint' in my last name. Except, well, for the scooter rides. Margaret found out, and we had a big fight. I'm surprised she didn't come over to the West Side to sock you."

"Why did you tell her?"

"I didn't. Leigh Ann is the only person I told. Elizabeth saw us that day. I denied it, but Margaret can read me like a cereal box. She always knows when I'm lying."

"That probably explains how my mom found out."

"What!"

"Uh-huh. Boy, is she ticked off at my uncle."

"Well, I don't think Margaret or Elizabeth would have told her. Maybe you're not as sneaky as you think. You probably walked in your apartment with the helmet on. So, how much trouble are you in?"

"Keep your phone charged, because you're not gonna see me for a while. I'm grounded."

"For how long?"

"Depends. How long do you think it will be till man lands on the sun?"

"Oy. But, Raf . . ."

"Yeah?"

"It was fun."

"Sure was."

Chapter 20

Oh, like your gym clothes smell like Chanel No. 5

Margaret is waiting impatiently for me to finish my breakfast, which I am trying to enjoy for once, rather than stuffing my face and running out the door. She's sitting across from me, drumming her fingers on the table and sighing loudly every few seconds.

"Are you sure you won't have some orange juice?" Mom asks her. "It's fresh-squeezed."

"You may as well," I say. "I'm gonna be a while."

"Thank you. I guess I will have some orange juice, Kate," Margaret says.

"Sophie, what did you do with my grabber?" Mom asks, reaching into the cabinet for another glass.

"Grabber? Oh, that thing. It's in my room. I needed it to get something off the top of a bookcase."

The ceiling in our kitchen is pretty high, and Dad installed full-length cabinets to store all his cooking gadgets and pots and pans. In order to reach the tip-top shelves, Mom needs this metal contraption with a handle that's about three feet long, with rubber-coated "fingers" that can grab hold of things.

Mom comes back from my room with the grabber and pulls down a little pitcher from the top shelf.

"I should get one of those for my mom," Margaret says. "It reminds me of that thing Jaz used to change the lightbulb."

"We use it all the time," Mom says. "I may need it later today to put Sophie's dirty gym clothes into a laundry basket. Lord knows I don't want to make actual contact with those."

"Mom. Please."

She holds up her hands. "Oh, I'm sorry. Did I offend the princess by suggesting that her gym clothes stink?"

Margaret is enjoying this a little too much. "Ewww. Sophie, you brought those home a week ago."

"Excuse me for being too busy to clean my room. Somebody keeps dragging me all over the city after school every day."

"And yet, my room is clean."

"That's because you're obsessive-compulsive."

"Well, you're both going to be late for school if you don't hurry," Mom says. She kisses me on the cheek. "I love you, Stinky."

"Thanks, Mom."

We make it to school with a few minutes to spare. Leigh Ann and Becca are waiting for us upstairs by the seventh-grade lockers.

"Lookie at what we have!" says Leigh Ann.

"Yeah, while you two losers were sleeping in this morning, Leigh Ann and I wrote a masterpiece," Rebecca adds. "Livvy is going to totally fall for it. It's as good as one of those Harvard things you're always yapping about, Margaret."

Margaret looks stunned. One does not joke about the Harvard Classics with her. "Let me see it."

Leigh Ann hands her the note, which alternates between Becca's and Leigh Ann's writing. It is supposed to look like something they wrote in class, passing it back and forth. I lean in to read it over Margaret's shoulder.

Hey LA, I did it! U know that big test in Lonneman's class Tues? I have all the answers.

OMG How?!

It wuz ez. Hacked into her computer after school. U can have a copy Just DONT TELL anyone, speshally sophie and the brain.

Y not?

Cuz they dont need it there like jeniusses and besides they never help me UR right they get A's no matter what. Anyway, marg is such a saint she'd probly tell Lonneman or Sister B. Promise?

Promise.

OK. Its on the top shelf of the locker under all the
books—make a copy if u want, but b sure 2 put it back.

"This is good," I admit. "I think Livvy'll buy it. I especially like the creative misspellings."

Becca pretends not to know what I'm talking about. "There are misspelled words?"

Margaret agrees with my assessment and hands the note back to Becca. "So, how do you get this into her sneaky little hands without her being suspicious?"

"We've got it under control," Becca answers. "L.A. and I sit right in front of Livvy in social studies. We're going to pass this back and forth a few times, making sure that Livvy sees us. After class, I'm going to situate myself right in front of her, and it's going to 'accidentally' fall out of my notebook. She'll never be able to resist reading it."

"Not bad, you two," Margaret says admiringly. "In the CIA, they call this kind of thing disinformation. Leigh Ann, I have to admit, I find this devious side of you most interesting. You definitely have a future in espionage."

At lunch, future spy Leigh Ann Jaimes reports that phase 1 of the plan went perfectly. After Becca dropped the note, Livvy pretended not to see it and covered it with her foot. When she thought no one was looking, she reached down and slipped it into her blazer pocket.

"And she had this smirky-jerky smile on her face," says Leigh Ann.

"Like the one you have now?" I ask. "Where is Livvy, anyway?"

Leigh Ann points with her eyes at a table on the opposite side of the cafeteria. "She's at her usual table, with the usual adoring crowd. They're all whispering about something. I swear, it looks like she's already told them. I can't believe that. I thought for sure she would keep it to herself."

Margaret shakes her head. "Not her style. This way, if she gives everyone the answers, she'll be the big hero. Don't forget, it's always all about Livvy."

"I hope Becca put the fake answer key in your locker," I say. "Because she is definitely going after it. I wouldn't be surprised if she makes her move today."

"It's there," Leigh Ann replies. "And the locker's unlocked. We always just leave the lock hanging."

"Speaking of leaving things hanging, Margaret," I begin, "when does the plan to catch Sergei go into effect?"

"Tomorrow," she answers. "Jaz says that Sergei shows up at Perkatory at about eight, so guess what? You and I are going to be there when he arrives."

"On a Saturday morning?" I whine. "How come they don't have to come?"

"Because they are busy doing other things on Saturday mornings. Important things. You would just be sleeping in."

"Sleep is good. Sleep is important. Doctors are always saying people don't get enough of it."

"Then go to bed early. Get all you want. But don't plan on getting much on Saturday night. We're all sleeping over at your apartment."

"We are?" Becca, Leigh Ann, and I say in unison.

"Uh-huh. Don't worry, I'll explain everything."

Sometimes having a genius for a best friend can be so exhausting.

"Um, Margaret, do I have any plans next March twenty-seventh, around three o'clock?"

"Well, actually, we do need to—" She stops, a big smile on her face. "Oh, all right, you've made your point. I'll go over to Mr. C.'s for the daily check-in."

"Awesome. That means we rehearse today," I say to Leigh Ann and Becca. "Let's go over to Elizabeth's right after school. Maybe we can actually learn a whole song."

An entire song. A short song.

Dare to dream.

When the dust from the dismissal-bell stampede of girls settles, Becca announces that phase 2 is complete. The Klack-Hack has taken the bait.

"I had my books arranged so that I'd be able to see if anyone touched them, and they have definitely been moved. The answer sheet is still there, but I'll bet you she made a copy and brought the original back so that I wouldn't know." She laughs her evil-genius laugh. "Hwaa-ha-ha! Livvy Klack is going down."

"Don't count your chickens, Bec," I say. "A lot can happen between now and Tuesday. And didn't you say the same thing about your supersecret anti-Vatican organization?"

"Don't be a buzz kill, St. Pierre. And for your information, I'm not done with the SAVO yet. You just wait and see."

"Oh, I'll wait, Chen."

Leigh Ann looks to Margaret, palms up, for help dealing with Becca and me. "Have fun practicing. I'll see you guys tomorrow," Margaret says.

Having the basement in Elizabeth's house all to ourselves for a couple of hours is just what we need. We crank the amplifiers up to a respectable-for-rock level, and Becca and I start to get the hang of playing together. About an hour into the practice, we make it through all of "Twist and Shout" without any (cringeworthy) mistakes and then congratulate ourselves with high fives and ear-to-ear smiles.

"Man, we should have recorded that," I say. "Margaret will never believe us."

"That was awesome!" Leigh Ann agrees. "We totally rocked it."

"Ready to do it again?" Rebecca asks. "When we can play it like that twenty times in a row without mistakes, then we'll be ready to play it in front of other people."

"Hello, girls," Elizabeth says, coming down the stairs. "Sorry to interrupt when you're practicing. You sound wonderful, by the way—now, that's my kind of music! There's someone here who says she was supposed to meet you—"

"Mbingu!" shouts Rebecca, who runs over to greet her tall, striking friend, who is wearing, appropriately enough, a bright red coat. "You made it! Everybody, this is the girl I was telling you about, from the art program. I didn't say anything 'cause I wasn't sure she'd come. This is Leigh Ann, and this is Sophie. She's the one who was totally rude to you on the phone."

"Becca! Jeez! I am so sorry about that," I say. "Rebecca dearest, you were going to explain that to her, remember?"

"Oh yeah."

Mbingu doesn't seem to know what to make of us, but Elizabeth helps things out by inviting everyone upstairs for a short snack break. "You girls need to get to know each other a little if you're going to play together. What better way to do that than over Oreos and milk?"

For all her wackiness, Elizabeth is very wise. By the time we polish off a package of Oreos and half a gallon of milk, we are bandmates.

"I do have one little problem with being in the band," Mbingu says, pulling a pair of drumsticks from her backpack. "These are all I have. No drums."

"Maybe we can borrow some for a while, until we get enough money to buy or rent used ones," I say. "We must know somebody with a drum set."

"My brother has some drums," Leigh Ann says. "He

doesn't have time to play anymore. I'll ask him if we can borrow them."

"Problem solved," Becca announces. "For today, you get to play on a plastic bucket, Mbingu. Kind of like those guys on the street. Elizabeth, you got one of those we could use?"

Back in the basement, we let Mbingu watch and listen as we play "Twist and Shout." By the time we're halfway through, she knows the beat and is pounding it out on the top of the bucket. And suddenly we sound much better.

Leigh Ann notices the difference, too. "Mbingu, that was amazing. Where did you learn to do that?"

"I don't know—I listen to a lot of music and just imitate what I hear," she says with a shrug.

"Well, keep doing it," I say.

We hammer through "Twist and Shout" five or six more times, until Leigh Ann has finally had it. "Okay, I need a break from that one. I'm going to lose my voice. Sophie, why don't we try your song for a while?"

Rebecca strums her bass. "You have a song?"

"Well, it's not really done, and I'm not too sure about the key, and—"

She cuts me off with another riff, louder this time. "Lemme see it."

I take a notebook out of my bag and flip through the pages until I find it. "The chorus is done, but I think it needs one more verse. I don't even have a title—I just call it 'The Apostrophe Song.' That dumb project of Mr. Eliot's was the inspiration."

"Play a little bit for us," Leigh Ann says.

"It has a punky, Ramonesy kind of beat," I say as I find my way through the first few notes. Mbingu is tapping out a rhythm right along with me. "Yeah. Something like that. And the chorus has a much quicker tempo. More like this."

Leigh Ann takes the notebook from me. "Play that part again so I can sing. Ready?"

"Ready, two, three . . ."

I wouldn't, oh no I couldn't,
And no I haven't and I don't.
He doesn't, no no he isn't,
No way, he didn't and he won't.
We shouldn't, oh no we aren't,
No we can't . . . no, no, no we can't.

"Sophie, that's awesome!" Leigh Ann says. "You have to finish it, 'cause I really want us to do this song."

Mbingu looks suspiciously at me. "This isn't some joke you're playing on the new girl, is it? You really wrote that? Because I like it!"

"You know, L.A. and Mbingu are right—it's got potential," Becca says. "When you said you wrote a song, I'm thinking it's gonna be some cheesy ballad about Raf's big brown eyes. But Sophie St. Pierre, punk princess? Who knew?"

"Who is Raf?" Mbingu asks.

"Sophie's boyfriend," Becca chides. "He's sooo dreamy."

"He's not my boyfriend."

Mbingu leans in to whisper to me: "But is he dreamy?"

"Definitely."

"Well, finish the song, princess," Becca says. "It's totally rockin' and we need it!"

Maybe there's hope for me yet as a bad girl? Move over, Sid Vicious and Johnny Rotten. Here comes Sophie Sinister!

Chapter 21

I'd like to thank the members of the Academy . . .

In a clear violation of the Geneva Conventions, Commandant Margaret drags her only POW—that's a prisoner of Wrobel—out of bed and down to Perkatory at 7:45 on the dot. I mean, it's Saturday, for cryin' out loud. Even worse, she woke me up right in the middle of a great dream. First, Raf, with slicked-back hair and a leather jacket, picks me up on his scooter and takes me to my dad's favorite café in Paris—a place I've been to many, many times with my parents. (I know that sounds like the most pretentious thing ever, but I swear it's not like that. It's just, my dad is French. So we go to France for a lot of family vacations. Makes sense, no?) We're sitting at a sidewalk table drinking *l'eau gazeuse* (water with bubbles), nibbling on a baguette, and chatting away *en français* about the beautiful evening. When Raf reaches over and takes my hand, I notice that I'm wearing the Ring of Rocamadour, and I just can't take my eyes off the gold band with its tiny cross of rubies. Behind me, someone is calling my name: "Sophie. Sophie? *Qu'est-ce que tu attends?* What are you waiting for?"

I look over my shoulder at the waitress, who has the face of St. Veronica (this I know from a very familiar painting in our church). She looks me right in the eyes and smiles sweetly.

"Bonjour, Sophie," she says. "Time to take the plunge. You are ready."

I try to say something—I don't know what—but my lips seem glued together.

Then the phone rings and jolts me rudely back to reality.

Ready for what? I wonder. Some part of me must want to achieve something important, but the semiconscious, sleep-deprived part sitting in Perkatory seems basically contented with the gigantic mug of steaming hot cocoa that Jaz has set in front of me.

"Mmmm. Cocoa good."

"So, you are alive," Margaret says. "I was beginning to wonder."

I shake my head. "No talk yet. Sophie need more cocoa."

The door jangles, and Margaret sits up stiffly when she sees who comes in. "Oh. My. Gosh. You are not going to believe who just came in."

"Mmfff. Who?"

"Your old friend Mr. Winterbottom. Winterbutt. Winterpatootie."

That brings me to life. I haven't seen ol' Winter-slimebucket since, well, since the week we recovered the ring, and he and I had a, well, interesting final encounter. And there he is, skin the color of an overripe banana, and dressed in a rumpled suit that hangs limply from his shoulders. "You know, I was just thinking about him, wondering what he's up to these days. Do you think he's working at another church?"

"Hmm. Seems doubtful." Suddenly she turns back to me. "I think he recognizes us. What's he doing? Is he coming over here?"

"Calm down. He's just ordering coffee from Jaz. Wait, now he's leaving."

"Well, that's strange. He left without any coffee or anything?"

A few seconds after he leaves, Jaz motions toward the door with her head, and a few seconds later, Sergei walks in. There's no doubt it's him; he is about five feet tall, and when he takes off his jacket, his biceps bulge through his skintight shirt like the Incredible Hulk.

And boy, is he all flirty with Jaz at the counter as he orders his caffeine cocktail. "Look at the guns on that dude. I wouldn't want to get into a fight with him," I say.

"Wait a minute. Did you really just say 'look at the guns on that dude'? Good Lord. Did you pick that up watching *WrestleMania*?"

I flex my muscles for her. "Nah. Been pumpin' some iron down at the gym."

Sergei sits right where Jaz said he would, two tables behind me and right next to the air vent. Margaret scoots her chair a few inches so that she can see him over my shoulder and slides an index card with some writing on it toward me.

"Your script," she whispers.

Ahem. Places, everyone. Quiet on the set. Time for yet another awesome performance from Miss Sophie St. Pierre. Actress. Guitarist. Vocalist. Composer. Lemon tart taster. Sigh. My public simply can't get enough. I just hope the script is worthy of—ahem—my extraordinary talent.

I wait for my cue from Margaret. Sergei settles in, reading the paper and humming quietly.

"I can't believe we have to go into school today," Margaret says, winking at me. "These morning practices kill me. What are you doing later?"

I check my script. "Oh, I have guitar at five, and then I'm going to a movie with Raf. How 'bout you?"

Margaret looks over my shoulder to make sure Sergei is listening. "Well, my violin lesson is at two, but I'm going to hang out next door, at Chernofsky's. I feel kind of bad for him ever since his assistant ran off with that violin. He seems kind of nervous, like the guy's going to sneak back and steal more stuff."

"But he, like, changed the locks and everything, didn't he?"

"Oh yeah. That's the first thing he did. I've been trying to tell him that there's no way the guy is getting back in there. New locks, new alarm codes. And it's a good thing, too—what?"

Margaret lowers her voice a step. "I'm not supposed to tell anyone, because he is a little wigged out by it, but one of Chiang Li's bows is in the shop. He showed it to me—it's worth about fifty grand."

The script tells me to react loudly—I can do that. "Fifty grand for a bow! You can buy a car for that."

"Shhh! I know, it's crazy."

"Whose bow is it?"

"Chiang Li. He's playing at Carnegie Hall next week, and I guess it needs new hair or something."

"He brought it to Mr. Chernofsky?"

Margaret shrugs. "He has a good reputation."

Sergei pushes his chair back and stands, draining the last of his coffee. Then he brushes past our table on the way to the counter to flirt a little more with Jaz. When he leaves a few minutes later, Jaz joins us at our table.

"Well?"

"I think he's our guy," Margaret says. "He was acting a little too much like somebody who's not listening."

"But what if he really wasn't?" I ask.

"Nobody's that good an actor."

"Ahem."

"Present company excepted."

"I would think so."

Jaz has been eavesdropping on our exchange. "You two should be on TV."

I stick my nose in the air as high as it will go. "I don't do television. I am a thee-ah-tuh actor."

"Oh, par-don moi, ma-de-moi-selle," Jaz says. "I deedn't know I was een the presence of one so great and powerful."

I hold my hand out to her, turning my face away. "I accept your apology. You may kiss my hand."

"All right, all right," Margaret says. "Applause. Curtain. We have work to do."

Mr. Chernofsky is leaning over his workbench, sanding the neck of a violin, when we come in. He looks up at us over his glasses and glances at his watch.

"So early, and on a Saturday."

"Tell me about it," I say.

"The early bird catches the worm," Margaret says. "Or in this case, the thief. Mr. Chernofsky, we have a plan to catch the thief in the act."

Mr. C. turns the piece of wood over and over in his hands, looking for imperfections.

"This thief, who is it this time?"

"Remember the guy we told you about? Sergei? He's going to break in here again tonight."

That gets Mr. C.'s attention. He sets the violin neck

on the bench. "Again? You know that he is the one who stole the violin?"

"Well, we don't have proof yet, but we kind of set a trap for him," Margaret says. "We told him, er, actually, he overheard us talking about this great bow you're working on here in the shop. We said it belongs to Chiang Li. We're going to put a repair tag with Chiang Li's name on my bow—the one that my 'friend' sent me—and we're going to leave it right out in the open."

"And then what? You are going to sit here all night and wait for him to come? No! It is too dangerous. You girls are too young for such a plan. I will not allow it. I will nail the hole in my ceiling shut and we will be done with this forever."

"No, Mr. Chernofsky, you can't! Listen to the rest of the plan first. We won't even need to be here. Not physically." She takes a miniature webcam out of her pocket and holds it out for him to see. "We're going to attach this little camera to your computer and hide it in your office. That way, we'll be able to watch what happens from Sophie's apartment. And we'll record it so that we can show it to the police."

He takes a handkerchief out of his pocket and wipes his forehead. He squints at the camera in Margaret's hand and shakes his head.

"Look, even if we're wrong about Sergei," I say, "and Ben—or someone else—did steal that violin, and nothing happens tonight, then we'll quit and let the police try to solve the case. But if we're right . . ."

"Okay. One night. But tomorrow I nail the door shut and hope for the best."

Margaret gets right to work setting up the camera and the link on the brand-new computer in the office. Perkatory has wireless Internet, so we go back there with Margaret's laptop to make sure everything is working.

"What are you two up to now?" Jaz asks, peeking over my shoulder at the screen. The ceiling and desk in Mr. C.'s office are clearly visible. "Looks like a weird movie."

"We're hoping it gets better later," says Margaret.

"Yeah, it's supposed to have a wow ending," I say.

On the way back to the violin shop, I ask Margaret the question that's been bugging me since we conceived the plan.

"Shouldn't we use another bow? Like a really cheap one? I mean, according to Ben, yours actually is kind of valuable. What if Sergei takes it and just disappears?"

"I thought about that, but if he knows anything at all about bows, he won't be fooled by a cheap one. We have to hope that mine is attractive enough. And besides, he's not going to disappear and desert Anna and Natalia. And don't forget his crush on Jaz. The power of love and all that. Have some faith, Soph."

The final step is to have Mr. C. fill in the information on the tag so that it looks authentic. When he's done, Margaret sets her bow on the top shelf of the rack in the front room with the tag hanging just so.

"Voilà. We're ready. When you leave this afternoon, make sure you don't touch anything in the office. I have the camera aimed perfectly, and it's completely hidden. We'll be able to watch him when he comes through the ceiling and when he goes back up again."

"Tomorrow we take the evidence to the police," I add. "And pray he hasn't sold that violin already."

"I have a customer coming in early tomorrow morning," Mr. C. says. "You will call me first thing, then?"

"No matter what happens," Margaret promises.

We're not quite out the door when he calls us back in. "Ach, I almost forgot. I have something for Margaret."

"You do?" we ask in perfect harmony.

"This came for you last night. Slipped under the door." He hands Margaret a large manila envelope, and for the first time in too long, I see him smile. Printed on the outside are Margaret's name and the words FINAL CLUES.

"What is it?" I ask.

"Just a guess, but it looks like it might be the final clues," she says.

"Brilliance!"

She carefully tears it open and takes out several pieces of paper. One is a photograph of a typical New York apartment building; the other six sheets are six-by-six grids with a letter in each of the thirty-six squares. Naturally, the letters don't seem to form words. That would be too easy, I suppose.

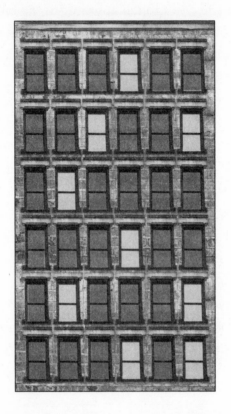

R	B	A	T	O	N
P	A	H	D	T	E
E	S	T	S	D	S
R	E	E	T	H	S
R	R	X	E	S	E
S	F	E	E	O	T

S	O	T	T	W	E
N	R	I	T	O	S
S	N	R	T	H	X
E	X	H	E	T	I
H	I	X	E	X	T
G	H	L	H	E	E

N	E	U	T	E	Z
M	P	H	T	B	E
E	M	E	R	F	O
I	O	V	A	R	E
T	N	N	H	E	I
C	A	R	N	T	A

D	Y	O	I	T	H
E	R	S	I	S	N
E	O	N	F	N	L
G	U	S	T	T	T
P	O	T	L	E	N
A	N	A	S	D	P

H	N	T	N	S	E
N	O	E	E	O	I
V	T	R	E	I	N
G	Z	H	H	S	T
E	E	E	V	R	R
E	I	E	T	G	W

B	I	L	O	N	G
D	R	I	E	G	S
S	T	O	T	S	R
S	E	O	H	N	F
S	E	E	P	T	A
T	H	R	D	E	D

A shake of the envelope and an index card falls to the ground. Margaret picks it up and reads,

> When you are ready to claim your violin, write the day and the time you will come see me on the back of this card and tape it to Fred Lebow's watch. I'll be waiting.

She carefully replaces everything in the envelope.

"Do you recognize the building in the picture?" I ask.

"Nope. Could be anywhere." She shows me the key that she keeps on a string around her neck. "I wonder if this is for that."

"I'll bet we know the answer by Sunday night," I say. "I'm feeling very confident."

"In the words of the esteemed Sophie St. Pierre, don't count your chickens."

Wise words, O Cautious One.

Later that afternoon, after a lengthy session with my mom and the rest of her string quartet, Margaret joins Becca, Leigh Ann, Mbingu, and me—a very different kind of quartet—at my guitar teacher's studio. We start off with "Twist and Shout" and quickly follow that with the first half of my song.

Gerry is sitting back in a chair, hands folded behind his neck and grinning as we hit the last notes.

"Tell me again how long you guys have been playing together," he says.

We look at each other, and I'm thinking he doesn't like what he's heard. "A couple weeks, I guess," I mumble. "Except for Mbingu. She missed the first couple rehearsals."

"Unbelievable," he says. "You're already better than some established bands. And, Sophie, I am really liking what you've done with your song. I have a few ideas for the bass line, so Rebecca will have a little more going on there, but you are on the right track with what you're doing everywhere else. Keep it simple."

"So you really don't think we stink?" Becca asks.

"Not at all," he says. "You're not perfect, but you've

got a nice clean sound. Just keep practicing, and play stuff you like. What do you call yourselves?"

"The Blazers," Leigh Ann says.

"Cool." He picks up the microphone. "And now the main event, the band you've all been waiting for . . . from New York City . . . the Blazers!"

And the crowd goes wild. Someday.

Chapter 22

In which we take one step forward, two steps on a slight diagonal, pivot on our heels, and repeat

Saturday night starts with us gorging ourselves on Dad's homemade pizza. As I'm cramming a second piece, Leigh Ann is already starting her third. Where does she put it? "Leigh Ann, I swear, the only time I see you eat is when you're here. Everywhere else you just peck like a little birdie."

"Ahgrow," she says. "Ahcanthelpit. Issogood."

Becca looks at me with a raised eyebrow. "Was that English?"

"Means she really likes my dad's cooking. She keeps asking if my parents can do some sort of mealtime adoption."

Leigh Ann nods eagerly. "Mmm."

Mom sets another whole pizza on the table before us and quickly takes away the empty tray. "My. Goodness. I might have lost a hand. Sophie, someone called for you earlier."

"I'll bet it was Raaafff," says Becca.

"Actually, it was your former swimming coach, Michelle. She's starting a new swim team at Asphalt Green, and she wants you to join."

"Really? Me?" In elementary school, I was on a kids' swim team, but with everything else going on in my life, swimming kind of got pushed to the side. It has been a few months since I've been in a pool.

"I think it would be good for you," Mom says. "You love to swim, and you are such a natural. Everybody says so. Michelle said you had tremendous potential."

"You never told me you swam like that," says Margaret.

I wave her off. "I'm not that good. Michelle must be desperate."

"You've always seemed . . . buoyant," Leigh Ann says.

Mom pats me on the shoulder. "You should definitely think about it. I don't know what you're waiting for. It's a great opportunity."

Weird! Mom just told me almost exactly the same thing that the Parisian waitress/St. Veronica told me in my dream.

"I promise," I promise. "Now let's talk about somebody else. Margaret, how did your practice go today?"

"Yeah, how was Andrew?" Becca taunts. "Is he just gorgeous?"

Nodding in agreement, Leigh Ann says, "He is."

"Uh-oh. Love triangle alert!" says Becca the Instigator.

Leigh Ann blushes. "I'm not interested, Margaret—honest! I was just . . . just confirming his cuteness."

Margaret holds up a hand to stop her. "It's okay, Leigh Ann. Becca's just teasing you and Sophie. Anyway, I don't think Andrew's interested in me. We had that one day when we did some texting, but he was all business at practice today. I mean, he's friendly—not acting like a jerk or anything—but he's not going out of his way to talk to me, either."

"Well, if he's not interested," I say, "he's an idiot and not nearly good enough for you."

"Thanks, Soph, but it's not like I'd be able to do anything about it anyway. Remember? My mother? My papa? My every-single-adult-relative?"

Mom laughs at that. "Don't forget, there's ice cream in the freezer when you're ready," she reminds us.

Pizza. Ice cream. The three best friends anybody ever had. Life is good if you're me.

Midnight comes and goes, but the SergeiCam show never changes. By two in the morning, we're all starting to fade. Leigh Ann and I are the most awake, so we volunteer to monitor the screen for at least another hour while Margaret and Becca sleep. We take turns keeping each other awake by telling stories, singing songs, and, in Leigh Ann's case, dancing around the room. Even after all that pizza, she is still so graceful and light on her feet that she barely makes a sound. Totally unfair.

As we sit cross-legged on the floor facing each other, I tell her about my latest ring dream.

"What was your answer?"

"That's just it—I don't know. I am trying to say something, but I can't talk. It's like my lips are glued together. I've been racking my brain trying to remember what I was thinking, but it's a blank."

"You remember the last time we all slept over—the night we were taking turns wearing the ring? You said that if St. Veronica was going to answer your prayers like it says in the legend of the ring, you wanted us all to be friends forever—no matter what else happened. Maybe you were trying to say something like that."

"Then why didn't I just say it?"

"Maybe you did, in your own way. Maybe in your dreams, you don't have to say everything. Just believing it might be enough."

"Could be. I'm not psychic, but it's like I know I'll see her again in my dreams. The way she looked at me and smiled—I wish I could explain how it feels. It's like, don't worry—everything is going to work out. But not in the way that grown-ups are always saying that. And I totally believe her."

"Wow, I wish she'd come and see me. I could use a little convincing of that myself."

"What's going on? Is your dad really going to take that job in Cleveland?"

"He still hasn't decided. I mean, I'm positive he's going to but just hasn't told me officially. He keeps saying he's thinking about it."

"Sorry. That stinks. It has to be hard for him, too—moving away from his family. Even, you know, with the divorce and everything. Tell you what. Next time I see St. Veronica, I'll tell her you need a little help," I say.

"Thanks, Soph," she says, sniffing a bit. "Hope it's soon."

A sliver of sunlight sneaks around the edge of the window shade and into my eyes, waking me from a deep, dreamless sleep. I lie there for a few more seconds, and then I suddenly remember the SergeiCam and jerk upright with a gasp.

Margaret, who is sitting at my desk, spins around when she hears me.

"Oh my God, I'm sorry, Margaret. I just closed my eyes for a second. . . ."

She shrugs. "It doesn't matter. I just fast-forwarded through everything after midnight, and there's nothing. He didn't show."

"You're sure?" I feel better that I didn't miss anything, but I know that Sergei not falling for the trap doesn't help matters. Any hope we have of recovering that Frischetti violin seems to be fading fast.

"Positive. Not even a mouse went in that office last night."

I rub the sleep out of my eyes. "Maybe he'll do it tonight."

"No, you heard Mr. C.—he's going to nail that trapdoor shut today. We had our chance. I should call him," she says, punching in the number on her phone.

A groggy Leigh Ann sits up. "What's going on?"

"She's calling Mr. C. Nothing happened."

"Hi, Mr. Chernofsky, it's Margaret. . . . What! How? . . . That's impossible! . . . No, there is nothing on the camera. . . . Yes, I'm positive. I checked twice. We'll be right there!"

Rebecca comes to life as Margaret shares the unbelievable news from Mr. Chernofsky: the bow with the fake repair tag—Margaret's bow—has vanished!

I tell Mom and Dad I'll explain everything later as the four of us run all the way to the subway. When we get to the violin shop, I realize not one of us has said a word since leaving my apartment. This has to be some kind of a record for four girls who don't hate each other.

After Mr. C. silently points out the empty space in the rack where the bow was resting, Margaret goes back into the office to check the computer and the camera. Then she walks around the rest of the shop in a daze, finally dropping into a chair in the front room, where she can stare at the spot where her bow should be.

"I just don't understand," she says, rubbing her temples. "We did everything right. How did it happen?"

"The doors were locked, and Mr. C. said the alarm was still set," I say. "Everything is just like it was yesterday except—"

"Except now I've gone and lost a really valuable bow. I suppose I'm lucky—at least it belonged to me, and not Mr. C. I don't think I could handle that. Somebody is outsmarting us. But who?"

Who on earth could be outthinking Margaret Wrobel?

Mr. Chernofsky sits down next to Margaret. "But there is good news, no?"

"There is?" she mumbles.

He nods. "Benjamin."

"What about him?"

"I think you are right. He was not the one who stole the violin after all."

"That's right!" I say. "Since you changed the locks and the alarm code, he couldn't have done it. Does that mean he can come back to work here? Ohmigosh, he will be so excited. I can't wait to tell him." Then, realizing what I've said, I quickly add, "I mean, that is, if I ever, like, see him again, ever."

Mr. Chernofsky chuckles. "So, it is as I suspected. You know where Benjamin is."

For the second time in less than an hour, all four of us are speechless.

He decides not to push the subject. "Well, if you ever see him, tell him to come see me."

I take charge. "We'll tell him right now, Mr. C. We

know exactly where he is. There's no sense in him acting like a fugitive if he isn't one."

Rebecca looks at Margaret and me. "Okay, it's all good for Ben. But what about the violin?"

"What do you think we should do?" Margaret says, eyes welling. "If you have any suggestions, I'm wide open. Obviously, I'm just a big failure. Finding the ring wasn't real detective work. We were just lucky. I officially quit."

"Come on, Margaret," I say. "That isn't true and you know it. And your theory about Sergei made perfect sense. The fact is, he could have stolen it just like you said."

"But he didn't and I was wrong."

"Even Sherlock Holmes wasn't right all the time, was he?"

"He's not a real person, Sophie."

Yeah, well, um, I don't know what to say to that. (Confession: I thought he was a real person.)

Leigh Ann takes the inconsolable Margaret by the arm. "Can we please continue this discussion over a bagel or something? You'll feel better after you eat something."

"You ate, like, half your body weight in pizza last night," I say. "I can't believe you're hungry again."

"I know. Your parents must think I'm some kind of freak."

"Are you kidding? They love you. Dad still hasn't forgiven me for saying that my favorite food is General

Tso's chicken from the Asian Garden. C'mon, Margaret, maybe Leigh Ann's right. We do think better when we're full."

I'm all for getting something to eat, but I have my doubts about the ability of a bagel to snap Margaret out of the funk she's in. This is the first time I've ever heard her say the words "I quit," and frankly, I'm not sure what it will take to bring her back.

Chapter 23

Perhaps she didn't quite understand the concept of quitting

Standing still for more than five minutes is considered wasting time in Leigh Ann's world. So when Elizabeth's basement is available on Sunday afternoon, she decides that playing some music will be a great way to forget about violins, bows, and codes for a few hours.

We find Ben in the kitchen baking gingersnaps, and although he's relieved that Mr. C. no longer considers him a dirty rotten thief, he is really upset by the news about Margaret's bow.

"Mr. Chernofsky said I should give you this." I hand him his button. "He wants you to come see him tomorrow."

Malcolm, who is dressed in his "courtin' clothes," as he calls his Sunday-best tweeds, shakes Ben's hand, and Elizabeth gives him a hug.

"Oh, Benjamin," she says. "Would you consider a trade? At least for a little while? Room and board in exchange for cooking a few meals a week for me? I'll even invite Malcolm over. I guess I can bear sharing you with him."

"Are you serious?" Ben asks. "Because if you are, I would be delighted. Your home is slightly more comfortable than my closet in the school basement."

"With way less rats," adds Becca.

"That's wonderful!" Elizabeth says, squeezing him again. "With you—and Malcolm, of course—I look forward to many future feasts." She winks at me over Ben's shoulder.

Sunday night comes and goes with no call from Margaret. No text messages, no e-mails. Nada. Nuthin'. What is going on with my no-problem's-too-difficult friend?

Monday morning. Six o'clock. Someday I'll learn to turn my phone off, or at least set it to vibrate, before I go to bed.

"Gralo."

"Wake up! I'm on my way. We have a lot to do!"

"We do?"

"Yes!"

Nine minutes later—a full two minutes ahead of her usual pace—Margaret whirls into my room, jumps on my bed, and shakes me.

"Come on, Sophie. I'm buying breakfast! Anything you want. You have ten minutes to get ready."

True to her word, we are out the door ten minutes later and headed for our favorite bagel shop.

"See, I've never been wrong so many times about one thing," she says between bites of a bagel that's gushing cream cheese from all sides. "So I stayed up all night thinking about it."

"Does this mean you're unretired?"

"I'm so back. And this case? It will be toast."

Ms. Lonneman must be worried that we're all going to fail her science test, because she spends the whole class period reviewing. And if she's worried, I'm worried. Margaret, who tends to be a tad jittery before test days, is far too serene, leaving me to wonder when the aliens who abducted the real Margaret on Sunday afternoon plan to bring her back.

And Livvy Klack and her circle of close fiends? No worries at all, mate! They are so confident that they spend the whole review period texting each other.

After school, Margaret takes us all on one more tour of the outside of the violin shop so that she can get a closer look at all the windows, but especially that round stained glass one. She gives the iron grate a good yank, but it doesn't budge. Apparently satisfied with its structural integrity, she then measures the distance between the window and the outside wall of the building next door. Not counting the church, they are the only two buildings on the block that don't share a wall, and

Margaret informs us that the space is three feet nine inches wide.

"Fascinating, Margaret," Rebecca says. "But why is that important?"

Margaret smiles. "You'll see soon. Now let's check out the inside."

A few seconds later, I push on the door to the violin shop and almost break my nose as Becca and Leigh Ann pile into me from behind. Then I notice the new sign (PLEASE RING BELL) and the button next to the door.

I press the button, and Ben comes out from the back, smiling when he sees me all smushed against the door.

"Hi, girls. I see you've discovered our new high-tech security system. I'll tell Mr. C. you're here."

"That's okay, you don't need to bother him," Margaret says. "Two seconds—I only need to check one thing."

"Be my guest. Are you hot on the trail of something?"

"Maybe. Hope so."

She does the *CSI* thing to the stained glass window: magnifying glass, tweezers, even the sniff test.

"She is smelling the window?" Leigh Ann asks me.

Without turning to look at us, Margaret says only, "All right. We can go now." Then she puts her magnifying glass and other detective tools back in her bag.

"Where are we going now?" I ask. "I need to study for science, and we have a ton of math, too."

Margaret calls Ben out of the back room. "Is anything going on here Friday at, say, seven o'clock?"

"You mean here in the shop? I can't imagine. We usually close at six-thirty. Why?"

"I may need to use this room for a little, um, let's call it a recital."

Ben looks baffled. "You're a very mysterious girl, Margaret Wrobel. And I am definitely looking forward to Friday."

If only he knew. (I know most, but I ain't tellin'!)

As I sit at my desk recopying my science notes and trying to imprint them on my poor overloaded brain, Friday seems a long way off.

But then the phone rings and everything changes.

"Tell me the truth, Soph," Margaret begins. "How close to being ready are the Blazers?"

"Define 'ready,' " I say.

"As in, ready to play in public."

"We only know two songs," I sputter.

"That's okay. It's perfect, even. So you are ready to play those two?"

"I didn't say that."

"But could you play them Friday? At Perkatory? I mean, if I can set it all up? It's *très* important."

So I take a deep breath. And I have this funny, déjà vu–ish feeling as I flash back to the dream where Raf and I are at the café in Paris. Is this what St. Veronica meant by taking the plunge? If so, does my entire future depend on it? Maybe we are ready. But what if we're not? I mean, what's the worst that can happen? We embarrass ourselves so profoundly that we have to go live underground in the subway tunnels with the alligators and mole people? Okay, that would stink, but assuming we're not that bad, then what could happen?

Well, one thing I do know: Becca will go ballistic if I agree to this without discussing it with her first.

"Hey, are you still there?" Margaret asks.

"Yep."

"Well?"

"Two conditions. One, you tell Becca."

"Deal. And?"

"Two—you spill all."

"Sophie, I have really, truly, positively figured out who did it and how they made my bow and the violin vanish into thin air."

"You got the how and the who?"

"Finally. We'll invite everyone to Perkatory at seven on Friday night for the world-premiere performance of the Blazers. You guys will play your songs, and then we'll gather everybody together—Agatha Christie–style— next door in the violin shop. And then the stumbling detective, *moi,* will unveil the murderer. Or, well, the thief."

"Wow, I mean, you're putting it all on the line, aren't you?"

"Uh-huh."

"And you're not gonna tell anything more to your faithful best friend, are you?"

"Nope."

As I turn my phone off and return to my science notes, I start to sweat. I mean, what have I done? Who was the crazy girl who promised Margaret that her band would be ready to play in four days?

And just like that, Friday seems a mere minute away.

Chapter 24

Not that there's anything wrong with Cleveland

Ms. Lonneman's science test covers everything she promised during her review, plus a clever little more. She has a knack for coming up with questions that make me doubt myself every time. Just when I'm feeling pretty good about my first choice, she throws in a "both B and C" or a "none of the above" or an "all of the above" just to jumble things up in my feeble brain. If I hadn't spent two and a half hours of my life recopying notes and studying my butt off (in between bouts of performance panic), that very brain would have melted into a puddle of gray goo.

When Ob-Livvy-ous and the rest of the Klack clique stroll into the room, confidence oozes from them like cream from an éclair. Mmmm . . . anyway, Livvy sits in the row next to me during the test, and she doesn't even break a sweat. After finishing up long before the period ends, she stares at the clock and taps out a rhythm on the desk with her pencil until Ms. Lonneman gives her a pointy look.

When the bell rings, I feel a little brain-drained, but noncrushed. Maybe not an A, but a B for sure, and on this test, I can live with that. Margaret gives me the "okay" nod, and Leigh Ann whistles a "whew" as we gather our bags to leave. The *clique de Klack* cackle like silly geese as they waddle out.

In the cafeteria, Margaret tells Becca and Leigh Ann that the Blazers will be playing their first gig on Friday. Becca's reaction? Let me put it like this: I am really happy there are four feet of table and Margaret between us. She swears. She pounds the table. She sticks her bottom lip so far out it's like a stubborn, fleshy shelf.

"Okay, I'm picking up on something," I say. "You're a teensy bit mad because I made a tiny decision without consulting you. But it's just two songs. And remember, Margaret is our manager. She knows what's best for us." I skate on the thinnest ice with this argument.

Leigh Ann steps in. "Actually, I think we can do this. Sometimes you do have to just, you know, dive into the deep end."

Rebecca takes a breath. "On one hand, I know we're not really ready, but on the other, I guess, yeah, ya gotta go for it."

Margaret is beaming. "Thank you, Rebecca, for that calm and sensible reaction."

"Too easy for you to say," Becca snorts. "You won't

be falling on your butt in front of a crowd. You'll just be sitting there with Andrew, laughing at us."

Margaret takes out a notebook and adds Andrew's name to a long list. "Thanks for reminding me. I'll invite Andrew to come on Friday."

"You can't!" I protest. "What if he brings Livvy? When she figures out what we did to her, she'll probably light my guitar on fire!"

Becca, who took Ms. Lonneman's test the period before us, giggles deviously. "Tell me again how cocky she was when she came into the classroom. I just love that part."

We have only an hour after school to practice, so we hurry over to Elizabeth's basement to twist and shout for Margaret, who is properly impressed and finally gets to meet our drummer, Mbingu. Even though Margaret is more classical than classic rock, she knows music, and with her suggestions, we're even better the second time through.

Then we play my song—which she loves!

"It's perfect. Don't change a thing. It is so punk!"

"You really think we sound okay?" Leigh Ann asks.

"You're awesome."

A few more times through the set, and we are feeling more and more like a band. Now that Mbingu has some actual drums, it is obvious how lucky we are to have her.

"That's it for me," Becca says, leaning her bass against the wall and unplugging her amp. "I promised my mom I'd be home by four. Mbingu, you headed downtown?"

She nods. "Is it okay if I go with you? My parents don't like me riding the subway alone."

"No problemo. You get off at Spring, right? I go to Canal, so I can protect you," Rebecca kids.

"I am so relieved," Mbingu says with just a trace of a smile.

"Yeah, I should go, too," Leigh Ann adds. "My dad's taking me out for dinner tonight to my favorite place. Which has to mean he is saying yes to Cleveland."

I put my arm around her shoulders. "I'm sorry. But don't worry—I have a plan to keep your brother nearby."

"Sophie, what are you up to?" Margaret asks.

"Hey, I'm allowed to have secrets, too. And right now I'm going home to snack and snooze."

"Can we just run into the school really fast?" Margaret asks me as we climb the stairs to Elizabeth's front hallway. "I want to see if Ms. Lonneman is there. Maybe we can find out how we did on her test."

It's a challenge to do anything quickly when Elizabeth is involved (she does like to talk), but we manage to thank her yet again for letting us use her basement, and Margaret invites her and Malcolm to attend our first show.

"Friday night, seven o'clock. At Perkatory. Wait till you hear these four."

"And what about you?" Elizabeth inquires. "Will you

be playing a little something for us, too? I've heard a lot about your violin playing, but I still haven't witnessed it firsthand."

A sly smile sneaks across Margaret's face. "Let's just say I have a very special performance planned."

"We wouldn't miss it."

The door closes behind us, and Leigh Ann and Becca are all over Margaret.

"What was that all about? What kind of 'performance' are you going to give?" Becca demands to know.

"Soon, my minions. Very soon."

I can wait for soon. But what's a minion?

Back inside the school, we scale the stairs to Ms. Lonneman's room on the fourth floor. Her door is open and Led Zeppelin is jamming on the classic-rock station. She jumps a little when Margaret knocks, then reaches over to turn down the volume.

"Sorry, girls. I am a child of the seventies. Love my Zeppelin, you know what I mean?"

"Definitely," I agree. "Jimmy Page is a god."

She looks at me with newfound respect. "You know who Jimmy Page is?"

"I kind of play guitar."

"She's a great guitarist," Margaret says. "In fact, she's going to be playing Friday. You know where Perkatory is, don't you? The coffee shop around the corner from the church?"

"Margaret," I interject. "I doubt that Ms.—"

"On the contrary, Miss St. Pierre. I would love to come."

"I have to warn you, we only know two songs."

"Who is the 'we' in that statement?"

"You know Rebecca Chen? Her and Leigh Ann Jaimes. And a friend of Rebecca's. And me."

"They're called the Blazers," Margaret says.

"Hmm. Clever name. Well, count me in—as long as the cover charge isn't too outrageous," she adds with a grin. "Did you girls come all the way up here to tell me that?"

Margaret sits at the desk right in front of Ms. Lonneman. "Actually, we were kind of hoping to find out how we did on the test today. Is that what you're grading?"

"It is indeed. I'm almost finished. That's the beauty of multiple-choice tests; they take forever to create, but they're easy to grade." She holds up a sheet of heavy paper with a lot of holes punched near the two long sides.

"What is that?" I ask.

"My magic grading tool. It fits right over the answer sheet. All I have to do is look to see if the spaces under the holes are blacked out. If they're clean, they're wrong."

"Just like the windows," Margaret says mysteriously. "Ms. Lonneman, your answer key just gave me the answer to a problem that has been driving me absolutely crazy. Thank you!"

Ms. Lonneman looks to me for an explanation, but I'm in the dark as much as she is.

"It's sort of complicated," Margaret says to Ms. Lonneman. "But about our grades?"

"I can play this game, too," Ms. Lonneman says with a gleam in her eyes. "It's complicated. I'll tell you tomorrow."

An incredible aroma of fresh-baked something greets me when I get home. Oddly enough, it's Mom, not Dad, in the kitchen, and every square inch of counter is covered with sugar cookies.

"What's going on in here?" I demand. "Does Dad know you're using his kitchen?"

"You'd better be nice to me if you want any of my cookies."

"Are you baking for the entire music school?"

"Sort of. We're having a big anniversary celebration Thursday, and I am the cookie committee. I suppose I should have gone out and bought them, but I had some free time for a change this afternoon, and I haven't done any baking in a while. Here, taste."

"Mmm. Cookie-licious!" I pour myself a glass of milk and sit at the table, also covered three deep with cookies. "Think you made enough?"

"The last batch is in the oven. Then I was thinking maybe we'd go out for dinner—just the two of us. Your dad has the late shift; he won't be home till midnight. How's your homework situation?"

"It's a light day. I had a free period and got my math and English done. Just a little Spanish—it'll take me maybe fifteen minutes."

"Why don't you do that right now while I clean up, and maybe we can even catch a movie. Check the paper for times."

Arms crossed, I confront her right there in the kitchen. "All right, Mom. What's going on? Are we moving? Did you get a job in Cleveland or something?"

Mom laughs. "Cleveland! What gave you that idea?"

"You baking cookies, dinner out, a movie—on a school night. What's up?"

"Hey, can't I spoil my daughter a little?"

"Ohhh. Well, if spoiling is what you have in mind, there's this awesome denim jacket in the window at—"

"I said a little spoiling. There'll be no completely ruining you."

"As long as we're on the subject of your unruined daughter, I have something to tell you."

"You're playing Friday night at Perkatory."

"Whoa!" I shout. "Jeez, I might as well live in some dinky little town. Everyone here knows everything I do!"

Mom almost drops a tray of cookies because she's laughing so hard. "It was Elizabeth Harriman. She called a little while ago to ask if she should bring something."

I get up and hug her. "I swear I just found out for sure today."

"It's okay, Sophie. I am so proud of you. What are you going to play?"

I tell her about the Blazers' tiny playlist. She can't get over the fact that I wrote a song.

"Maybe we'll have a look at this denim jacket after all."

"Really?"

"We'll have a look. By the way, did you ever call Michelle? If you're going to join the swim team, I think you need to be at the pool on Sunday afternoon."

"I'll call her right now."

"What are you going to tell her?"

I raise my hands over my head in the dive position. "Mom, I'm taking the plunge."

Chapter 25

Not my best work, but it beats the heck out of a poke in the eye with a big stick, or so I would guess

"Some of you did very well on the test, maybe even surprisingly well in some cases," Ms. Lonneman announces at the start of science class. Livvy and her crew turn to one another with smug smiles.

"However," she continues, "some of you ladies have a little explaining to do. I'm not an expert in the field of probability or statistics, but I can't help but wonder at the likelihood of a number of students—good students—receiving such similar scores."

Livvy raises her hand. "Maybe they studied together." She turns and smiles oh-so-sweetly at me.

"Miss Klack, perhaps you will understand my concern better after you see your test." She passes the papers back without a word.

Margaret holds hers up for me to see. A perfect one hundred. Leigh Ann's turn. Ninety-eight. Ms. Lonneman hands me my test. Ninety-six! Yes!

Livvy and friends, on the other hand, have gone silent. Livvy spins around, scowling when she sees my score. Then she sees Leigh Ann's paper. Her jaw practically bounces off her desk; her eyes, they become mere slits; and her face, it gets redder and redder as she glares at Leigh Ann, who looks innocent as, well, a schoolgirl.

"The following students will stay for a little chat after school today: Miss Klack, Miss Aronson, Miss Peters, Miss Welles, and Miss McCutcheon."

Yikes. I imagine how that conversation will go. ("But, Ms. Lonneman, the answer key that we stole out of a locker—the one that we thought was the real thing, stolen from your computer—turns out that it was a fake. So we're victims, really.")

Brrrinnnng! The three of us RUN down the stairs to the cafeteria. Rebecca holds up her own test—an eighty-six—and grins. "How did our dearest darling do?"

"Shame on you, Rebecca," Margaret scolds. "And you, too, Leigh Ann. Those poor girls trusted you!" She holds the straight face for a half second longer, then cracks up. "Can you believe how gullible they are?"

"It was a beautiful plan," says Becca, high-fiving Leigh Ann.

I put an index finger to my lips. "Shhh. Here they come." Livvy leads the way, with her four stooges in tow.

Becca, she cannot resist. "Hey, Livvy! How'd ya do on the science test? Me? A little ol' eighty-six."

"Do not gloat," Margaret warns. "That's just what got Odysseus into all that trouble."

Becca leans back in her chair. "What are you talking about?"

"*The Odyssey*? Remember? After Odysseus blinded Polyphemus—you know, the big Cyclops—by jabbing that big stick in his eye, he acted just like you. He couldn't stop himself from bragging about how he did it and rubbing the guy's face in it. The Greek-derived word for that kind of excessive pride is 'hubris.' And because of that, the gods turned on Odysseus, and it took him twenty years to get home."

"Are you saying it's gonna take me twenty years to get back to Chinatown? Because, you know, I can walk there in, like, an hour if I have to."

I pat Rebecca on the shoulder. "Just know that you probably haven't heard the last of Livvy Klack."

We decide to celebrate our minor act of revenge in a let's-not-tick-off-the-gods way, with ice cream and baked goods at my apartment after school. God knows we have cookies. When we get there, there's a package wrapped in bright red paper on my bed with a card stuck in the ribbon.

"Look, your parents got me a present!" Rebecca says. She picks it up and shakes it.

Margaret takes it from her. "Easy, Becca. It might be fragile."

"This is strange," I say. "It's not my birthday, is it?"

"I don't think so," Margaret says.

"Maybe it's not for me."

"See? I knew it was for me!" Becca exclaims.

I tear the card open and read:

> *Dear Sophie,*
> *Just a little something for making us so proud.*
>
> *Love,*
> *Mom and Dad*

I blink back a tear, stuff the card into my pocket, dig into the wrapping paper, and stop cold when I see the store's name on the box. "No way." I lift off the top and there it is: the coolest denim jacket ever. It is faded perfectly, with three different-colored bands sewn into the left sleeve, just above the elbow. We're talking rock-star cool.

"That's the one you were—" Leigh Ann says.

"I know. Mom and I were out last night, and I showed it to her, but she said it was too much. 'Maybe for Christmas' was all she said." Suddenly I feel very self-conscious, and I put the lid back on the box.

"Try it on!"

"C'mon, I want to see it on you!"

"I feel kind of stupid now," I say. "It just seems kind of rude, opening a present in front of everybody. It would be different if it were my birthday."

They jump me and start pounding me with pillows, wrapping paper, my blazer, anything within reach.

"God, could you be a bigger loser?" Rebecca chides. "Rude? If you don't try that jacket on in the next five seconds, I'm taking it."

I put it on. "There. Happy?"

"Look in the mirror," says Leigh Ann. "Raf is going to flip when he sees you in that thing."

I can't help smiling when I see my reflection. "Whatever you do, don't say that in front of my dad. He'll never let me out of the apartment." I take the jacket off and lay it gently on my bed.

Parents! Go figure.

Rebecca is already on her way into the kitchen, shouting, "What about this ice cream you promised? Whoa! Are these cookies all for us?"

"No!" I shout back. "We're only allowed to have the ones in the cookie jar."

"Why, are these too good for us?" Becca says.

"Becca! You're being a brat," says Margaret. "Sophie, come in here so that I can tell you guys how I solved the puzzle with the picture and all the grids."

"You mean . . . the . . . *dun, dun, dun* . . . final clue?" I ask.

Margaret takes the envelope with the clue out of her bag and spreads the papers on the table. "I went crazy looking at all these grids, trying to find words in every possible direction. I even went to the library and took out a few more books on deciphering codes, but nothing worked. And then . . ." She stops to take a big spoonful of ice cream, leaving us hanging.

"Margaret!" we shout.

"Okay, okay. When I saw Ms. Lonneman grading those tests with that tagboard answer key, it hit me.

Windows. At first I thought this photograph of the apartment building had something to do with all the clues with
addresses and apartment numbers, but I was wrong—
again. The picture was telling me how to decipher the
code, how to read the grids. It is the key to the whole
thing."

"Ohh," we say together, not understanding even the
tiniest bit.

"See, the picture is a kind of code machine called a
grille, or a grid, all by itself. I learned about them in one
of the library books. They were used by real spies back
in World War I. Now look at the picture again.

"Do you notice anything special about the windows?"
she asks. After a few seconds of silence from us, she adds,

"Like how many there are or
how they are arranged?"

We bend over the table,
elbowing each other to get a
better look and trying to be
first to answer.

"Thirty-six windows. Six
by six," Rebecca says, sticking her tongue out at me.

"Precisely. What else
about this clue is six by six?"

I win this round. "Ahhh.
These grids with all the
letters."

"Now for the bonus round. How many of the windows have lights on?"

"Nine," Leigh Ann answers.

"Yep. Nine out of thirty-six. Exactly one-fourth. Now the tricky part. I took a sheet of paper exactly the same size as the grids with the letters and divided it into thirty-six squares, again just like the grids. Then I cut out the squares that correspond to the locations of those windows, like this." She holds up her own grid with nine square holes.

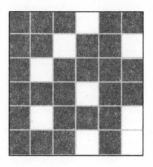

"And here are the first two grids."

R	B	A	T	O	N
P	A	H	D	T	E
E	S	T	S	D	S
R	E	E	T	H	S
R	R	X	E	S	E
S	F	E	E	O	T

S	O	T	T	W	E
N	R	I	T	O	S
S	N	R	T	H	X
E	X	H	E	T	I
H	I	X	E	X	T
G	H	L	H	E	E

"Now watch what happens when I set my grid with the holes on top of the first one with the letters, like so."

			T		
		H			E
	S				
			T		
	R				E
			E	T	

"Sophie, read the letters off from left to right and top to bottom. Leigh Ann, do me a favor and write them down as she reads them off. Ready?"

"T-H-E-S-T-R-E-E-T," I read.

"The street," Rebecca says. "Now what?"

"Now comes the beautiful part. Leave the grid with the letters alone, but turn the one with the holes a quarter turn clockwise, and you get the next nine letters."

	A		D		
				D	
	R	E			S
	S	F		O	

I read the next nine letters. "A-D-D-R-E-S-S-F-O."

"And another quarter turn for the next nine," Margaret says.

R		A			
P				T	
		T			
				H	
R			E		
		E			

"R-A-P-T-T-H-R-E-E."

"One more turn, and we'll be done with this letter grid."

	B			O	N
E			S		S
	E				
		X		S	

"B-O-N-E-S-S-E-X-S. Got all those, Leigh Ann?"

She spins her paper to show Margaret the full message so far:

THESTREETADDRESSFORAPTTHREEB
ONESSEXS

Margaret uses a pencil to divide the letters into words.

THE/STREET/ADDRESS/FOR/APT/
THREE/B/ON/ESSEX/S

"Everybody still with me? Good. Now, since the message is longer than thirty-six letters, it continues on the next grid, which has all new letters."

Leigh Ann is checking out the grid with the holes. "Uh-oh. I forget which side is the top."

"That's easy. Just look at the windows in the picture. Turn the grid until it looks just like that. Pretty cool, huh? As long as you have the key, why don't you take the rest of this one?"

Leigh Ann aligns the two grids and reads off the first set of letters, which Margaret writes down. "T-I-S-N-E-I-T-H-E. Is that right so far?"

Margaret nods and watches with a satisfied smile as Leigh Ann turns the top grid and reads off the next nine letters. "R-T-H-E-H-I-G-H-E. And the next nine are S-T-N-O-R-T-H-E-L. One more turn, and we get O-W-E-S-T-X-X-X-X."

"Those *X*'s are just fillers at the end of the message," Margaret says. She takes her pencil to the row of letters and divides them, leaving us with this clue:

THE/STREET/ADDRESS/FOR/APT/THREE/B/
ON/ESSEX/ST/IS/NEITHER/THE/HIGHEST/
NOR/THE/LOWEST/XXXX

"I already solved the other two, but here they are if you want to solve them for yourselves," Margaret says.

N	E	U	T	E	Z
M	P	H	T	B	E
E	M	E	R	F	O
I	O	V	A	R	E
T	N	N	H	E	I
C	A	R	N	T	A

D	Y	O	I	T	H
E	R	S	I	S	N
E	O	N	F	N	L
G	U	S	T	T	T
P	O	T	L	E	N
A	N	A	S	D	P

H	N	T	N	S	E
N	O	E	E	O	I
V	T	R	E	I	N
G	Z	H	H	S	T
E	E	E	V	R	R
E	I	E	T	G	W

B	I	L	O	N	G
D	R	I	E	G	S
S	T	O	T	S	R
S	E	O	H	N	F
S	E	E	P	T	A
T	H	R	D	E	D

I move the grids around myself to make sure I really understand how it works. "So it uses every letter on the grid exactly once? How is that possible?"

"Funny you should ask that, Sophie. You see, that's the really amazing part, and the thing that makes this code so hard to crack. The holes have to be arranged in a very special way for the grid to rotate properly." She opens a beat-up paperback about secret codes to show me a six-by-six grid that is numbered like this:

5	6	7	8	9	5
9	2	3	4	2	6
8	4	1	1	3	7
7	3	1	1	4	8
6	2	4	3	2	9
5	9	8	7	6	5

"See how there are four squares numbered one, four numbered two, all the way up to nine? Well, in order for the whole thing to work, you have to number your grid exactly like this and then cut out one of the ones, one of the twos, one of the threes, and so on."

"Oh, I see why that works," I say. "All the fives are in the corners, and the eight is always four spaces from the left in the top row, no matter how you spin the grid. Same with all the numbers."

Margaret holds up the photo of the building. "All that makes this even more unbelievable. Somebody went to a lot of trouble to Photoshop this picture so the lights would be on in the right nine windows. It boggles the mind."

"Oh, my mind is boggled, all right," Becca says.

Margaret's eyes sparkle mischievously. "Brace yourselves. There's more."

Chapter 26

One is good with pita bread; the other goes better with a big slice of humble pie

A few minutes later, I open a new document on my computer and start typing in the clues we have gathered from the four different challenges.

The piano player lives on Hester Street, but not in Apt. 4M and not at no. 127 or no. 301 (the orphan clue).

The bassoon player lives in 2J, but not on Grand or Essex (the first-letter clue).

The xylophone player lives on Bleecker Street, but not at no. 288 (the first pigpen clue).

The violinist does not live in the building located at 456 Grand or in Apt. 7A (the second pigpen clue).

The street address for Apt. 3B on Essex Street is neither the highest nor the lowest (the first grid clue).

And for those of you who didn't figure out the other two grid clues on your own, here they are:

The man in Apt. 5C at no. 301 is not on Spring Street and doesn't play the flute.

Neither 288 nor 770 is the address of the building on Spring Street.

When I finish, Margaret slides onto the chair next to me and makes this chart:

Instrument	Address	Street	Apt.
Bassoon	127	Bleecker	2J
	288	Essex	3B
	301	Grand	4M
	456	Hester	5C
	770	Spring	7A
Flute	127	Bleecker	2J
	288	Essex	3B
	301	Grand	4M
	456	Hester	5C
	770	Spring	7A
Piano	127	Bleecker	2J
	288	Essex	3B
	301	Grand	4M
	456	Hester	5C
	770	Spring	7A
Violin	127	Bleecker	2J
	288	Essex	3B
	301	Grand	4M
	456	Hester	5C
	770	Spring	7A
Xylophone	127	Bleecker	2J
	288	Essex	3B
	301	Grand	4M
	456	Hester	5C
	770	Spring	7A

"Guys, Sophie's going to print out three of these—the chart and the seven clues—one for each of you to take home and solve. Remember that there are five musicians, and for each one, there are five possible addresses, streets, and apartment numbers. Slice o' strudel for three smarty-pantses like you!"

" 'Pantses'? Really?" Rebecca says. "And what about you?"

"I worked it all out last night," Margaret says. "But I knew you'd want to be able to solve it on your own. Much more fun than having someone else just give you the answers. Just ask Ms. Klack."

"I think my brain just got smaller," Leigh Ann says.

"I've been feeling that way for the past five years," I say.

Margaret ignores our self-pity party. "What you're looking for is the address and apartment number of the violin player so that you know where to take the key. But see, you won't know that until you have solved almost everything else. I have so much confidence in you all that I'm leaving a note saying we'll all come to the apartment on Sunday afternoon."

"Aren't you supposed to leave the note on somebody's watch?" I ask.

"Fred Lebow's. You know that statue of the guy who is looking at his watch in the park at Ninetieth Street? That's him. How does one o'clock Sunday sound?"

I quickly calculate the travel time needed to get to my other commitment for the day. "Can we make it noon? I need to be at Asphalt Green for swim team at three."

"If I can't solve the puzzle, can I still come?" Leigh Ann asks.

"You can solve it," Margaret says confidently. "It really is simple compared with figuring out how someone was able to walk through the walls at Mr. Chernofsky's."

"Why, Margaret Wrobel," I say. "I do believe you are bragging."

Rebecca joins in. "Yeah, isn't this that hummus thing you were talking about?"

"That's hubris. Hummus is that spread made out of chickpeas—you know, tastes good with pita bread. But the answer is no. I'm simply confident of my abilities, that's all. There is neither hummus nor hubris."

"Still, I think I might bring some pita with me on Sunday," I say.

Thursday is a blur of classes, band practice, homework (thanks, Mr. Eliot, for assigning an essay due on Friday—that's a big help, really), constantly checking myself out in the mirror in my new jacket, and texting back and forth with Raf about a million times. As if he weren't in enough trouble already, his mom got a call from his French teacher saying he was in danger of failing.

I call him immediately. "Raf, *je parle français*. I can

help you. Why didn't you tell me you were flunking? I'm never going to see you again."

"I failed one stupid test. And I got a ninety on the next one."

"So, what about tomorrow? Can you get ungrounded? The Blazers are playing at Perkatory."

"Don't worry. When I tell my mom I'm going to see you and Margaret, she'll let me go. She thinks you're a good influence on me. Wait until I tell her it was your idea to take the scooter across town. I'll get a ridiculous curfew—probably, like, nine o'clock—but I'll be there."

Friday nights are usually quiet at Perkatory, but with word out that the Blazers are doing a free concert, tables start to fill early. (And if you pull this leg, it plays "Stairway to Heaven.") Seriously, Aldo, the manager, seems pleased. He should be; he's selling a lot of coffee, and he doesn't have to pay us a dime. Now all we have to do is not chase everybody out the door by stinkin' the place up.

Livvy and two of the Klackettes are taking up precious real estate at one of the best tables. Although Ms. Lonneman couldn't technically prove that the girls had cheated, parents were called, tears were shed, and punishments were handed out. Becca heard through the grapevine that Livvy was grounded for months, had her cell phone taken away, and has to spend an hour after dismissal every day tutoring kids in the lower school. And Becca's story about a second grader puking on Livvy's brand-new shoes? Just a tiny bit delicious.

Livvy is her usual charming self to Margaret when she and Andrew arrive together. She asks Andrew—loudly enough for us to hear—why he's "slumming" with a bunch of losers.

And that, finally, is the last straw for Andrew.

"Livvy, you moron, Margaret is my friend. I know friendship is a strange concept to you, but do me and everybody else a big favor and just shut up."

We cheer wildly as Livvy and her "friends" skulk out the door. Margaret immediately snags their table for my parents, Becca's mom, and Leigh Ann's family, all of whom walk in a few minutes later. Margaret invites Jaz, who has the night off, to sit with her and Andrew, and when Mr. Eliot comes in (sans phantom wife, yet again), he sits with Sister Eugenia, Ben, and Mr. Chernofsky. Then Ms. Lonneman, who waves as she hurries inside, joins them, too. Just as I'm starting to worry that Raf isn't going to make it, he and his friend Sean—who looks like he stole Bart Simpson's hair—show up and squeeze in at Margaret's table.

Malcolm and Elizabeth share another prime table with Caroline and her husband, Roger, and daughter, Caitlin. I do a minor bit of meddling when I rearrange people so that Malcolm, Caroline, and Alejandro Jaimes can be seated near one another. "Malcolm and Caroline are both professors of archaeology at Columbia," I say to Alex. "You know, it's the only Ivy League school right here in New York. Malcolm, I'm sure I've mentioned Leigh Ann's brother, Alejandro, to you. Oh! And what a coincidence! He just got asked to take part in some math program at Columbia. Probably has a million questions for you."

And so my work there is almost done.

Leigh Ann drags me back to our "backstage"—a closet-size storeroom—where Becca is psyching herself up. "Guys, we have a little problem," Leigh Ann says. "Mbingu's not here. I tried calling her, but I can't get through."

"Have you heard anything, Bec?" I ask.

"Nope. Haven't talked to her since rehearsal the other day."

"Well, what's the plan if she doesn't show?"

"If who doesn't show?" Mbingu sticks her head in the door, smiling sheepishly.

"Mbingu!" we all shout.

"I'm so sorry! My papa surprised us—he arrived from Tanzania a day early—and I almost forgot! I ran from the subway station."

"Did your parents come?" I ask. "I can make some room for them up front—"

"No, they need some time to relax together. Papa has been away for six months."

"Wow. What was he doing?" I ask.

"He still works there. He is a safari guide—you know, driving people around to see the lions and giraffes."

"So, have you ever seen a lion that was, like, not in a zoo?" Becca asks.

Mbingu laughs. "Many. And leopards. And cheetahs."

"That is so cool. The only wild animals I've ever seen are pigeons and rats."

"That's not true, Rebecca. Sometimes there are squirrels. And seagulls!"

"And cockroaches!" Then she reaches into a plastic grocery bag and tosses something to each of us. "If you don't like 'em, we don't have to wear them," she says with a very un-Rebecca-like shrug.

I hold up a lipstick red, long-sleeve T-shirt painted to look exactly like my school blazer. It has the pockets, the crest, the buttons, and a triangle of plaid "skirt" showing at the bottom; it even looks like there's a white button-down blouse with a red tie underneath. I was planning to wear my new denim jacket, but this thing is just way too perfect not to wear, and besides, it's not just about me. It's about the band.

"Holy smokes," Leigh Ann and I say together.

"You like 'em?"

"You made these?" Mbingu asks, incredulous.

"They're awesome," Leigh Ann says. "They must have taken forever."

More shrugs. "Eh. Gave me something to do instead

of homework. I hope you don't mind—I added the ties. Makes it a little more—you know, punk. And check out the crest."

"Semper Rock," I read.

"It's the only Latin word I know."

"Becca, you never cease to amaze me. All that grumbling and complaining, and look at you!"

"Yeah, well, I'm still annoyed with you." She tries, but fails, to keep a straight face.

We pull the shirts over our heads and smile, smile, smile . . . and, um, smile.

"You know, we are totally ready for this," I say.

"Let's rock," Rebecca growls.

But first, a group hug. Hey, rockers do that. Don't they?

Chapter 27

Venimus, vidimus, rockimus
(that's "We came, we saw, we rocked," for you non–Latin speakers out there)

Okay, first, about that group hug. I know what you're thinking, and I agree 100 percent. We have some cooling up to do if we're going to be real rockers.

We take our place on the "stage" (aka a corner of the coffee shop). I throw my guitar strap over my shoulder and try not to look at the crowd. Everyone is clapping and shouting our names, but the blood pumping through my brain is making so much noise I can't hear a thing. Leigh Ann, who has been through dozens of dance recitals and has starred in several school musicals, calmly steps up to the microphone, looking like she's been doing this all her life, which, in a way, she has.

"Hey, everybody. Thanks for coming to check us out. I'm Leigh Ann, and this is Sophie on guitar, Becca on bass, and Mbingu on drums, and we are . . . the

Blazers." She takes one step back to make sure Becca, Mbingu, and I are ready. "Two, three, four . . ."

It's the Blazers' first public performance, and "Twist and Shout" goes almost perfectly. At first, I'm in such a state of sensory overload that everything seems blurry—my vision, my hearing, even my sense of touch. My fingers feel a little rubbery, and I flub a couple of notes. Halfway through the song, though, I start to have fun. I sneak a peek at Becca, who, despite her attempts to be the cool, unflappable bass player you've seen in a million bands, is grinning uncontrollably as she plays and sings along with Leigh Ann. My fingers begin to belong to me, and my pulse finally slows enough that I can hear not only my own playing, but the sound of the crowd singing along. And suddenly—I'm at Madison Square Garden, and twenty thousand fans are standing and cheering as we play the final notes of our opening number. Oh yeah. I like this rock-star stuff.

We exhale and do fist bumps all around, and then Leigh Ann returns to the microphone. "This next song was written by our very own Sophie St. Pierre." I try my hardest to fight off my very un-rock-star-like blushing and smiling when Margaret and Raf start chanting, "So-phie! So-phie!"

I signal to Mbingu to start playing, and then Leigh Ann sings:

You can bring me flowers, but I'm not gonna cave,
Give me magic powers, I still won't misbehave.

Take me to France and Spain, don't mean a thing,
Stand outside my window, play guitar and sing.
You can do most anything, if you've got time to
    waste,
Just another desp'rate boy, and not the first I've
    faced.

I wouldn't, oh no I couldn't,
And no I haven't and I don't.
He doesn't, no no he isn't,
No way, he didn't and he won't.
We shouldn't, oh no we aren't,
No we can't . . . no, no, no we can't!

Show up in Daddy's car at seven-forty-five,
Top's down, the music's up, you even let me drive.
Tires flat, out of gas, just get me to the dance,
I'm tellin' you right now, there's not a snowball's
    chance.
Have to give you credit, you just refuse to quit,
Keep tryin', boy, no doubt you've got some style
    and spit.

I wouldn't, oh no I couldn't,
And no I haven't and I don't.
He doesn't, no no he isn't,
No way, he didn't and he won't.
We shouldn't, oh no we aren't,
No we can't, but then he did!
He held my hand, he closed his eyes,
He kissed me once, he kissed me twice,
Threw me clear off the track,
And then, oh then,
I kissed him back!

We practiced it so that the song ends the instant Leigh Ann shouts that final line—and we totally nail it! There is this moment of (stunned?) silence, followed by cheering and clapping and a few shouts for encores, which is a small problem for a band that knows only two songs.

"Um, unfortunately, we don't actually know any more songs, but thanks for asking," Leigh Ann explains. "And we promise we'll be back."

"We don't care," my dad yells. "Play that one again!"

Parents!

The rest of the crowd likes the idea, though, and starts to chant, "Blaz-ers! Blaz-ers! Blaz-ers!"

Leigh Ann turns to Becca and me; we shrug and kick the volume on our amps up a notch. Gotta give your fans what they want.

The second time through is a little louder and a little sloppier, but no one seems to mind. We take our bows and run off the minuscule stage to be congratulated, hugged, and kissed. Malcolm, who swears that he saw the not-yet-famous Beatles play in Hamburg in 1962, tells us that we are definitely "the next big thing."

My parents—you know, my classically trained violinist mom and French chef dad—are in a state of shock. Mom gives me a big hug and then pulls back to give me one of those I'm-so-proud-of-you-I-think-I'll-cry looks. "I had no idea you were so good. When you said you girls were going to play, I thought . . . well, I don't know what I thought, but it sure wasn't this. You were amazing!"

"So you're really okay with me quitting violin?" I ask.

"Honey, I just want you to be happy doing whatever you're doing. Now, about this song you wrote . . ."

Uh-oh.

Matters are made far worse by the arrival at my side of one Rafael Arocho.

"Perfect timing," I say under my breath.

"Hey, Mrs. St. Pierre," Raf says good-naturedly. "What'd ya think? Not bad, huh?"

Mon père glares at *l'imbécile.*

"I mean, they were totally awesome!" Raf corrects.

Dad nods. "Much better. Now, young man, I think you and I should have a talk about this song my little baby girl wrote." He puts his arm around a suddenly uncomfortable-looking Raf.

"Dad!" I scream. "Don't you dare. Mom, stop him. Please."

Margaret saves the day—and perhaps Raf's life—by moving to the microphone and asking for everyone's attention. "Excuse me, everyone—I have a little announcement and a request for some of you, but first I just have to say one word about my best friends: WOW! I hope when the Blazers are rich and famous, you guys will remember your old friend Margaret."

"Margaret who?" Rebecca shouts.

"Exactly," Margaret says. "As I was saying—I think

everyone here knows that not long ago, a valuable violin was taken from Mr. Chernofsky's shop next door. The police have been working on the case, but we Red Blazer Girls have been conducting our own investigation as well, and during the course of that, a second theft occurred, of a bow, for which I take all the blame." She pauses for full dramatic effect. "Tonight, however, I am pleased to announce that we have solved the case. We know who stole the violin and the bow, and how the thief pulled it off."

People turn to one another in a sudden burst of conversation and questions. Becca elbows me. "We do?"

"Just go with it. Act like you know everything Margaret knows."

She stares blankly at me. "As if."

"I'd like to ask everyone to move next door to the violin shop, where I will reveal the identity of the thief," Margaret continues. "Oh, and by the way . . . it's someone in this room."

Instant silence, followed by a moment right out of the movies. Eyes dart around the room, from table to table, trying to guess the identity of the violin villain.

"How exciting! I feel like I just stepped into an Agatha Christie novel," Elizabeth gushes. "Goodness— it's not you, is it, Malcolm?"

He smiles slyly, with a quick raise of his eyebrows, but like a great poker player, he reveals nothing.

Margaret asks a still-speechless Mr. Chernofsky to open up the shop, and Ben offers to help set up a few chairs.

"To make this scene completely authentic," he says, "we ought to have a parlor room full of wing chairs and English antiques, but we're going to have to make do with some of these metal folding chairs."

The other Blazers and I follow Margaret up to the counter, where Aldo teases her about taking all his customers away.

"Just for a little while," she explains. "They can come back afterward."

"So, this band of yours," Aldo says. "Who does the talking for you?"

We all point to Margaret. "She's our manager," I say.

"Well, manager, do the Blazers have any other engagements for next Friday? There's five free sundaes in it for you."

"What do you think?" Margaret asks. "Are the Blazers ready to turn pro?"

"Oh yeah," says Becca.

Margaret shakes hands with Aldo. "I just have one little favor. You know that long pole that you use for changing lightbulbs? Can I borrow it for a few minutes? And promise me you won't lock up for a while, okay?"

"I'll be here for another hour at least. And one lightbulb changer coming up."

Chapter 28

Ah, Mademoiselle Wrobel! Monsieur Poirot and Miss Marple are waiting to welcome you into their club

We settle in at Mr. Chernofsky's.

Margaret begins: "First, please note a few details about the security system Mr. Chernofsky has in place. Because he often works on very valuable instruments, his insurance company requires it. There are bars on all the windows. Each set is securely bolted to the brick. Each windowpane is also connected to the alarm system, so even if the bars were removed, a broken window would set off the alarm. The front and back doors both have extra-secure dead bolts and are also alarmed. Now, Mr. Chernofsky—at the time of the theft, who knew the alarm code?"

Mr. C. rubs his beard, thinking. "Besides me? Just Ben."

"That would be Benjamin Brownlow," Margaret explains, pointing Ben out to everyone. "Your new assistant."

Lots of suspicious looks at Ben.

Margaret holds up her hand. "Don't jump to conclusions like I did. I figured it had to be Ben, too. He knew the value of the violin, so he had motive. He knew the alarm code, so he had opportunity. And then there was the matter of his button. Ben always carries around a plastic button from an old coat—sort of a good-luck charm—and on the morning when Mr. C. discovered the theft, he also found that very button on the floor right next to the spot where the violin had been. It seemed like an open-and-shut case. But, and not for the last time on this case, I was wrong. We discovered that Ben had—well, let's just say he had an airtight alibi. Sorry, Ben."

"No harm, no foul," he says with a good-natured wave.

"Which brings us, as they say on TV game shows, to door number three—this one." She walks across the room to the door that leads directly into Perkatory—the door that can be unlocked only from inside the violin shop. She pulls on the doorknob once to show that it is locked. Then she twists the knobs on all three dead bolts and pulls the door open, revealing the back of the identical door to the coffee shop.

"As you can see, these dead bolts are accessible only from inside the shop. There is no place for a key, and it's the same thing for the door into Perkatory." She closes the door and makes a big show of relocking all three dead bolts, then makes it clear that they were locked the morning Mr. C. discovered the violin was gone.

"And that leaves us with one more option, the site of

my second big mistake on this case. If you go into Mr. Chernofsky's office, you will see a trapdoor in the ceiling, just big enough for a small person to fit through, that is there for access to pipes and wiring. Once I had eliminated Ben from my list of suspects, I started to obsess about that trapdoor, thinking that if there's one down here, there's probably one above it, and they're probably connected somehow. Kind of like those air ducts in the movies. Then we found out that a relative of the two women who live upstairs is a world-class gymnast and only a shade over five feet tall—small and agile enough to fit through the opening. Once again, I was sure we had our man. We set up a little trap using a webcam, making sure that he knew all about a valuable bow that was in the shop. We sat up all night staring at a computer screen, waiting for Sergei—that's his name—to come crawling through the ceiling like a squirrel. But guess what? He never came. And boy, do we owe him—and those two lovely women, Anna and Natalia—an apology. All that wouldn't have been so bad, but when Mr. C. told me that the bow—my bow—had been stolen right from under our noses, I figured my career as a detective was pretty much over. But then Sophie's mom saved the day."

"I did?" Mom says.

"Yep. I was waiting for Sophie—as usual—the other day, and you used that handy little gadget that lets you grab things to get something out of one of the high cabinets in your kitchen. And coincidentally, we had been at

Perkatory the day before and Jaz was using this contraption," she says, holding up the lightbulb changer from Perkatory. "It has a suction cup on one end that you can use to change lightbulbs, and it extends to about twelve feet long. And suddenly I knew. Well, I was ninety-nine percent sure I knew, anyway. So I came back in here, made a couple of quick measurements, and took a really close look at one very important detail I had overlooked before."

Raf clears his throat during Margaret's dramatic pause. "And are you planning to tell any of us? Or are you just gonna talk all night?"

"Patience, Rafael. I'm not merely going to tell you, I'm going to demonstrate how it was done, so even you will be able to understand," she adds with a wicked grin.

I scan the assembled audience once more to see who looks nervous, suspicious, or anything out of the ordinary. Malcolm catches my eye and winks. Hey, what's that about?

Margaret's eyes twinkle as she gives me that just-trust-me look of hers before asking Mr. C. to lock and bolt the doors and set the alarm after she leaves the shop. He seems a bit unsure, but when she is gone, he does as she asked, and the room grows strangely quiet.

Leigh Ann leans over to whisper to me and Becca, "Who do you think it is?"

"Well, my dad looks pretty guilty," I say. "Look at him fidgeting in his chair. And he needs a shave. The guilty person always needs a shave."

"What if it's a woman?" Leigh Ann asks.

"Well, I think it's Mr. Chernofsky," Becca says, folding her arms for emphasis.

"That's ridiculous," I say. "Why would he steal a violin from his own shop?"

"Duh. Ever hear of insurance? He tells everyone the violin is valuable and then arranges this whole phony break-in so that he can collect the insurance money. I'm telling ya—I saw the same thing in a movie. Everybody trusted the sweet, old old guy . . . until he robbed them blind."

"Gosh," I say, "if it happened in a movie, it must be true."

Leigh Ann shushes us. "I think I hear something. Outside that window." She points to the round stained glass panel that is situated directly across the room from the door leading to Perkatory.

"What the heck is she doing?" I ask.

"Seriously," Leigh Ann says, "I know she's skinny, but no way is she going to squeeze between those bars."

Everyone leans forward in their chairs, straining to see what the shadow behind the window is going to do next. For the next minute, it sounds like a mouse is scratching at the pane, trying to get in. Then we watch with open mouths as one section of glass—a cobalt blue triangular piece about three inches across—pops out of its lead frame, looking for a second like it is going to fall to the floor. As if by magic, however, it stops in midair before it is slowly lowered to the floor with the help of a piece of string and the rubber suction cup from the light-bulb changer.

"Okay, I'll admit it. So far I'm impressed," Mr. Eliot says. "Assuming, of course, she hasn't set off a silent alarm somewhere."

"We would know if she had set off the alarm," says Ben. "It is anything but silent."

Silent seconds pass as we all stare at the hole in the window. Then, like one of those snakes coming through the wall in *Raiders of the Lost Ark,* the fully extended and wobbly aluminum pole of the lightbulb changer begins to slither its way through the opening and into the room. Two feet . . . three . . . four . . . and more and more, finally coming to rest on the floor against the bottom of the door to Perkatory, ten feet away.

I can almost feel the smile on Margaret's face as she maneuvers the end of the pole up to the first of the locks. It is then that I notice that the end of the pole (where the suction cup would normally be) has a notch cut into it. She misses a couple of times, but on her third try, the notch lands perfectly on the little wing-nutty-looking handle that you turn to lock and unlock the dead bolt. A confident twist of the pole, and . . . TA-DA! The bolt opens with a satisfying *clunk.* One down, two to go.

"Oh. My. God," Jaz says quietly. She is leaning against the back wall, and I almost forgot she was in the room.

"Pretty crazy, huh?" I remark to her, but she doesn't respond.

The pole, which seems to have a life of its own, moves up to the second and third locks, finishing them off in no time at all. *Clunk. Clunk.* (With a few more hours of practice, I think Margaret could change contact lenses with the thing.) And then we wait. The pole rests comfortably on the floor while everyone resumes chatting.

"I still don't get it," Leigh Ann says. "When Mr. Chernofsky came in that morning, he said the locks were definitely locked. I don't see how she can—"

Becca cuts her off. "Never mind that. What about the big hole in the window? The cops would have noticed that."

Malcolm, however, has complete confidence in my best friend. "If I know Margaret Wrobel, she has an answer for both of you. Stay tuned."

The words are barely out of his mouth when we hear the locks on the Perkatory side click open, and Margaret strolls into the violin shop, takes a violin from the rack of inexpensive student rental instruments, and carefully places it in a case, snapping the lid shut. From her pocket, she takes out a plastic button, just like Ben's, and places it on the floor right by the violin rack. Then, with a quick wave, she disappears out the same door.

"Is that it?" Becca asks as we wait once again for something to happen.

"Hang in there," I say. "I have a feeling the best is yet to come."

A minute later, it feels like we're watching the same

movie in reverse. The bulb changer begins to levitate again, moving up to the three locks, locking each in turn, and then disappearing back out the hole in the window. When it is gone, the piece of glass attached to the suction cup begins its slow rise to the window frame. As it approaches the opening from which it came, I can't help myself—I jump up to see just how she's going to pull this off. How is she going to reattach the glass? Bubble gum?

Close.

The pointy white nozzle of a tube of silicone glue—like the clear, rubbery stuff that goes around your bathtub—comes through the hole. As Margaret holds the blue triangle of glass firmly in place with the suction cup, she squeezes a line of the clear glue around its perimeter and then oh-so-carefully pulls the string, and with it the glass, into place. From inside the room, it is absolutely impossible to tell that the window has been tampered with.

"Holy crap," Becca says.

Exactly.

Becca, Leigh Ann, and I arrive at the same conclusion at precisely the same time. We spin around to stare at Jaz.

A loud knock sounds from the front door, and I gasp before realizing it's just Margaret. Mr. Chernofsky lets her in to a chorus of cheers and applause that rivals what the Blazers received. (Not that I'm, you know, measuring the difference or anything like that. Merely an observation.) Jaz is totally quiet. Then she stands as the crowd settles down, holding her chin up defiantly.

"You can't prove anything," she says boldly.

"That may be true," Inspector Wrobel says, "but I'm willing to bet the police will be very interested— interested enough to make your life miserable for a while. That is, unless, say, a certain violin and my bow were to just happen to . . . reappear in the next few minutes. In that case, I think we would all be willing to forget what happened. Chalk it up to 'youthful indiscretion' like they do with politicians' kids. What do you think, Mr. Chernofsky? Sound good to you?"

Mr. C. nods, and Malcolm clears his throat, addressing Jaz directly in that firm, authoritative voice of his. "Young lady, if you have possession of the violin and bow that disappeared from this shop, it is certainly in your best interest to return them immediately. You have already caused a great deal of trouble, and now you have an opportunity to set things right without significant consequences—other than the loss of trust these fine girls may have had in you."

Everyone fixes on Jaz as she considers her options. A faint, disbelieving smile creeps across her face.

"One question," she says to Margaret. "How did you do it? It was . . . perfect."

That famous all-knowing smile of Margaret's. "Nothing's perfect. In the end, it was simple logic. The dots were all there, I just had to figure out how to connect them. The lightbulb changer. Ben's button, which he last saw in Perkatory the morning Sergei was there—a morning you were working. Just a guess, but he probably dropped it, and when you realized he worked here, you knew you had a red herring that would point right to him. And you were also working that day we overheard him on the phone, so you knew the violin was special. Once you knew it was a Frischetti, I'm sure it didn't take much effort to figure out how much it's worth. When we set up the operation to catch Sergei, you knew the location of the hidden camera because you saw us testing it. Remember, you even said something about it looking like a weird movie. The only thing I wasn't sure of was how you knew about the locks and the window, and the distance between them. Mr. Chernofsky, though, remembered that you had been in the shop. It was a few weeks ago. He was in the workshop and didn't hear you come in. He found you snooping around, and you told him a tale about a violin that you wanted to have appraised—but you never came back. You must have already been planning a break-in when fate brought that Frischetti into the picture. As for the rest, the locks were easy once I saw the bulb changer and the freshly cut notch in the end. I'll admit that the window had me stumped for a while, but when I came back for a closer look, I noticed that the blue piece of glass sounded different when I tapped on it. The silicone glue is like rubber; it doesn't get brittle like other glue. It sounds different. It even smells different. From the outside, I could see where you had scratched the lead when you pried the glass free, and on top of that, some of the glue had seeped out. Fresh glue."

Jaz shakes her head in amazement.

"Now I have a question for you," Margaret says. "Why? I mean, why a violin, of all things to steal? If you're smart enough to plan all this, you're smart enough to know that it would be almost impossible to sell it for anything close to what it's really worth. In the end, it would hardly have been worthwhile. Why take such a big chance?"

Jaz's eyes narrow as she turns to find someone in the crowd. "That's easy. Because of him." She points right at a very surprised Ben.

Raf rubs his hands together. "The plot thickens."

"Me? What did I do? I don't even know you," Ben says.

Jaz takes a step toward him. "Oh, not much. You just ruined my life, that's all. Three years ago, I was all set to go to NYU. I was accepted, found an apartment in the Village with great roommates . . . and then . . . and then . . . nothing! It all came crashing down, and I'm left working in some crummy coffee shop and living and going to some rinky-dink college in . . . Queens."

I feel Leigh Ann squirming to get up and defend her homeland. "What *is* it with people slamming Queens?"

"What on earth does any of that have to do with me?" Ben asks.

"One word. TechnoQuake."

By the number of blank faces around the room, it's clear that Ben and Jaz are the only two people for whom that one word means anything.

"I thought that might ring a bell. My father was one of your best customers. He put his life savings—my college money—into TechnoQuake stock, which you sold him, and which you went to prison for."

"So all this was about revenge?" Margaret says.

Jaz nods. "I had to. He made my life miserable. It was my turn to do the same to him."

"What about the three years he spent in prison?" I ask. "Doesn't that count as miserable?"

"Look, I'm truly sorry your life isn't going the way you planned," Ben says, "but in case you haven't noticed, I'm not exactly living the high life, either. I gave back every penny I made from that stock, and until a few days ago, I was living in a closet in a basement with a bunch of rats."

Leigh Ann pokes me. "I knew it!"

"And I know you won't believe this," Ben continues, "and it certainly doesn't excuse my actions, but I didn't know I was selling your father stock in a doomed company. The TechnoQuake executives lied to everyone."

Jaz is unmoved. "What, you expect me to feel sorry for you?"

"Not at all. If you want to spend the rest of your life hating me, fair enough. But don't drag innocent bystanders into it. Mr. Chernofsky and Margaret haven't done anything to you, but as it stands, they've both lost something valuable because of what you did."

Malcolm stands, addressing Jaz again, and for the first time, I see him as Professor Chance. "If I may, young lady, I would like to offer a little advice; ignore it if you will, but know that I give it with the best of intentions. Life, as a wise man once said, is what happens while you're busy making other plans. I know of no one whose life has turned out exactly as planned. Yes, you had a bad break. But it is time to get on with your life. Do you have any idea how fortunate you are? You're young, presumably healthy, and obviously bright. You live in a city of infinite opportunities. Instead of making excuses, make something of yourself. Anyone with the ingenuity to plan and carry out what you did here is certainly capable of great things. It's up to you to make your life extraordinary. Sometimes we just need a determined girl in a red blazer to remind us how important that is."

Malcolm's little speech has the stuff.

"All right, all right, I'll return them," Jaz says quietly. "And you're serious, no police?"

"No police. I promise. As long as everything is undamaged," Malcolm says.

"They're fine. Okay, I just need to make a call. They're not here, but very close by." She turns to the wall to call her coconspirator. I'm unable to hear most of what she says, but before hanging up, I hear her snap, "Just bring it to the coffee shop. I have a buyer right now."

We follow Jaz back to Perkatory, and guess who strolls in ten minutes later, violin case in his hand, looking for Jaz?

Mr. Winterbottom!

Malcolm greets his old nemesis with a huge grin. "Well, this is just perfect. Gordon, I can't even say I'm surprised to see you. After all, who has more experience in shady dealing than you?"

"Malcolm Chance! You again." And then he sees Margaret and me. "And—and you."

Always polite, we wave at him. "Hi, Mr. Winterbottom."

"What was the arrangement, Gordon? You sell the violin for the girl and you get to keep half the money?"

Winterheinie grunts, tucks the violin case under his arm, and turns like he's going to make a run for it. Except with those smoker's lungs of his, he's not running anywhere. I'm guessing a brisk walk would probably be fatal.

"Don't do that, Gordon," says Malcolm. "Just hand them over and I'll make you the same deal I made your little friend: no police."

He thinks about it for a second, sets the case on a table, snarls something about Malcolm under his breath, and stalks out as the rest of the crowd returns to Perkatory.

Moments later, Mr. Chernofsky smiles broadly as Margaret hands him the case containing the violin and her bow. He caresses the top, then opens it and gingerly hands the violin to Margaret.

"Maybe you will play us a little something," he says.

Becca starts chanting, "Mar-ga-ret! Mar-ga-ret! Mar-ga-ret!"

"Something Polish," Mr. C. suggests. "Perhaps a little Chopin?"

Margaret clamps the shoulder rest in place, tightens the horsehair of the bow, and pulls it across the strings, closing her eyes and smiling to herself as music fills the room.

All in all, it has been a very good day for the Red Blazer Girls.

Chapter 29

One last letter

I'm dreaming about the Blazers. We're rehearsing in Elizabeth's basement, and Mbingu is tapping out some new rhythms for a song we're working on. *Tap, taptap. Tappity-tap, taptaptap. Taptaptaptaptap.*

I open my eyes, but the tapping continues. Odd. My eyes slowly come into complete focus, and across the room, I spy my "blazer" shirt hanging from the back of the desk chair. Odder still, there sits Margaret, pecking away at my computer keyboard.

"Wh-what are you doing?" I ask.

"Finally. I thought you were going to sleep all day," she says.

"What time is it?"

"Seven-fifteen."

"Unnnhhh. How did you get in here?"

"I knew your mom would be up. Get dressed. We're going out for a bagel—I have to tell you something."

Five minutes later, we're on our way out the door. When we hit the sidewalk in front of my building,

Margaret grabs my jacket, stopping me. "I can't wait. If I don't tell somebody soon, I'm going to burst!"

"Something else happened last night?" After the celebration at Perkatory, Raf had to run to catch a crosstown bus—yeah, that's right, a bus—in order to make it home for his ludicrous nine o'clock curfew. Margaret then ditched me to walk home with Andrew, leaving me alone with my parents. On a Friday night. Heavy sigh. To make matters worse, on the way home they threatened to keep a far closer eye on me after hearing my song.

But enough about stupid, stupid, stupid me.

"So, tell me, tell me, tell me! What happened?"

She buries her face in her hands. "Arrghh. I'm so embarrassed! We were walking home, and having a really nice conversation, and then—then we got to my building."

"And?"

"We were just saying, you know, good night, and how we'd see each other today at our lesson, and then . . ." She reburies her face, groaning.

"Margaret!"

"I kissed him!"

"What!"

She nods. "I. Kissed. Him."

"What did he do?"

"He was so surprised he didn't do anything. And then I ran inside, so even if he wanted to do something, like . . . like—"

"Kiss you back—"

"It was too late. And . . . and . . . and this is all your fault!"

"What did I do?"

"You told me I need to take more chances. Try new things. The whole time we were walking home last night, that's all I could think about. I mean, I'm almost thirteen! And then—I just went and did it. And I didn't even wait around to get kissed back." She sighs, quite dramatically. "My life is ruined. He'll tell everybody, and I'll be the nitwit girl who kissed and ran."

"Not gonna happen. He likes you. Look how cool he was at Perkatory, telling Livvy off like that. I think he might even be—just barely—good enough for my best friend."

"You really think so?"

"I know so. I'm willing to bet you're going to know what it feels like to be kissed very soon."

"But how can I possibly face him today?"

"Easy. Just be yourself."

"Well, I am never doing that again."

"Listening to my advice?"

"Well, that, too. But I meant kissing a boy."

"Margaret, Margaret," I say, shaking my head. "Of course you will!"

After my guitar lesson, I get down to the serious business of solving the logic problem. Since printing out the clues and the chart, I haven't even looked at the thing, but I'm determined to do it myself.

And I do. Not quite "easy as brioche," as my dad would say, but nothing I can't handle once I put my mind to it. Once I'm positive I have the solution, I call Margaret.

I wasn't home when she and Andrew saw each other for the first time since the Kiss. Dad took me out to a local pub so he could watch a French soccer game and I could chow down on a colossal cheeseburger. Right now, it is details I am hungry for.

"So, how did it go today?"

"Um, great. I think. Andrew was totally cool. He didn't say anything about, you know, what happened, but we talked after the lesson. He asked me to this concert at Lincoln Center next weekend."

"Yay! That's excellent! A date!"

"And get this: my parents said I can go! Of course, it starts at two in the afternoon."

"Hey, it's something," I say.

"Are you ready for tomorrow?" she asks.

"I know where the violin player lives."

"That's good. Okay then, I'll meet you there tomorrow, a few minutes before noon."

"We're not going together?"

"Nope. Becca and Leigh Ann will meet us there, too. This way, we're all equal. We're a team, but we can do it ourselves if we need to."

"But what if some of us are wrong?"

"That's a great question, Sophie. See you tomorrow!"

• • •

Sunday morning, I leave the apartment at eleven, thinking that I will lurk outside Margaret's building and follow her. The doorman, outside hosing down the sidewalk, smiles and waves when I approach.

"You just missed her," he informs me. "She went thataway about five minutes ago. She said you'd be by."

Oh, she just thinks she is so clever. Grrrr.

I take the subway down to Fifty-ninth and then hike up to Sixty-third to transfer to the F train, which I take to Delancey Street.

I'm non-ultrafamiliar with this part of town, so it takes me a minute to get my bearings. As I'm looking up the street, I spot Leigh Ann trying to read a map. I sneak up behind her and boom, "CAN I HELP YOU, MISS?"

"Jeez, Sophie! Don't do that. I swear, my heart stopped." She puts her hand on her chest to slow her heart down, closes her eyes, and takes a deep breath. Very actressy.

I take out the paper with my solution and show it to her. "Is this where you're going?"

She looks incredibly relieved. "Hey, guess I really did it! And if we're both wrong, at least I'll have someone to be lost with. Where's Margaret?"

"Somewhere ahead of me. I've been trying to catch up to her, but I keep missing trains by, like, two seconds." I point across the street. "We need to go that way."

As we wait for the light to change, Leigh Ann slips

her arm through mine. "Hey, thanks for Friday—you know, for introducing Alex to Malcolm and Caroline. He said he had such a nice time with them that Columbia is definitely moving up on his list."

"So there's a chance. That's good, right? How 'bout your dad?"

She shakes her head. "Nothing new. He's moving right after Thanksgiving. I'm starting to be okay with it."

"Really?"

"I mean, I don't want him to go, but when we went to dinner, he explained that it is a fantastic opportunity for him, and he says it's only for two years. I felt bad, because when I told him how I felt about everything changing so fast, he looked like he was going to cry. But we had a good talk, and I decided that I'm going to be mature about it." She stands up straight, her chin high in the air. "After all, I am almost thirteen."

"I'm glad I still have a little time as a tween," I say. "This 'growing up' stuff sounds like it could be hard."

"Tell me about it. Oh, and somebody sent him all this information about Cleveland. You wouldn't know anything about that, would you?"

"*Moi?*"

"I knew it was you! Anyway, thanks! He already found a school nearby with a great summer dance program—so I'll probably spend most of my summer vacation with him."

"See, that'll be nice," I say, throwing my arm around her shoulders.

A few minutes later, we catch up to Margaret, standing on the sidewalk in front of a run-down-looking apartment building.

"Ah, here comes that famous bass player," I say, spotting Becca.

When we're all together, we all show our solutions on the count of three, like poker players revealing their hands.

"See?" Margaret says. "A cinch!"

I look up at the building. "You really think this is the place? It almost looks abandoned."

"This is the right address. And I left a message on that Fred guy's watch telling him when we'd be here."

As she starts for the door, I see it. Peeking out of Margaret's bag is the latest issue of *Seventeen*. But that is a conversation for another day.

"Umm, I know this is kind of late to be asking this," Leigh Ann says, "but how do we know this is safe? It looks a little sketchy to me."

"She has a point," I agree. "What if we open the door and there's a guy standing there with a million pins sticking out of his head or something?"

"Or there's, like, a basket full of bloody body parts in the middle of the floor?" Becca adds.

"You watch too much television. I gave my parents the address, they know where we are. And look, there's four of us. If anything about it doesn't look right, we won't go in."

A trio of grunts and nods—grods.

"So," Margaret announces, *"allons-y!"*

We march single file to the door. Margaret takes the key from around her neck and inserts it in the outside door. I hold my breath as she turns it, and the door swings open. We take one last look at each other and step inside.

The staircase is really dark and creaks loudly with every step. There's no sneaking up and down the stairs in this building. We stop in front of the door to the apartment where the mystery violin allegedly. resides.

I have 9-1-1 punched into my phone, with my thumb on the SEND button, as Margaret knocks on the door.

"Come right in," says a strangely familiar voice.

"Hey, that sounds like . . . ," Leigh Ann starts.

Margaret turns the knob and pushes the door open.

Not in ninety-three years would I have guessed what awaits us.

"What the—"

Despite the seedy appearance of the building's exterior, the apartment is surprisingly pretty and bright . . . and packed wall to wall with people I know.

For starters, all of our moms—all wearing some version of a red blazer—are sharing the couch. Behind them are the dads and Alex, who is talking to Caroline. Becca's little brother and sister are sitting on Malcolm's and Elizabeth's laps in matching wing chairs. Mr. and Mrs. Chernofsky have claimed dining-room chairs, as have Ben, Mr. Eliot, and Sisters Bernadette and Eugenia. And finally, in the shadow behind the door stands

Raf, the first boy I ever kissed—the boy who now thinks it is acceptable to keep secrets from me!

"What is going on here?" I demand. "Mom. Dad. How did you . . ." I fix on Raf. "And you. I saw you Friday, I talked to you yesterday!"

Raf flashes one of his famous smiles at me and—wait, remind me why I was supposed to be mad at him?

We are still standing one step inside the door, too freaked out to move, despite the many beaming smiles.

"Ladies, please come in," Malcolm says. "We've been expecting you. Make yourselves comfortable. May I get you something to drink?"

"Oooookaaaayyyy," Margaret says. "But—"

Malcolm cuts her off. "I promise an explanation—after libations." He hands each of us a plastic champagne glass full of ginger ale and then holds up his own glass—which I suspect contains something a bit stronger—to make a toast. "To the Red Blazer Girls on the successful completion of another case."

"Cheers!" shouts the crowd.

Still confused and a little embarrassed, we seat ourselves while Malcolm takes some papers out of an oversize envelope.

"All right," he says. "I think we've challenged these young ladies enough for one day. I have a little story to tell and a letter to read to you. My good friend Harvey Woldowski, who was also my college roommate and is now an attorney, had a client for many, many years named Janos Bartoszek. This Bartoszek fellow was a

Polish immigrant who first came to Harvey because, at the time, he was the only lawyer with a Polish name he could find. Janos worked at Carnegie Hall and lived in this apartment for nearly fifty years. A few weeks ago, he died at the age of eighty-three. And then, as you will see, things got interesting."

Malcolm takes a sip of his drink before continuing. "Many years earlier, Mr. Bartoszek had given a letter to Harvey, to be opened upon his death. This very letter." He puts on his reading glasses and begins:

To my dear and loyal friend Harvey Woldowski,

If you are reading this, it means that my time on earth has come to an end. But do not weep for me. My life, like so many millions before, was filled with happiness and sorrow, and joy and pain, and much, much more. If you must shed a tear, shed it for my family—my mother and father, and my sister, Anna— whose lives were stolen in the insanity of World War II. I have never told their story to anyone, and perhaps it is time.

Before the war, my father was a professor at a small conservatory of music in Warsaw, and through him, my sister and I grew to love music. Anna played violin like an angel. I played piano, but not nearly as well.

After the Germans marched into Poland in 1939, the officers often came to the conservatory recitals in the evenings. Anna was a favorite performer there. One young German officer, a promising violinist himself, befriended Anna, asking her for pointers and bringing her chocolates and other scarce items in return. Father was afraid for her but dared not speak out, for we had all heard rumors about the camps where those who spoke against the Germans were sent. This went on for several months. Then we learned that the officer had received a promotion and suddenly had much more power and influence than before. One evening, after dinner and too much wine, he accused Father of being a Communist. Now, Father had friends who were Communists, but he was indifferent to their politics and never attended any of their meetings. He tried his best to convince the German that he was a music teacher and nothing more. This ambitious young officer, however, had other ideas in his terrible, corrupt mind. He had fallen in love with Anna, but when she refused his attentions, he decided that he would have his revenge by taking something precious to her—her beloved violin.

When Father was a boy, the violin was given to him by a wealthy patron, and he passed it on to Anna on her twelfth birthday. I had seen the officer looking at it, and when she let him play it, the desire to have what did not belong to him began to eat away at what was left of his decency. The next weeks were a nightmare that I have relived over and over. Based on the false accusations of the young officer, Father was arrested and sent to a camp. When Mother refused to give the names of all of Father's friends, she was arrested and sent away, too. I tried to get Anna to run away with me, to hide in the countryside, but she still had hope that Father and Mother would be released, and she refused to leave. When the Germans came for her, she didn't scream or cry. She simply handed the violin over to the young officer.

"Play it in hell," she said.

I never saw Anna again. Nor Father and Mother.

After the war, I learned that they had all died in the camps. For a long time, I was simply lost, wandering from village to village. Eventually, I found my way to America. After almost ten years in New York, doing odd jobs like tuning pianos and driving taxis, I got a job at Carnegie Hall. I started out as a janitor, but when they learned that I knew about musical instruments, I was tuning pianos and assisting visiting musicians. And then fate stepped back into my life.

It had been twenty years since I last saw him, but I could never forget that face. The young German officer, no longer young and handsome, now fleshy and red-faced and even more arrogant than before, was in New York for a concert. He did not recognize me, even when we found ourselves face to face in his dressing room. When he was a young man, his playing had been far inferior to my sister's, but there he was, playing to a large crowd at Carnegie Hall. Playing my Anna's violin. All I could think was that Anna should be alive and on that stage, bowing and humbly accepting the crowd's cheers, instead of this arrogant, thieving pig.

And so, on January 16, 1959, I went into his dressing room and took back what belonged to Anna. It was quite simple, really. The hall was especially crowded and warm, and during the intermission, Wurstmann—that was his name—stepped outside to cool off. I ran to his room, threw his coat over the violin case, and calmly walked out the stage door and across the street to a diner where I often stopped for coffee. In the restroom, there was a small closet, and I put the violin, still wrapped in the coat, on a shelf, out of sight if anyone should happen to look inside. Then I rushed back across the street, blending in with the crowd and reentering the hall unnoticed. Within moments, Wurstmann realized the violin was gone and began shouting loudly in German, but by that time I was rearranging music stands and chairs on the stage and talking with my coworkers. The police searched the hall and questioned everyone who worked there, me included, but the door had been unlocked, leaving the police to believe that someone had simply walked in from the street, taken the violin, and vanished.

All this happened more than fifty years ago. Once a year, on Anna's birthday, I take out the violin and play a little song, a Polish folk song that was our favorite when we were children. The rest of the year, it sits on a shelf where I can see it . . . and remember.

And now, the point of this letter.

You have been a good friend to me for many years, Harvey, and I have one final request. I would like you to find a young girl—a girl like Anna, who plays the violin like an angel—and I want you to tell her my story and entrust her with Anna's violin. I will trust you to find a girl who will always cherish it, for it must never be sold, but simply passed on to its next caretaker. Thank you, and God bless you.

Your friend,
Janos Bartoszek

In which the truth comes out and our friends and families are exposed for what they really are: outstanding, unsurpassed, superlative, preeminent, and brilliant (thank you, "Word Power"!)

When Malcolm finishes reading, he removes his glasses and wipes his eyes. He then folds the letter, places it in its yellowed envelope, and turns to Margaret.

"Harvey told me about Mr. Bartoszek and this letter the very day you and your friends recovered the Ring of Rocamadour. Call it fate, call it providence, or divine intervention, a coincidence—but whatever you call it, it was clear to me that you and Anna's violin are destined to be together. Mr. Chernofsky, would you do the honors?"

"It will be my pleasure," Mr. C. answers.

Margaret opens her mouth, but no words emerge as Mr. Chernofsky holds out a violin case to her.

"You have earned this, Margaret," Mr. Chernofsky

says, choking up just a little. "And now you must never forget Janos Bartoszek's story. Every time you play, Janos and Anna and their parents are all playing along with you."

Margaret holds the case as if it were made of spun glass, seemingly afraid to move, afraid even to breathe.

"Go on, open it up," Malcolm says, smiling.

She flips up the latches and lifts the lid of the case. Her eyes grow wide as she struggles to comprehend what she sees.

"But . . . wait, this isn't possible," she stammers.

"What isn't possible?" I ask, looking over her shoulder.

It is the violin, the very one Jaz stole from Mr. C.'s shop and the one we—well, Margaret, actually—recovered Friday night. The one on which she played "Ave Maria" so beautifully that day in the shop. The one with the tag saying it belonged to David Childress of the Longfellow String Quartet.

"So all this time," Margaret starts, "and all those clues that led us here . . ."

Malcolm bows deeply. "Those were my handiwork. I knew you and the violin were perfect for each other, and Harvey agreed but had to clear up all the legal paperwork before we could turn it over officially. We had to make sure there were no claims on the violin from insurance companies or even the Wurstmann family. I know how you love a challenge, so I thought some new puzzles would keep you interested for a while. On top of that, Anna's violin hadn't had a good checkup in about fifty years. We wanted it to be in perfect condition when you got it—cleaned up, with new strings and such, so we gave it to Mr. Chernofsky for a good going-over."

"And that's when things got complicated," Elizabeth adds. "Not that it was Anton's fault. No one could have foreseen it being stolen in such a . . . creative manner."

"I think you can imagine how we felt when it disappeared," Malcolm says. "Especially Mr. Chernofsky. That caught us completely off guard. We didn't know what to do."

"But the Red Blazer Girls swooped in and saved the day," Mr. Eliot gushes.

Wow. I mean, he has gushed before, but never about us.

Margaret lifts the violin out of its case. Her eyes well up and she sniffs back tears as her parents come closer to hug and kiss her.

Her father's smile fills his face as he squeezes her. "You see? I tell you that one day soon you will play at Carnegie Hall. Now you have a violin that will show you the way."

"That's right, Margaret," I say. "This thing has already been there, done that. Now it's your turn."

"I'm still confused about one thing," she admits. "Actually, I'm confused about a lot of things, but one in particular. I left the message that we would be here today, that we had solved all of the clues, on Thursday afternoon. We didn't get the violin back until Friday night. If you didn't have the violin, what were you planning to do when we showed up here today?"

"Wow," I said. "That is a good question." I turn to Malcolm for an explanation.

Ever suspicious, Rebecca says, "You guys set up the whole robbery thing with Jaz, didn't you? It was just another test for Miss Sherlock here. I always knew there was something funny about it."

"I wish I could say you're right, Miss Chen," Malcolm says. "But believe me, that whole vanishing violin act was a complete surprise. My friend Harvey was definitely not pleased that his client's final wish would not be fulfilled. No, it was all too real. But in answer to your question, Margaret, we did come up with a Plan B. Frankly, when we learned the violin had been stolen, we didn't hold out much hope for its recovery. After all, the last time it was stolen, it was gone for fifty years! I called a meeting of everyone who's here today, and we made a decision. Mr. Chernofsky had one other violin available—a beautiful example of his own work, a masterpiece that he offered at a fraction of its real value. We asked Kate St. Pierre to give it a test-drive to determine whether it would be suitable for your needs, and she gave it a glowing review. And I should tell you: every single person in this room—even your young friend Rafael—promised to pitch in to pay for it. You are a very fortunate young lady, Margaret, to have friends and family like these."

Poor Margaret. She's practically hysterical, sobbing

and hugging her f's and f. I take the violin out of her hands so that it doesn't get tear-warped, and then step back with Leigh Ann and Becca to watch and wonder as we try to put all the pieces of this strange case together.

As the hysteria begins to settle down, people try to persuade Margaret to play something on her new, second-best friend. (I'm numero uno—it's in my contract.) She's in no shape to play, however. Not yet.

This gives Elizabeth a chance to stand and get everyone's attention.

"If I could just have my girls join me here for a moment. Margaret, Leigh Ann, Rebecca, Sophie. Please."

I see a bag in Elizabeth's hand and swap my worries for greedy anticipation. You see, it's not just a bag; it's a little blue bag. A Tiffany blue bag. Oh, calm down, I tell myself. Just because it's in a Tiffany bag doesn't mean it's from Tiffany. It could be bagels and cream cheese, and that would be nice, too. Right?

Elizabeth pulls the four of us together, facing our friends and families, while she stands behind us, arms on our shoulders. "These four girls have done more for me than you can imagine. In just a few weeks, they managed to find the ring that was hidden so cleverly by my father and helped bring my daughter and granddaughter—and this old coot, Malcolm—back into my life. As you know, the ring they recovered, one of the two Rings of Rocamadour, is now in the Metropolitan Museum, where it belongs."

Dad leads everyone in a cheer, and as ever, I am Ms. Uncontrollable Blushface. A peek in Raf's direction (he's keeping his distance from my dad) confirms it: he is loving this moment.

"However," Elizabeth continues, "before we delivered the ring to the museum, I took it to an old friend who owed me a favor." She reaches into her little blue bag and hands each of us a tiny, blue-wrapped box. "Girls, from Malcolm, Caroline, Roger, Caitlin, and me, thank you again, from the bottom of our hearts. Wherever life takes us, I know we'll always remember the wonderful thing you did for my family. And I hope these help you remember how grateful we are. Go on, open them up."

My pulse is pounding in my ears as I tear away the paper. Inside is a blue cardboard box, and inside that, a black jewelry box. I flip the lid up and my jaw drops open. It is the Ring of Rocamadour: that familiar gold band with its cross of rubies. Becca, Leigh Ann, and Margaret hold out their boxes; they each have one, too.

"They're perfect copies," Elizabeth explains. "Made by a friend of mine at Tiffany's. And guaranteed to be the only ones ever made. That was part of the arrangement we made with the museum—that the ring would never be duplicated except for these four."

Here's something else that will never be exactly duplicated: the feeling I have at that moment as I slip the ring onto my finger and look up at my three best friends.

Chapter 31

Maybe not worthy of a chapter all to itself, but epilogues are like that sometimes

After the celebration, I take a cab uptown with Mom and Dad so that I can quickly change and head to Asphalt Green for my first practice with the swim team. Michelle, the coach, greets me enthusiastically as I come through the door to the pool. She is in her fifties, swims a couple of miles a day, and still has energy to burn.

"Great to see you, Sophie! I am so glad you decided to join us. You girls have so many things going on these days that I truly appreciate your commitment. I don't know if I can promise it will be fun, because it requires a lot of work, but it will be good for you. For the record, I wasn't just trying to flatter you when I said you have real promise as a swimmer. You were one of my strongest juniors. You look like you've grown a few inches, which will help, too. I think we're going to try you out in the one hundred and two hundred individual medleys and some of the relays. How does that sound to you?"

"Sounds great." I look around the pool deck at a sea

of unfamiliar faces. "Is there anybody here from my old team? I don't see anybody I know."

"Nobody from your junior days, but there's one other girl from your school who will be joining us. In fact, you two will be on the relay teams together. Ah, here she is right now."

I turn in the direction Michelle is pointing and find myself face to face with—of course—Livvy Klack. My face reveals all, and Michelle immediately says, "Oh good, you do know each other."

"Oh, I know her," Livvy says. "Don't I, Sophie?"

"Um . . . yeah."

"Excellent," says Michelle. "Why don't we get started? Let's do an eight hundred warm-up, and then we'll take it from there."

I start to bend down to feel the water temperature before jumping in, but stop myself halfway. Nope. I promised I would take the plunge, and here I am—hot or cold, Livvy or no Livvy.

And with a splash, I dive into the deep end of the pool.

Appendix: How to Solve the Final Logic Problem

Start by making a copy of the next page—you don't want to write in a nice, new book, do you? I didn't think so.

How to use the chart: Once you determine a street, address, or apartment number, circle it. If you know that a musician *can't* live at a specific location, cross it out. The crossing out part is *very* important! Many of your answers will be revealed by your new best friend, POE (no, not Edgar Allan). "POE" stands for "process of elimination." If you eliminate all the wrong choices, you will be left with only one possibility—the correct answer!

First, read through the clues for the given information.

Instrument	Address	Street	Apt.
Bassoon	127	Bleecker	2J
	288	Essex	3B
	301	Grand	4M
	456	Hester	5C
	770	Spring	7A
Flute	127	Bleecker	2J
	288	Essex	3B
	301	Grand	4M
	456	Hester	5C
	770	Spring	7A
Piano	127	Bleecker	2J
	288	Essex	3B
	301	Grand	4M
	456	Hester	5C
	770	Spring	7A
Violin	127	Bleecker	2J
	288	Essex	3B
	301	Grand	4M
	456	Hester	5C
	770	Spring	7A
Xylophone	127	Bleecker	2J
	288	Essex	3B
	301	Grand	4M
	456	Hester	5C
	770	Spring	7A

The piano player lives on Hester Street, but not in Apt. 4M and not at no. 127 or no. 301 (the orphan clue).

The bassoon player lives in 2J, but not on Grand or Essex (the first-letter clue).

The xylophone player lives on Bleecker Street, but not at no. 288 (the first pigpen clue).

The violinist does not live in the building located at 456 Grand or in Apt. 7A (the second pigpen clue).

The street address for Apt. 3B on Essex Street is neither the highest nor the lowest (the first grid clue).

The man in Apt. 5C at no. 301 is not on Spring Street and doesn't play the flute.

Neither 288 nor 770 is the address of the building on Spring Street.

1. *From clue 1 we know that the piano player lives on Hester. Put a circle around Hester in the piano player's row. And if the piano player lives on Hester, that means no one else*

can, right? So cross out all the other Hester Streets. That same clue also tells us that the piano player does not live in Apartment 4M, or at address numbers 127 or 301, so cross out those possibilities for the piano.

2. Using clue 2, circle Apartment 2J for the bassoon player, and cross out Grand and Essex. Then cross out all the other 2J's.

3. Clue 3 gives us the xylophone player's street—Bleecker. Circle it, and then cross out all the other Bleecker Streets, and cross out number 288 as a possibility for the xylophone. By process of elimination, you should see that the bassoon player lives on Spring Street, because it's the only choice left! Go ahead and cross out all the other Spring Streets.

4. The fourth clue tells us about the violinist. In his row, cross out 456, Grand, and 7A. The violinist must live on Essex, and when you cross out the only remaining Essex Street, we see that the flute player lives on Grand, and we also know that the address is 456. Be sure to cross out all the other 456's. At this point, you have a street for every musician. We're almost there!

5. Clue 5 is very important. Here we find that the violinist's apartment on Essex Street is 3B. Circle it, and cross out the remaining 3B's. Then cross out the highest (770) and the lowest (127) for the violinist, according to the clue.

6. The sixth clue reveals that 301 is not the address at Spring Street and that the person at 301 is not the flute player. We also learn that the apartment at 301 is 5C. Because you know that the bassoon player lives on Spring Street, cross out 301 and 5C for him. The next part is a little tricky: At this point, the only musicians that could live at 301 are the violinist and the xylophone player. But since you already know that the violinist lives in Apartment 3B, he can't live at 301, so cross it out. That means that the xylophone player must live in Apartment 5C at 301 and the violinist must live at 288. Circle those answers, and then cross out the other possible addresses and apartments for the

xylophone player. *By POE, you've also revealed the piano player's apartment to be 7A. Circle that, and cross out all other 7A's, which, in turn, reveals that the flute player lives in 4M. Circle that answer.*

7. *According to clue 7, the building on Spring Street (the bassoon player) is neither 288 nor 770. Therefore, the address must be 127.*

Aaand, the answers are:

Hey! You're not trying to sneak a peek at the answers before you finish reading, are you? I didn't think so. Because I just *know* you wouldn't want to do anything to disappoint me, would you?

Seriously, *don't* do something you'll regret later! I have total faith that you have the, um, smart-itude to solve the problem without resorting to peeking. So sharpen your pencil and get to work!

Oh my goodness. You again? Haven't we been through this already? NO PEEKING! On the other hand, if you *have* read the whole book *and* figured out where the violin was—good for you! You may turn the page!

Bassoon: 127 Spring Street, Apartment 2J
Flute: 456 Grand Street, Apartment 4M
Piano: 770 Hester Street, Apartment 7A
Violin: 288 Essex Street, Apartment 3B
Xylophone: 301 Bleecker Street, Apartment 5C

Did you solve this? Nice work! Maybe you should think about getting your own red blazer.

About the Author

Michael D. Beil's first Red Blazer Girls installment, *The Ring of Rocamadour*, was hailed as "a PG *Da Vinci Code* . . . with a fun mystery, great friends, and a bit of romance" (*School Library Journal*).

Mr. Beil is a former attorney who now teaches English and helms the theater program at a New York City high school. No mere mild-mannered academic, he has also sailed, written plays, and climbed Mount Kilimanjaro. He finds literary inspiration in horror films, Encyclopedia Brown, and *Rumpole of the Bailey* and earnestly hopes that readers will try to figure out the puzzles and codes in *The Vanishing Violin* even faster than the Blazers' brainy Margaret.

Mr. Beil has every confidence in his readers' tenacity and, uh, smart-itude.

In a starred review, *Booklist* called for "more Red Blazer Girls, please!" Mr. Beil suspects that further mysterious mayhem is inevitable. He and his wife, Laura Grimmer, share their Manhattan home with two dogs and two oversized cats.